HONOUR KILLING in A

'I loved it. Beautifully written, like ¡ novels, so engrossing that your mind does not baulk at the remarkable sequence of events near the close, you are drawn right through to the very end, which is poignant, quite unexpected yet very satisfying. There is no tame happy ending, but there is much happiness.'

—Rev Jock Stein, MA BD Cantab. Minister and Theology Publisher, Kincardine

'A riveting read, showing in a dramatic and exciting way, through the lives of two young people, how religious and cultural differences can be overcome and how the idea of paradise can change with different circumstances. This engrossing story is full of emotional highs and lows while the shocking and gruesome events in the final chapter leave the reader totally overwhelmed. A gripping and inspiring tale.'

—Christine Boyd, Primary School Teacher, Glasgow

'Award winning author, William Scott, has reached new heights with this powerful novel that will hold the reader spellbound. In a style reminiscent of John Buchan at his best, the author tackles head on the subject of honour killings, and produces a devastating ending which will shock the reader.'

—David Torrie, an editor, DC Thomson Publications Dundee

i

'I finished this in two sessions. I found it moving, profound and gripping; the best fiction I have read for some time. Modern cultural and religious dilemmas are shown to be solvable in a fascinating way. I particularly liked the final chapter; the puzzle of the Russian femme fatale solved in a pleasing if gruesome way.'

—Tom McCallum, MA, Classicist, Stromness

'Your book has been read by me at almost one sitting. I found it very interesting, easy to read, very enjoyable and a book I did not want to put down. Well done, you.
'Not only is William Scott a very talented, dedicated and engrossing writer of Scottish History, he is also an accomplished writer of fiction. His novel *Honour Killing in Argyll & Bute* is a fast moving and absorbing story about the clash of cultures in our modern fundamentalist world. Log on to this book.'

—Colonel Bruce Niven, MA, MBE, PPA, ex Chief of Staff, S.A.S., Geographer, writer, Everest climber, Gurkha Commander and Leadership Trainer, Singapore

'A great read, in which mathematical and philosophical insights are seamlessly intertwined within a fascinating study into the fallacy of known paradise.'

—Gordon McConnell, BA, BSc, Principal Maths, Ayrshire

OTHER BOOKS BY WILLIAM SCOTT

Fiction

The Bannockburn Years, Luath Press

A Bute Crucifixion

Non Fiction

Bannockburn Revealed

Bannockburn Proved

History and Imaginative Reconstruction

The Bute Witches

First Published by Elenkus,
PO BOX 9807, Rothesay, Isle of Bute, PA20 9YA,
Scotland, United Kingdom.

Email: elenkus@yahoo.com
Website: www.elenkus.com
Telephone: 01700505439
Mobile: 07842 404268

© William Wallace Cunningham Scott

All rights reserved. No part of this may be copied or transmitted in any form without the express permission of the author

ISBN 9780952191056

The right of William Wallace Cunningham Scott to be identified as the author of this work has been asserted by him in accordance with the Copyright, Design and Patent Act 1988.

HONOUR KILLING In ARGYLL

By

William Scott
BA,BSc,MEd,FIMA,FSAScot

Subtitle:

PARADISE DEMOLISHED

ELENKUS

MMVIII

The duty of every real writer is to provide original solutions to important problems in an interesting, entertaining and accessible way.

This is a novel. Except for the big scientists, mathematicians and the professor of religion mentioned, four of whom are known to the author—with two of whom he has spent significant time—the characters are invented. The big men cannot object to their presence in a book with such an obviously decent objective, especially when their presence at Harvard, Oxford and Cambridge means that the invented characters would necessarily have come across them.

The suicide bomber believes he will go to Paradise and Paradise is precisely defined. Show him that his idea of Paradise is incorrect and you will divert him from his act, especially if his authority is literal, the exact, reported, word of God—not subject to interpretation.

If he is not sure where he is going, he is not likely to blow himself to pieces. It is only the certainty of a well-defined paradise as a reward that makes him act as he does.

1

In a small community on the west coast of Argyll in Scotland, occurred an event with the power to affect the conduct of nations.

Unaware of what was to come, Hector McIvor was speaking to his assembled family at Tigh-na-mara, his rambling, two storied house sited out on a finger of the land between two narrow sea lochs. Outside, sheets of rain descended from a leaden sky, blasting the land and the sea in salvoes that slanted from the north as if fired from the great mountains close at hand. Hector was at the head of the table dressed in a grey polo-neck sweater and brown corduroy trousers, both stained with hardened paint of several colours.

Around the dining table with the remains of a meal on it, were Rose, his wife, his two daughters, Margaret and Jane, and his son, Robert. In contrast to her golden-headed husband, Rose's dark-hair was streaked with grey and she wore a beige dress which clung to her very slim figure. The children were in the school uniform of white shirts, black and gold school tie and black sweatshirts with the gold logo of the school.

'The trouble with people,' Hector said, 'is that they grow up with crazy ideas in their heads which make them impossible adults. By then, there is no shifting them— the ideas, I mean.'

'Isn't this another of your own crazy ideas?' said Robert. Everybody laughed.

'Not on this occasion,' replied Hector, smiling. 'Look at the Catholics and Protestants here in the sixteenth and seventeenth centuries. They killed each other for having a slightly different faith. They both believed in God and Jesus and the gospels and the commandments, especially the one about not killing other people. And yet they did! —For a trifle.

'Even today in Ireland—just a few years ago— it was the same: thousands blown up or murdered for a trifle of a difference of faith. And what they believe, both sets, probably isn't true. Imagine killing somebody because he worships in a slightly different way from you— especially when you are supposed to love one another! That is the madness of it. They are both supposed to love everybody and they kill each other instead and call it *defending the faith* when killing is so totally opposed to what they believe as the innermost core of their faith.'

'What is the answer, then, Dad?' said Robert, golden haired, like his father.

Jane said: 'Get hold of them in childhood and make sure they have no crazy ideas.'

'How can you do that?' said Robert. 'They'd never let you in.'

'In the schools, that's where you must begin.'

'You mean stop the Catholic and Protestant schools? Make them all the same?'

'Yes.'

'But,' said Rose, 'every parent should have the right to educate their child in the faith of his father and mother.'

Robert replied: 'You mean they have a right to inculcate their own crazy ideas in the heads of their children just because they are their own?'

'Yes.'

'But that makes children just chattels.'

'Who else should have the right to decide how children should be educated but their parents?'

'Some parents are not competent to decide.'

'The state then?'

The argument continued for a while and eventually ceased as such things do when everybody got up to be about their business. The children went off to do their homework, their father settled down with a newspaper and a dram and Rose saw to the dishes, everyone having stacked their plates at the hatch in the wall that led to the kitchen.

As she washed the dishes by hand Rose looked out upon a garden of shrubs set in lawns of roughly cut grass and, further off, a long finger of the sea which stretched for two miles eastwards to the village of Kinoidart and another mile after that. It was a narrow finger not much above 100 yards in width but it twisted and turned, only widening at the village into a bay four times as wide, a natural harbour sheltered by a wooded hill on the west. The land on either side of the finger of the sea was not at all high. So it could not be thought of as a fjord. It was better for being low-lying, she thought, for it was more accessible, even though few people lived there. There were many woods and she thought the area beautiful. It was the usual Scottish conjunction of water carving shapes amid a landscape replete with meadows and woods and, far off, great islands rising like leviathans out of the sea and, not far away to the north, even greater mountains, often snow topped, that could occasionally be glimpsed on an infrequent clear day.

The garden, sheltered to the west from the worst winds that blew off the Atlantic by a coppice of trees, was her pride and joy. Every year, now that the children were grown, she opened up a fresh flower-bed and experimented with roses and herbaceous, trying to nourish them into life because of the warm Gulf Stream, and despite the frequent torrential rain. Only the grass was not her province. Robert took care of it, when he remembered.

It often surprised her that she had come here, that she lived in such pleasant surroundings. She had fallen in love with an artist, a man with a mission, who earned his bread by teaching in the school far to the north. Everyday for years he had journeyed back and forth by car to spread his message among 'the great unwashed', as he would refer to them. Recently, he had retired early to devote himself to painting full time. How they would manage to put the children through university on his reduced income was unclear but he was sure of his talent and knew he must develop it now before it was too late. So every morning, instead of going to school, he would shut himself in the studio upstairs and set to.

Always profligate with paint and canvasses, now that he had all day to paint, his expenditure was far worse. He was never satisfied, forever throwing canvases away onto an ever-growing heap and starting anew. He had been at it for nine months and had finished nothing yet to his satisfaction.

'But that looks very fine,' she had said so often, really enjoying something he'd done. 'Couldn't we sell that one?'

But he would only shake his fair-haired head sorrowfully and turn it to the wall. 'I'm not making homely scenes of little houses by the loch side with a skein of smoke drifting into an azure sky. That's what sells. It's what people want.'

'Then why not give them what they want?'

'It's not art. I can do better.'

'I don't understand you. We need the money.'

And he would take her by the shoulders and look into her eyes and try to explain. 'It is not the job of an artist to make people feel comfortable but to shake them up, change the way they view the world and themselves. Provoke them into self-development. I need to find my own style and I haven't done it yet. If I try and sell these things, I sell myself short. Don't you see? I will become known for them. But what I want to achieve is different, something original, something powerful. I have to find it in myself first before I sell anything.'

'How are we going to pay for Robert at university next year?'

'I don't know. He can take out a loan.'

'But he will be crippled by it before he's even got a job.'

'It's what they do, some of them. I don't know the answer. I just know I have to go on developing.'

'You're selfish then? You'd put your development before his?'

'If you like. I could really do something important, Rose. Don't you see? I have a duty to try. I'd be an ass if I carried on at school just to earn the cash to finish off the education of the kids. I would never achieve anything then. I can do it, Rose. I know it in my soul.'

'But what if you are the only soul that knows it? If you never sell a painting?'

'Then at least I will have tried.'

'How can you think that's right? How can you put yourself first?'

'I have as much right to develop my talent as to pay for Robert's. He'll manage, I tell you.'

'Well, I think you should have been selling paintings before you gave up teaching and retired early on a pittance. You should have known you could make it first.'

'You can't know that kind of thing in advance, I tell you. And you can't do it part-time. It's a 24-hour affair. You'd only end up doing the teaching badly because you were so set on the painting.'

This much she understood for her Hector was restless, now, to get on with his work, his quest for the holy grail of art. It had taken a grip on him she could see. He was up at all hours and she despaired of the life they had enjoyed before, a normal one, with distinct hours to themselves. They'd scarcely made love once a month since he'd taken up his new career, as he insisted on calling it.

On the other hand there was Robert at sixteen and his talent was obvious. The parents' meetings had only confirmed what they knew instinctively. Robert was already a scientist with a voracious appetite— for physics especially. Every present, every prize that came his way, every pound that fell into his pocket, had to be translated into a book; often an original work like Newton's *Optics* or *Principia Mathematica* or Faraday's Experiments or Einstein's papers— a translation from the German by a Professor in Ireland[1].

Robert had got to the point where school was almost an irrelevance, a place he was obliged to attend as a staging post while waiting for university. There, increasingly, he did not fit in. He had no time for the games others thought natural, never socialised in the town or even the village, never went to school functions except if there was a concert when he would be wanted to play the violin, the only hobby he would allow. Rose worried about this dedication. It seemed unnatural, as if part of him—the human element— was being swamped by the pressure within to develop his mind. And it was a mind that could inflict serious injury, for it was razor sharp, respected nothing but the truth. Tact, any

---

[1] *The Einstein Decade*, by Cornelius Lanczos, Dublin Institute for Advanced Studies, pub Paul Elek (Scientific Books Ltd) 54-58 Caledonian Rd. London, N1 9RN. 1974. The original papers published in Annalen der Physik are translated therein.

form of charity for weakness, especially deficiencies of insight or reasoning, was despised by Robert whom she had seen destroy almost everyone he came across. It was just a matter of time before he demolished his father, she knew.

Then there were the girls. Margaret was three years younger than Robert, a red-haired, seriously freckle-faced, blossoming young woman with a growing talent for music—the bassoon, in her case. The cost of instruments and lessons was becoming a nightmare. Would there be any money left for Jane, newly arrived in the secondary and, therefore, about to be exposed to things that cost real money?

Not for the first time, she began to consider the possibility of applying for a job. Anything would do. And it might mean travelling to the county town, the only place, apart from Oban with enough shops where she might find employment.

She was proud of her family, proud of their ideals, ambitions and abilities— even if she doubted that everything would turn out for the best. She should have been very happy at the prospects and the way of life she enjoyed, precarious though it seemed.

If she had known what some mysterious force in the universe had in store for her and the family, she would have rejoiced in her present predicament for its potentialities, despite all its dangers.

2

It began on the school bus, which was boarded by her three children after a walk to the foot of the track to the house by the fjord where, as usual, they were collected before being conveyed to school.

At first there was an unaccustomed silence as the habitual commuters all in black and gold with matching ties and white shirts, surveyed the newcomer. She had dark hair and dark eyes and was quite tall. What stopped them in their usual high-jinks was the clothing she wore. The dress, a large dark-brown sack-like garment, called by some a djellab, by others a djellaba, began at the top of the neck and continued all the way to the ankles, which remained covered. The shoes were flat with short heels and a dull black matt colour. A white garment—called a tudong—covered all of the head and shoulders except for a round space in which the face could be seen. It was an unblemished and symmetrical light-brown face but not especially pretty.

One of the boys, Jim MacLean, decided to have some fun and took the seat behind her. Carefully he lifted up the tudong so that he could see her more clearly, at least from the rear. The hair was smooth as silk to the touch and seemed to shine.

Like the lightning strike of a snake, a hand came around, grasped his fingers and, surprisingly strong, began to bend them. He yelled and then screamed, tearing his hand away. The girl said nothing, continued to stare straight ahead.

'Fucken hell!' said McLean, ruefully, getting up, wringing his hand and returning to his seat near the back of the bus. 'I was just having some fun.'

Again the new passenger said nothing. When the bus stopped at the playground, she sat in silence until everyone else had departed before getting up to leave.

'My name is Raissa Hussain[2],' she told the school secretary at the reception area. 'I wish to join the school.'

She was interviewed by a senior teacher and answered questions directly. Finally, Miss Spence, a tall brown-haired lady in a grey trouser-suit, said. 'You will have to stop wearing these clothes. There is a school uniform and a policy about it. If you want to come here you will have to obey our rules.'

'I'm not sure my grandfather will allow that.'

'Then you will have to go to some other school. Perhaps an independent one. But that will mean boarding. There are no fee-paying schools around here. This is the only secondary on this side of the county.'

'My family live in Kinoidart. We have a business there and there isn't money for private schools.'

'In that case, Raissa, you will have to wear what the other children wear. Either that or up sticks and move down south where there are day-schools in which the students wear clothes like yours.'

Raissa was left to think about this while Miss Spence went to talk to the Headmaster who decided to see her himself. John Simpson, bespectacled and clad in a dark-blue pinstripe suit was sitting at his desk and frowned at the interruption to his paperwork: 'You could complain, of course, and you might get some support from the newspapers and television people. We've seen this before. But it wouldn't do you any good here and that's where it counts for you. If you begin by causing trouble it will not go down well with your teachers. It could affect your performance. They might take no notice of you in class, might not encourage you in the ways that are most productive. The main thing is that these clothes create a barrier between you and the other students.

---

[2] Pronounced 'Raeesa'

That is not a good idea for you. You need to integrate here to be successful. Attending a school is a social experience. Wearing different clothes like these simply makes your social development uncertain—maybe impossible. Do you understand?'

Raissa nodded. 'Would it be enough if I did not wear the tudong?'

'You mean the head-covering? No. You need to wear the same clothes as everyone else. A school blazer or sweat shirt, a black skirt or trousers and a white shirt and a school tie.'

'—And black tights,' Miss Spence reminded him, 'and black shoes—with one inch heels, mind. No higher.'

'I don't possess these things.'

'Then you would have to buy them in the town like everyone else.'

Raissa sat thinking for a time.

'What will happen if I do not wear these clothes you speak of?'

'You will be barred from the school; not allowed to register or be educated here.'

'And if I don't attend school?'

'Since you are of school age but over 16 you are unlikely to be approached by the truant officer. Probably nothing will happen. But you would not be educated further. You could apply for a further education college but that would mean a longer journey and, perhaps, overnight stays. Even then, the level of education there is far below what is available here.'

After some further discussion, it was plain that Raissa had read some books which were unexpectedly advanced. 'Give her a test, Miss Spence. See what she's made of.'

Miss Spence, who was not greatly enamoured of this girl, took her to her office and gave her an O level prelim in maths to deal with. Raissa polished it off in half an hour, getting everything correct.

'Where did you learn to do this?'

'Here and there. Wherever my family was living at the time. But mainly from books. I have read many books. It is what I like to do.'

Anxious to find something to criticise, Miss Spence said: "you should say 'my family were living'".

'No, 'family' is a singular, not a plural.'

As they returned to see the Headmaster, Miss Spence reflected on her put-down and was irritated but also impressed. There had been no malice in it. The girl simply stated a fact. On reflection, Miss Spence realised that she was correct.

'A very singular person, Headmaster,' was the verdict.

'Well, what are you going to do?' said he with a smile, to the brown-faced pupil before him.

'I want to come here. Very much,' she replied. 'If you will tell me where I can buy the school uniform, I will go and do this. I have money.'

'Very well then, problem solved.'

But Raissa made no move to leave. 'There is just one other thing. My family must not know that I am not wearing the clothes of our culture. Will you tell them?'

Simpson looked at Miss Spence. 'What do you think?'

'A letter will be sent out saying you have registered here and are expected to obey the school rules along with a leaflet detailing what is expected.'

'Does it say anything about clothes?'

'Yes, it does.'

Raissa thought for a moment. 'Perhaps they will not read it. They do not read well.'

'They will know as soon as they see you in your uniform, how it is,' said the Head.

'Then I must not be seen wearing it.'

'How will you manage this?'

'I will have to change clothes before I get to school or after I leave home, whichever is most convenient.'

Simpson said: 'I'm not sure we can go along with this. Your parents may come to parents' meetings. Someone might tell them. It might not be possible to hide this. I am not sure it is right to deceive them.'

'Do you mean you intend to tell them?' said Raissa, almost tearfully.

'We are responsible for your education and we have a duty to convey to your parents anything which they ought to know.'

'Even if it is not in my best interest as a student? If it meant I would be prevented from coming to school?'

'That's a tough one, Raissa,' said Simpson, gently, with respect. 'Some things we do not tell parents, that's true. It depends on the parents. I take it your parents are anxious to preserve your culture. Yet we have to try to integrate you into ours. I can't guarantee what we would feel it necessary to tell them. I can assure you that we would not want to do anything against your interests. That would be our main concern.'

Then, with the inventiveness that characterised everything she did, Raissa, asked: 'What happens if someone on the school bus needs the toilet?'

The Head and Miss Spence looked at one another unsuccessfully for an answer.

'Would the bus have to stop?'

'I suppose it would,' he said.

'Since the journey takes nearly an hour, with all these children to be collected, this must happen from time to time. Where is there a public toilet between Kinoidart and Oban?'

'Good question. I don't think there is one.'

'Then what happens if there is a problem en route?' Raissa persisted.

'Anyone caught short will tell the driver and the lady of the next house will be asked to provide her facilities.'

'Then that is what I will do. Either stop the bus and change in the toilet of a house on the way or change at school as soon as I get here. Would that be acceptable?'

'You mean put on the clothes of our culture as soon as you arrive here at the school?'

'Yes, if that is the only solution.'

'And change back before you return? What do you think, Miss Spence? Is this practical?'

'I don't see why not.'

'It means you would not be wearing school uniform on the bus,' the Headmaster said, thoughtfully.

'Does that matter?' said Miss Spence.

'No, I think we might stretch a point,' said Simpson turning briefly to look at Miss Spence. 'We have a person here who is anxious to learn, if I am not mistaken, and who deserves to have what we offer. I expect you are yourself in some difficulty over this and I sympathise. You have tried very hard to accommodate our rules at some inconvenience to yourself. Miss Spence, why don't you take Raissa down town and arrange for her to buy the uniform?'

And so it was done. 'I have never been to a school like this before!' she exclaimed as they left in the teacher's car.

In the Jean Shop in Argyle Square, all the clothes were chosen, tried on and collected with Miss Spence's approval. Black trousers, a black sweatshirt with the colourful school logo and a black and gold school-tie were chosen, followed by a white shirt and a black fleece, again with the logo, were parcelled up along with the Somerled clan T shirt—Raissa having been allocated to that house by Miss Spence.

At the cash desk, Raissa's face glowed with excitement. 'That will be £81, declared the sales lady.'

Raissa's face fell. 'I don't have that much.'

'How much do you have?'

'Only fifty pounds.'

'Well, I don't see what you can do' said Miss Spence. 'And you still don't have socks and shoes. We will have to buy them elsewhere. That's another £20. You need £101 altogether.'

'I have more money at home. I will bring it tomorrow.' To the sales assistant, she said: 'Would you please keep these for me to collect tomorrow?'

When this was agreed and they were outside the shop, Raissa turned to Miss Spence and said: 'Where in the town can I sell things?'

'What kind of things?'

'Jewellery. Gold necklaces.'

'You don't have the money, do you?'

'I can get things which are worth money, the same thing.'

'You should ask your parents.'

'I know, but I can't. I would have to explain what it was for.'

'What are you going to do for the rest of the day?'

'You mean that I can't wait in the school for the bus?'

'Well, you can't join a class until you're registered and you can't do that until we are satisfied that you will attend in accordance with the rules. For that you need a uniform and it doesn't look as if you can afford it.'

The girl was floored by this—on the point of tears, thought Miss Spence, but recovered almost immediately: 'What happens when someone is too poor to afford the uniform?'

'They get help. But since your father has a business, that isn't likely. If you take that course, his affairs would have to be investigated to see that he can't afford to pay. You wouldn't want that, I suppose?'

'No, it will have to be managed some other way.'

They got into the car and drove off. Arrived again at the school, they sat together. 'Is there a pawn shop in town where I can exchange things for money?' said Raissa.

'I don't think there is. I would have to ask around. I don't think you should use it even if there is. You could lose a lot of money.'

Raissa looked at her with frustration and astonishment. 'What could be more important to me than knowledge? There are things I need to know, training I must have.' And then, very quietly, reasonably, levelly and even respectfully, she added: 'There are things I was born to do. I feel it strongly. And I can only do them if I first come here. You have what I need. There is nowhere else.'

Miss Spence was taken aback—again. 'Come with me. We'll see what the Head has to say.'

With Raissa at her side, Miss Spence soon stood again before the Headmaster's desk. 'She doesn't have the money. Not all of it. Not half of it. She is talking about pawning her gold jewellery. She won't qualify for a grant since her parents are in business and anyway that is impractical: they would have to be told what it was for and their affairs would have to be looked into. Isn't there something else we can do?'

Simpson looked at Raissa and said: 'Why are you so anxious to come to school?'

'Tell Mr Simpson what you just told me, out in the car.'

When Raissa had done so, he sat back in his chair and put his hands together in the prayer position while he considered the matter.

'Well, I'll say, this, young lady, we don't usually have children who are as eager to come here as you are. That puts a special lustre on this. How much money is she short?'

'Fifty one pounds.'

'What do you suggest, Miss Spence?'

'I could pay it myself.'

'You would do that?'

'Oh, yes. This is a deserving case.'

'How would you pay it back, Raissa?'

'I don't know. It could be years before I earn any money. I could ask that any presents I receive are cash and I would hand it over immediately. I'm afraid I can't guarantee anything.' Then, after a pause: 'Maybe I could win some prizes. If there was cash, I could hand it over. If not, I could sell them for cash and pay it that way.'

'You think you could win prizes here?'

'Oh yes.'

'Why do you think that?'

Raissa seemed surprised that there should be any doubt. 'I never forget anything. I never have difficulty understanding things in books. I read books very quickly.'

'But what kinds of books?'

'Any kind, so long as it's interesting. Textbooks, novels, non-fiction.'

'How many books do you read in a month?'

Raissa was puzzled by the question. 'I have read three books in a day and started a fourth.'

'But in a month?'

'Usually I don't have that number of books. So I am sometimes reduced to reading the same ones again. I suppose that doesn't count.'

The Headmaster smiled.

'But can you solve problems? That's what exams are full of.'

'Of course. I never found a problem yet I couldn't solve.'

The Headmaster and Miss Spence looked at each other with disbelief. 'Maybe you haven't seen any hard ones yet.'

'Try me,' declared Raissa confidently, yet without arrogance. As if she were just stating a fact.

'You have a 3 gallon can, a 5 gallon can and a river,' said the Headmaster. 'How do you make 4 gallons?'

Raissa did not hesitate. The answer seemed to be present, already formed in her mind. 'Fill the 3, pour into the 5. Fill the 3 again and pour off until the 5 is full. That leaves 1 in the 3. Empty the 5. Pour the 1 into the 5 and then fill the 3 and pour into the 5. That makes 4. Or you could start by filling the 5. Then you would pour off the 5 into the 3 until it was full, leaving 2 in the 5. Empty the 3, pour the remaining 2 in the 5 into the 3, leaving space for 1. Refill the 5 and pour out until the 3 is full. That leaves 4 in the 5.'

'You got me,' said the Headmaster, smiling. 'Have you seen this problem before?'

'Certainly not.'

'What is thirteen squared?' said Miss Spence, whose subject was maths.

'One six nine,' was the reply, made without pause for calculation.

'Did you memorise the thirteen times table?' asked Miss Spence.

'Certainly not. What for?'

'How did you do it so quickly?'

'Thirteen squared is thirteen times ten plus three and that is obviously a hundred and thirty plus thirty nine. I.e. one six nine.'

'What law were using?'

'The Distributive Law: a bracket b plus c bracket is a times b plus a times c.'

'I think we have to help this young lady. What do you say, Miss Spence?'

'It would be a crime not to.'

'Well, then, Raissa, here's what we'll do. Miss Spence and I will chip in fifty one pounds between us and you will go and buy your uniform. You can pay us back if and when you get any money. But you will repay us best by doing well here.'

Miss Spence led Raissa back to the car, drove her to the shop in town, parked outside and then counted out the necessary shortfall in bank notes. 'You are sure you have fifty pounds?'

'Yes.'

'Then here's the rest. Go get it, Raissa.'

It took ten minutes before Raissa emerged dressed in the new uniform, smiling radiantly, with her other clothes in a plastic bag. After another visit to get shoes and socks, Miss Spence judged her fully qualified to take up a place in the school.

Registration took place on arrival and Raissa was taken around the campus, shown the classrooms in which she would receive instruction, introduced to each class and given the textbooks. By lunchtime she had been introduced to her registration group and given a timetable.

In the classes that afternoon she was completely silent, absorbing everything: the classroom, the other students and the teacher. She asked no questions. At the end of school, she waited until the others had left and then changed in the school toilets. By the time she emerged into the playground, the school bus had left.

Miss Spence, observing her from the window of her office where she was in conversation with the Headmaster, said: 'Well, that's just dandy. She's missed the bus, she knows and isn't upset at all.'

'What will she do?'

'Come and ask for a lift. She won't have money for a taxi.'

But that was not the solution Raissa chose. Instead, with the plastic bag containing her school uniform in one hand and a pile of books under the other arm, she set off striding purposefully, once again dressed in the clothes of her culture, towards the main road back to Kinoidart.

'What is she up to?'

'I expect she's decided to walk home. That's one very determined young lady.'

Twenty minutes later after Miss Spence was able at last to leave, she drove along the road to Kinoidart and eventually drew up beside the striding figure of Raissa.

Opening the car door, she said: 'Do you know that it's eighteen miles to Kinoidart?'

Raissa smiled. 'No problem, as you say here.'

'Get in,' replied Miss Spence.

After Raissa was settled, Miss Spence said: 'Were you going to hitch a lift? You weren't really going to walk that distance, were you?'

'Why not, if I have to? Where I have been, such distances on foot are nothing much.'

'But it would take you 4 hours!'

Raissa turned to her and said quietly, 'I have been waiting all my life for a good school. What is 4 hours?'

3

Wisely, Raissa made no use of the toilet-stop idea, correctly realising that the children from Kinoidart would realise what she was doing and discuss it among themselves—especially if it happened every single day. It was impractical, would make the journey for everyone even longer. The information could get back to her parents, especially since they ran the village shop. And yet, it was not the habit of her people to encourage idle chatter with the Christians. Providing goods and services was one thing, but fraternisation was not allowed. There was also the problem of concealing the school uniform from her family. Raissa's solution was to store them in the locker after school, having changed back to the clothes of her culture. The bus driver had been ordered to wait until she boarded, for they knew by now that, if it left without her, she would walk home and anything might happen to her on the way. The school could he held responsible. But it was too late to renegue. A deal had been made; an offer accepted; money had changed hands.

An assistant-head teacher had pointed out the existence of directive 157 which governed procedures in matters of this kind but, after some reflection, the headmaster, with the support of Miss Spence, was able to say: 'There is a grey area surely, but this is a special case. We have a duty to cater for such a potentially outstanding student.'

During the following month or two everything settled down. Raissa seemed to enjoy her work, her assignments were always handed in on time and she was behaving like a model student. Except in this: she did not socialise at all, which was hardly surprising, thought Miss Spence, since she was for the first time in an environment where there were other young people of her own age. During any kind of free moment or interval for lunch, Raissa would make for what soon became her favourite location: the library, in a corner out of sight of everyone, especially everyone who might constitute a distraction. Strictly speaking, she should have been excluded from the library at certain times, especially when it was unmanned because of staff shortage, but Miss Spence decided to overlook this in her case and, telling no one, left it open for use on all occasions.

Once, she happened to take a class in the library which had no teacher that period and set them to do their usual work while doing some of her own. It was while stretching her legs after finishing that she chanced upon Raissa. The girl's head was down, fascinated by what she was reading and, as Miss Spence watched, the pages were being turned with surprising speed.

'She is a page reader!' said Miss Spence to the Headmaster later.

'But what was she reading?'

'I've no idea,' laughed Miss Spence. 'I was so shocked, I forgot to enquire.'

Everything came to a head suddenly after the term exams. When the papers were handed back in the physics class, there was general consternation when it was announced that two students had scored 100%. Robert MacIvor and Raissa Hussain. It was at that moment that each looked up and took notice of the other. Robert surveyed this girl who had challenged his superiority. Raissa, who had nurtured the idea that she was mentally matchless, was equally struck by the competition. Suddenly, there was a great deal of interest in the other results by students and staff. Who was the best scholar now? For years, everyone had deferred to Robert. But had he been surpassed?

To general amazement, when the maths results were read out the result was the same. Both had a perfect score. In Chemistry it was the same. After that they diverged. The next result was Philosophy which only Robert studied. He was awarded 92% for the essay questions there. Raissa took Biology and scored 100% again. Latin and Greek, which Robert alone took of the pair, produced marks of 100%. One subject alone remained and, because of the time required to mark so many essays, they had to wait a fortnight for it: English, in which Robert must have a distinct advantage. He was given 91% and Raissa, 93%.

The talk in the staff room was of this dusky girl with dark hair who had appeared out of the blue, stepped into the Fifth year without any preparation and out-performed every native speaker in what to her was a foreign language.

When John Simpson stopped Raissa in the corridor to congratulate her, she smiled demurely and at first said nothing. But curiosity got the better of him. 'How do you account for it? You've only been here a term.'

'Maybe it's because it's all I want to do. I just love it.'

Later that day, he pursued the question further with the Head of English. 'How did she, a foreigner, beat Robert at English? Explain that.'

'She has experience which is uncommon. It comes through in everything she writes and she writes so well. She uses prose as a technical device like music to create an effect. Everybody else just tells a story. She not only creates a gripping read, she conveys it vividly in a quite original manner. Everything she does is a fresh surprise. She is amazing.'

'Will she do English, then, later?'

'Not a chance! She is hooked on science. Obsessed.'

'How can that be?'

'She is already reading Einstein's papers.'

'Who put her onto them?'

'Nobody. She found a copy in the library. The one Robert made us buy for the school.'

The Hussain family had never seen a report card before. Since it had to be signed, Raissa had no option but to hand it over to be read, though she would rather have kept the matter of her success under wraps in case it drew attention to her schooling. The family knew children had to go to school by law, though not that she, being above the age, could have stayed at home. Had they known, she might have been kept back to serve in the shop. Since she was a female, nothing much was expected of her.

The head of her family was her grandfather who had arrived in the country later than the others, once they had become established. This was Suleiman, a grey-bearded patriarchal figure who could have earned good money as a look-alike in London cinema-land for some important biblical figure like Abraham or Moses. Suleiman was six feet two and lean, with a full head of hair the same colour as the beard. He had a high, august forehead, prominent cheekbones, a straight commanding nose and rather sleepy blue eyes from which he looked out upon a world very different to the one he had known in youth— a world of deserts and caravanserais, long journeys by camel, threatened by thirst, locusts, disease, banditry and even war. Except on special occasions, he moved and talked slowly and never entered the shop which was the lifeblood of his enterprising son, Ahmed, a very different version of his father but with dark hair, balding, and an increasing paunch due to his lifestyle as entrepreneur, constantly resorting to the provisions which were his livelihood. The truth was that Suleiman did not really understand the shop.—Oh, he understood trading well enough. But he was more hunter-gatherer than shopkeeper. The acquisition of money and what it could buy had always been far behind the adventure of the journey, the sights seen, the dominance achieved—over the other elements of the world, including weather, drought, pestilence, flood and mostly, other men. A good rifle and a biddable camel— or better, a string of them— and a good fire at night against the chill of the desert wastes, was his idea of paradise—and maybe a harem of women and numberless streams of cool, fresh water—these were the ideals of Suleiman's life.

Now that he found himself in a country full of streams his taste for water had departed. There was more water in Argyll than he had ever imagined possible. Rain fell continually on the high mountains and you could hardly journey a league without falling into a loch or a river. It was no place for camels. He longed for the dry air and space of the desert instead of this humid, rain-forested place in which you could hardly see a hundred yards for trees and kept bumping into people who were so different from all those he knew. They puzzled him so. He had no idea how to treat them. Mostly, they ignored him as if he were a temporary visitor from outer space. Since he habitually wore a white turban there was even a vague resemblance to the proverbial space-man.

Ahmed had been different from the beginning. Things attracted him, any kind of thing, and he early became a swapper of things he had and grown tired of, for others he liked the look of. This led him to realise that the brightest things of all—coins—could be accumulated if one were sufficiently skilful. It was a matter of knowing your customer, understanding his need and his greed, fencing with him to estimate what he would pay or take for the goods and then closing with the offer he couldn't refuse and standing fast.

Ahmed had been in the U.K. for several years, having arrived when it was easier to gain admission, on the back of a relative who had been admitted years before and set up a shop. Before that they had been in several places, Tajikistan, among others, including most of the countries round about. The religion of the family was some small sect for which an English name does not exist. It was related to many of the religions of the region and had borrowed freely from among their customs. Everybody deferred to 'The Great One,' the originator of all things. A few luminaries had, down the ages, received important spiritual insights about how men and women should live in the desert climate and these formed the rituals of the sect, which had been written down over the centuries and copied for general use. Praying three times a day was mandatory: before breakfast, lunch and dinner. No other meals were allowed. This was done facing the place of burial of 'The Great One' in the mountains not far from their Himalayan neighbours. Every time you referred to Him, you were supposed to say: 'Be thou at ease,' as if he were present and in the discussion, overhearing every word; or 'May he be at ease', if he were not, forms of words which, however, Ahmad had almost given up after years in a country which had no such requirement and valued efficiency above spirituality.

By this time, inevitably, Raissa had naturally learned to put off her religion with her clothes every time she put on the school uniform. Her time at school was preoccupied by lessons and books and assignments. The idea of stopping to pray before lunch was unthinkable. Anyway, lunch was a sandwich eaten at a desk while reading.

Her mother, Nemissa, was herself preoccupied with her two younger children, both at the local primary school, at which school uniform was not expected.

It was to Nemissa that she gave the report card. She was standing at the sink in the kitchen while the youngsters sat next door with Suleiman watching children's TV, about the only thing he enjoyed about his adopted country. So much TV had made of him an expert in the spoken language though he was unable to write and not good at reading. Having travelled so much, he had of course a gift for assimilating languages, these being necessary for bartering for weapons, women, food, water and especially, camels.

'What is this?' asked Nemissa, when the card appeared.

'It tells you about my performance at school.'

Nemissa dried her hands on a dishcloth and opened the report. 'I don't understand this. What is this Physics?'

'It's a subject, mother. Most of them don't know either, though they do it. You have to sign it.'

'Well, you better show it to your father.'

When Raissa did so a few hours later before dinner, he read it carefully. 'It seems to be quite good. The teacher says: excellent. But why only 93% in English? All the others are 100%.'

'Nobody ever gets 100% in it.'

'Why not?'

'I am not sure. Maybe because there are no right answers for comparison, only good ones and bad ones.'

'Do you like the school?'

'Yes. You have to sign it to say that you have seen it.'

When Ahmed had done so, Raissa put it into her satchel and said no more. After everybody had washed, family prayers followed, everyone on the carpet of the sitting room, facing India which was roughly the right direction. Then they sat together, cross-legged, on the floor and ate with their fingers from dishes spread out on a sheet between them, which mother and daughter fetched from the kitchen. It was the only time that Suleiman felt normal. It had always been this way in the desert, often under a sky filled with stars. The rain of Argyll, he reflected sourly to himself, made that impossible. The stars were often hidden by clouds. The rain and wind and cold would spoil the food in a moment if they were outside. Still, if there ever was a warm dry evening, which he had been told there was at times, but doubted, he would have them decamp to the back garden.

He noticed the corpulence of Ahmed whose belly seemed to roll on the carpet every time he bent forward in the prayer and wondered. How was this possible on the strict regime of meals they had? It never occurred to him that Ahmed was secretly snacking on the provisions for sale in the shop.

Raissa did not think about the prayers to The Great One very much. It was something you got used to doing; a ritual that brought order to the day. And when a passage from one of the holy books was read out by the principal male present, who happened to be Suleiman for the time being, she would think about her physics. The stars outside above the omnipresent clouds, she knew, were numberless, most never even noticeable with the naked eye. How did this amazing thing come to be? It was extraordinary. Einstein had the key, she believed.

When the prayers were over, Nemissa and Raissa would clear up while the others would watch television. Then Nemissa and she would put the youngsters to bed. As soon as possible, Raissa, who had her own room, would retreat to it again among her books. Television did not interest her much. If she had seen it, she would, perhaps, have learned that other people had gone beyond Einstein: Hawking, Penrose and others, and before them, Niels Bohr, Richard Feynman and Paul Dirac. The school was never likely to put her in their direction.

The family at Tigh-na-mara, out on the Atlantic coast was not so very different. Dinner was a family affair around a table looking out onto the trees which had been planted to protect the house from the winter gales. The three children sat between their parents. There was wine instead of water and knives, forks and spoons instead of fingers. There was no prayer before the meal because neither Hector nor Rose thought it necessary. They did not go in for God, except as an occasional swear word, usually by the former when something went wrong with a painting— a frequent occurrence. If anyone qualified there for the appellation 'The Great One,' it was surely Hector himself. He was a man full of stories and, since he read the Times and the Herald every day, full of judgements about politicians and their problems and even about sport in which he took an inordinate interest like most

Scotsmen. The difficulty— impossibility, he would say— of a Scottish team able to win at Twickenham was never far from his thoughts. But he was not fanatically anti-English like most of his tribe. Separation was not on his agenda and he viewed the possibility as a probable disaster.

And yet, increasingly, the status of Hector as paterfamilias, fountain of opinion, Lord of All He Surveyed, out on that rocky shore, at least, was under threat as Robert's quizzical mind applied itself with ever increasing depth and demand for rigour to the issues that wafted around the table. But, after many a difficult session at the table when Rose worried about the impending destruction, one evening Robert found himself for once on the back foot.

'I hear there is a competitor in the school these days,' said Hector.

'Yes,' said Rose, brightening. 'What is she like this brilliant girl?'

Robert masticated in silence for a time, considering, and eventually replied: 'I don't really know anything about her. We are in the same class most of the time. She answers very well and gets wonderful marks but that's all I know.'

'Would that not be a friend for you, then, if she is so clever?' said Rose.

'I don't really need a friend. I have so much to occupy me.'

'But it would be nice to have someone to talk to about it? Someone who understood and had the same interests?'

'Yes, I expect so. It might be useful to talk about one's pet subjects.'

'There you are then,' said Hector. 'You might find the conversation stimulating for a change. Isn't that what you always say? That nobody round here has anything worthwhile to say and you get bored by their company?'

'I suppose so.'

'Then why not invite her along here some afternoon at the weekend?' suggested Rose. 'She only lives two miles away. That's just a stroll.'

'I couldn't do that. I don't know her at all and it isn't likely she would agree. I couldn't ask someone who might not want to come.'

'Nothing ventured, nothing gained, Robert.' Rose persisted.

'You don't understand. She lives in a different world. That first day she turned up, she was dressed in a colourless sack that covered her from head to foot. There is even a helmet-thing to make sure her hair is covered over. Can you imagine that? It was quite a nice day, really. Warm too. Imagine being covered up like that on a hot day? Crazy.'

'You shouldn't write somebody off just because of her clothing,' said Rose.

'It's what the clothing means, don't you see? That is just the sign of other differences.'

'Well, that might be refreshing,' said Rose. 'It could be interesting to meet someone from another culture, so very different.'

'I don't disagree, mother, but it is not that simple. When you get to know people really well, there are bound to be consequences from these differences you both started out with.' A prescient remark, as time would reveal.

'Well, I think you should ask her out and hang the differences. It could be fun.'

'That is impossible. She is not amenable to conversation, shuts herself away among the library books whenever she can and has only one thing on her agenda.'

'And what is that?'

'Beating me in the exams.'

Hector laughed. 'Is that what you're doing then?'

'I don't follow?'

'Is that why you are always in your room swotting over some book?'

'Certainly not!' he replied angrily, at the deep injustice of this suggestion. 'I've always been like that. Before she ever arrived.'

'So you won't ask her, then?' said Rose.

'Not unless the circumstance arises and if I want to. And that isn't going to happen. She shuts herself off from everyone. Nobody is her friend and she is totally self-sufficient.'

4

For a time, this is how it was: Raissa was totally self-sufficient. Until one day, in the bus, Robert was reading a textbook by Richard Feynman and Raissa had chanced to sit across the short aisle from him.

Feynman had been the youngest physicist at Los Alamos during the years of the first atomic bomb. When the key of the safe containing the atomic secrets was mislaid he had picked the locks and gained access for a prank— which provoked apoplexy among the security people, terrified of them falling into enemy hands— and performed other wonders of ingenuity. When the Apollo space rocket went on fire, killing its occupants, he was the scientist who correctly realised that the rubber rings closing off the fuel had failed due to the rubber deteriorating. After World War II, at Caltech, two doors along from Murray Gellmann, discoverer of the quarks, Feynman had realised that the mysteries of colliding particles in Quantum Mechanics could be described far more easily by simple diagrams than by the complex mathematics of Neils Bohr. And so Feynman became the founder of Quantum Electrodynamics, an important advance on what had gone before. His three introductory university textbooks were unusually accessible— which is why Robert was so engrossed.

Raissa couldn't help but see the equations and diagrams and was instantly fascinated. Having nothing with her to read that day except school books, the knowledge that there was within a foot or two another book filled with things she knew not of, acted upon her like a powerful magnet. She stared and stared, trying to understand what lay so close.

Yet having difficulty because of the angle of the pages to her line of sight.

Behind her there were sniggers until at last someone tapped Robert on the shoulder and announced. 'The Paki fancies you, Robert.' There was some laughter at this.

Robert looked up from the book, turned and identified the interrupter, turned again and noticed Raissa staring at him with reddening cheeks. Turned again to the child behind and said: 'I don't think she is a Paki, as you put it. And,' looking down at the book and realising the real matter of her interest, 'I don't expect she fancies me. It will be my book that has caught her attention.'

Robert returned to his study of Feynman's university textbook and Raissa pulled out a schoolbook. For a minute or two, they each read with concentration. Then Robert looked up and across at Raissa. 'Would you like to see this?' It was an instinctive reaction. If you love ideas, the idea of sharing them is instinctive.

'Yes, I would. But I wouldn't deprive you of it.'

'Well, we could read it together. Only, you will have missed some of it.'

'I don't mind,' she said. So Robert moved his seat to join her.

And so the journey continued with the pair of budding scientists reading the book together.

After a few minutes, and wanting to turn the page, Robert said: 'Are you ready to go on?'

'Yes, I have been waiting for you.'

Robert blushed and turned the page. He never asked that question again because, as experience showed, it was never necessary: she read pages while he read paragraphs.

When the bus reached the school Raissa thanked Robert and went off to change her clothes before the first class.

All the rest of that morning— a time when they would not meet in class— he found his mind wandering to think about her. Of course it was a worry to find someone quicker than you were. That was the clear meaning of the experience with the book in the bus. Was she pretending to understand? No, he decided. She really was intelligent. What would be the point? It could be exposed so easily. It would just take a question.

He just knew that she would have the answer or, if not, there would be an excellent mitigating circumstance. Her marks in the exams allowed no other conclusion.

When they did meet in the afternoon in the maths class, the worry was still there and to general astonishment he fluffed a couple of answers. 'Mind not on the game today, Robert?' was the teacher's response.

The next day was the same and the next and the next. He realised that he had lost the plot. The matter was raised in the staff room and Miss Spence decided to take an interest. She waylaid Robert in the corridor and said: 'I wonder if you would come along to my office for a chat?'

'What about?'

'You and your work.'

Robert was sufficiently worried to answer: 'If you like.'

When they were settled on either side of her desk, Miss Spence began: 'So there really is something the matter.'

'I don't understand you.'

'You would never have agreed to come here if there wasn't. Spit it out.'

'I don't know what to say.'

'You mean you are too proud to say, is that it?'

Robert blushed, considered, and then with the relentless honesty of mind which was a characteristic of him, replied: 'Yes, you are right.'

Miss Spence sighed with relief. 'That's all right then. We can do something about it now. You remember this in future, if there is ever a problem: get it out. Don't suffer in silence. Too much depends upon you being at your best. Do you understand?'

'I think so.'

'You are very clever, Robert, but that is never quite enough. You need to take the right decisions, work very effectively and then, perhaps, just perhaps, you will develop into something really worthwhile. That's what we all want here: to see you make the most of yourself.'

She gave him time to adjust to this and said nothing, hoping he would lead. But he couldn't.

'What has got into you?'

'I am not myself. I can't concentrate. I keep thinking of other things. It's dreadful.' He put his hands over his mouth as if the effort of saying any more was too much.

'It's Raissa, isn't it?'

'Yes.'

'What is the trouble?'

'I suppose I am afraid.'

'You are intimidated by her intelligence?'

'Yes. She's quicker than me. I've never been in this position before and I don't like it. I can't seem to handle it. I know it isn't very manly and I'm very sorry if I have let you all down.' He described the experience on the bus with the Feynman book: out it flowed in a rush, like a dam breaking.

Miss Spence smiled, encouragingly. 'That's a marvellous response, Robert. It does you credit. As a human being, I mean— the one thing you do not value very much. You should, you know. It matters just as much as having a mind.'

They looked at each other for a few minutes without speaking. Then Miss Spence said: 'What do you think you ought to do?'

'I don't know.'

'Well, put it this way: what if you knew someone who was brilliant, like you— for that is what you are, Robert— what would you say to him?'

'That he must come to terms with the problem. Otherwise he'll never develop as he should and make the contribution to the world that he is capable of.'

'Right. And how should he come to terms with it?'

'I'm not sure.'

'The first thing is to be brave enough to do the right thing.' She gave him time to absorb this. 'Can you do this? It will take courage.'

Robert thought about this and then nodded. 'I will try.'

'Well, what would you tell this other brilliant talent that he ought to do?'

'I really don't know.'

'Accept that she is quicker. For that's all it is, Robert. Raissa reads more quickly than you do. Maybe she picks up things quicker than you do. But that isn't everything.'

'How do you mean? Isn't it enough? It means she can learn faster than me. That means she can learn more than me in the same time!'

'Exactly, that is it precisely. But, as you should know, it is not the fastest learner that makes the discovery. It is the person who sees deep into the problem and goes deeper than anyone went before. That is the original mind.'

Robert all of a sudden sat upright and brightened immediately. Then he stood up. 'Miss Spence, thank you very much. I think I will always remember this conversation. You have really made a difference to me.'

'One thing more, Robert. Don't you think you should befriend Raissa? Once you get to know her you will feel less intimidated.'

'—Or more!' replied Robert with a rueful smile. 'I shudder to think what else she can do. But I take your point. I have to do my best and it is better to know her as she really is than worry about nameless assets she possesses that I don't.'

Of course Robert made no move in her direction. They boarded the bus separately, sat separately and got off separately. And so it went on for a time. Robert's work improved but did not reach the raging level of confidence he had once possessed. It was as if he were condemned to live in the shadow of her quicker intelligence. Raissa's hand was raised at every question and she was streets ahead of everyone else and never wrong. Indeed, her answers were increasingly received with awe by her teachers. She would see things that the authors of the textbooks had never imagined or conceived. Robert became dispirited, his efforts lacked their former piercing rigour and it showed in his face and in everything he did.

Miss Spence decided to talk to Raissa and called her into her office one day. 'I wondered how were you settling in. Whether you were happy here?'

Raissa smiled radiantly. 'Yes, Miss. I have never been so happy in my life.'

'How are you managing with the language and the differences in our culture?'

'Very well, I think.'

'And at home, how are matters there?'

'Very easy. I am not much troubled. I have a few chores to do and I serve in the shop occasionally at week ends but I have plenty of time for things.'

'What things?'

'The things I want to do. My work. I enjoy it very much. My books.'

'And how about the bus? Are the other students difficult in any way?'

'No Miss. They treat me quite well.'

'Good. I wondered what you make of Robert MacIvor? He also travels on the bus.'

'Yes, I know.'

'Well, what do you make of him?'

'I don't know him.'

'You must know something about him. You are in the same class half the time. And in the bus.'

'He seems a very good student.'

'Would you say he is happy?'

Raissa considered the question for a moment. 'No, I suppose he is not. He is not as he used to be, I think.'

'Have you any idea why this might be?'

'No, I can't say I do.'

'Some of us are worried about him. I wonder if you might do me a favour?'

'Yes, if I can.'

'Befriend him. I think it would help him to have a friend. He seems not to have many friends. A bit bookish, like you. Maybe you could talk to him. You might like it and it might do him a lot of good.'

Raissa thought about this. 'It is not usual in my culture for a student like me to make advances to a student like him.'

'Yes, I can see that. But you would not be making advances.'

'He might not see it that way. I expect others would think that was what I was doing.'

'But if you made a useful friend, one you could share your enthusiasms with, it might be a price worth paying. What do you say?'

'I see what you mean, of course. It's just that I have never thought of approaching anyone before like this.'

'—Still less a young man of the same age. I understand. But that is not what you would be doing. You would be approaching him for his good not your own.'

'I don't know how.'

'All you have to do is engage him in conversation if you chance to meet him. Ask him if he liked the last lesson and discuss it with him. Any lesson will do. One thing will lead to another if I am any judge. You should have a lot to say to him. He will understand everything you say and he will have things to say himself. Try it. For me. Please. You would be helping him. He needs a friend and you are the most suitable person around.'

Of course, Raissa never did. No one in her culture would have contemplated such a move. It was unthinkable. Promises did not come into it. She had no experience of what she was supposed to do.

And so, for a time, there was little change.

But one day just before the start of the English class, Robert was sitting two rows behind and to one side of Raissa and he couldn't help noticing what she was doing: like a man in a race who cannot win because he is always looking at his opponent and takes his eye off the finishing line.

She was reading, as usual, filling every moment of the day with the relentless search for ideas—a state of mind he understood very well. Though he did not realise it, being too far away, Raissa was engrossed in a maths text-book somewhat in advance of their official stage of development.

Many functions can be expressed as power series, she read. A general power series, starting with a constant and increasing every step by another factor of x, was written down with variable constant coefficients and then differentiated term by term. Then, in each case, x

was given the value zero. This meant that every term but one vanished, leaving only the variable coefficient. In this way, one after the other, the coefficients of the series were directly obtainable. And this meant that any function[3] could be expressed as a series very quickly. This, she learned, was MacLaurin's Theorem, the theorem— the world class theorem!— of a man from Glendaruel in Argyll, not far away, as she was very soon to learn.

With growing excitement she saw this applied, first to the exponential function and then the exponential with ix in place of x [where i = √ -1] was written down almost immediately and what a wonder that was. But then the functions sinx and cosx were obtained by applying the theorem and in a flash, a flash of acute surprise, Raissa saw that cosx +isinx was identical to the exponential function with ix as the variable. It was a miracle! Who would have imagined such a connexion between three such apparently different sets of functions! The book did not take the matter any further—right away, at least. The mind that wrote it was not as good as hers. But she saw in an instant that if you replaced x by iπ then $e^{i\pi}$ = -1+0. That is, e to the power iπ plus 1 = 0. Mathematically, $e^{i\pi}$ +1 = 0.

Raissa jumped up in her chair and then stood up with an expression of unbounded astonishment on a face radiant with joy. Here was an equation of great simplicity which expressed the relation— EXACTLY!— between the 5 most important numbers that there are! Numbers that are, two of them at least, as incomprehensibly complicated as any in the universe! Utterly irrational and even transcendental[4]!

She felt as people report they do when they see God—or at least as Archimedes did when he discovered the law of displacement while lying in his bath. Mindless of his nakedness he had to tell someone. He

---

[3] In principle, at least. The series must converge for the values given. Some do not. But many do. Colin MacLaurin was appointed Professor of Mathematics at Edinburgh University on Sir Isaac Newton's recommendation.

[4] Transcendental: never the solution of an algebraic equation with rational coefficients.

had to run down the street naked shouting; 'Eureka! Eureka! I have found it! I have found it!'

Raissa was in the same state of amazement. She had to tell someone. She looked around her and saw her fellows. Whom could she tell? There was only one person in all that school who would understand what her understanding had that moment achieved: Robert. Robert would see what she meant.

She seized the book off the desk and in two strides was at his desk where she threw it down. 'Have you seen this!' she shouted. 'It..it..it's so woooooonderful!'

Robert, at first appalled by the sudden, seemingly aggressive move in his direction, relaxed, grinned broadly and stood up. They forgot everything, all proscriptions against contact between boys and girls in school— especially in a public place!—all taboos about contact between different races and cultures. They were enchanted with their shared love of these amazing ideas and Robert lifted his hands and laid them gently on her shoulders and, after a moment, she returned the complement. They stood for a full minute staring into each other's shining eyes and beaming face. And then the teacher entered the room and said: 'Well, I never! What is going on here?'

And Robert ignored the question, never even heard it put, never saw the teacher standing at the blackboard waiting for a response. Nor did she.

'Look!' he shouted. 'That's not all. Look here'— and he stooped to write on his English jotter. 'Replace x by $-x$ and $\exp(-ix) = \cos x - i \sin x$!'

'This means that:
$(\cos x + i \sin x)(\cos x - i \sin x) = e^{ix} \cdot e^{-ix} = e^{ix-ix}$ [adding indices] $= e^0$ which equals 1.

'Therefore, $\cos^2 x + \sin^2 x = 1$'

'That's lovely!' declared Raissa. 'Really beautiful. Who would have believed it? And so simple!'

They stood gazing in wonder at the result for a time and then became aware of the silence around them and looked up and saw the class, open-mouthed at this remarkable behaviour and then the teacher, standing by the blackboard, anxious to begin the lesson and quite unable to do so. Both faces reddened with embarrassment and, without another word, they quickly resumed their seats.

The lesson passed in a dream for them and they went their separate ways afterwards, only meeting up on the bus, where, as usual, they sat apart.

The next morning, it was the same. They occupied their usual seats and tried to ignore each other. And so it went on. And then one day, Robert came upon an argument in a book on philosophy he thought especially brilliant and he looked up and turned to her with a face shot with ecstasy, nearly weeping at the insight. Across from him Raissa saw it, recognised the symptoms and was compelled to get up and go to him—a thing unimaginable before— and enquire. 'What is it? What have you just seen?'

Without discussion they went to sit together near the front in empty seats, a pair of seats together, and Robert, almost in tears such was his delight, told her about *The Naturalistic Fallacy,* the idea that the word 'good', must be capable of definition and that anyone who sought to be a good person could not succeed without first discovering this definition and then applying it. How could you know what to do to be good unless you knew what the word meant? 'The idea is 2,500 years old—longer! Plato tried to do this in Athens in the fifth century BC and Socrates, his teacher, before him. And many thought they had done it, right down to John Stewart Mill and the Utilitarians. And they were all mistaken! G.E. Moore proved them all wrong!'

'But how? I don't see!' said Raissa. 'Didn't they define good as the greatest good of the greatest number? Whatever is good for the greatest number is the good thing to do.'

'But listen,' said Robert. 'Here is AJ Ayer's[5] version of the disproof. If 'good' is definable. Let it be identical to C. Then, we should be unable to make a statement of the kind: 'C is good,' for it could mean nothing. It would be a tautology. However, we make such statements all the time. We say this is good and that is good and even the greatest

---

[5] Ayer was a professor at Oxford, author of *Language Truth and Logic,* his Phd thesis, a demolition of Logical Positivism, a doctrine he had encountered in Vienna. Also *Problems of Philosophy et al.*

good of the greatest number is good. But they all have meaning, these statements. Yet if C really was identical to 'good', the statement should be meaningless.'

Raissa was poleaxed. 'How extraordinary!' she said in a hushed voice.

'So the search of philosophers for centuries was shown to be an utter waste of time by one man in 1903[6].'

Gradually, the two students began to sit together quite naturally and no one thought very much about it. Even the idiot proletariat realised that the attraction had nothing to do with the normal interests of the young. In the bus, the girl was so shrouded from head to foot in dark clothing that the idea that there might be some sexual content to the connexion was ridiculous. So no one made that connexion. Nor was there any such connexion. It was an association of like minds and nothing else.

Every day in the bus each would tell the other what he or she had been learning the night before, or what they had been working at. Gradually, the very problems that perplexed them assumed a greater and greater proportion of the time, for there were puzzles that seemed to defy solution; had defied solution for all eternity.

It was only natural that sooner or later one of them would refer to the heavens, to the great universe of space and then it was that a radical disagreement occurred. To Raissa, the author of the universe was The Great One. To Robert, there was no author. Each tried and failed to convert the other and after a while they had to agree to differ. It seemed that Raissa had an awareness of The Great One which Robert wholly lacked.

'I don't see how you can believe in a God who made everything. What evidence have you for this?'

Raissa was equally perplexed by his attitude. 'Look around you! What do you see but wonders? The land, the woods and streams and beaches and islands. How can you think that this came here by chance?'

---

[6] The year of publication of *Principia Ethica*, G.E. Moore's book on the subject.

'How can you imagine that some big guy up in the sky with a big white beard called it into being? That is ridiculous.'

'What about the marvellous things humans have done because of their creation by The Great One?'

'What about the millennia of rottenness and murder they have gone in for? They have only learned not to kill each other after centuries of failure and they are still learning yet, for they still murder each other, hundreds of thousands a year, either deliberately or by omission.'

There was nothing to be done about the disagreement except agree to disagree, at least for the time being, but every so often the subject would raise its head like a swaying cobra between them, threatening to strike one or other or both.

5

As the time of The Highers[7] was upon them, their studies began to focus exclusively on the work of the courses, which meant there was less to enthuse over. They were much taken up with answering exam papers because they were expected to by teachers. Then, all too suddenly, the exams were upon them and revision went on constantly, whole days spent at home revising before attending school only on the days of the exams.

Finally, it was over and there was a slack period for a few weeks while the papers were marked. It was a time once again for wide reading for the sheer pleasure of it and conversations started up again. At the prize-giving, Robert was made dux medallist because he had taken more subjects and Raissa, though of a slightly higher standard in a few, proxime accessit. Then the school broke up for the summer holiday.

Most days, Raissa, clad in the shapeless clothes of her culture, would serve in the shop by the quay and since it was arranged as a small supermarket, she had not much to do except man the check-out. Most of the locals shopped there habitually because it was far more convenient than the equivalent in Lochgilphead or Oban and these were augmented

---

[7] In Scotland, the exams secondary school-children take around the age of 17 before entering university.

by fishermen, yachtsmen and even campers, now that the weather had improved. Even so, there was much time for reading between customers and even some free time. Ahmed could hardly conduct his private struggle with the more delicious groceries while his daughter was around the shop. So he had a vested interest in being there on his own. Robert would work at his studies until about eleven each morning and then walk the two miles into Kinoidart to get the newspaper and, then it was, he would engage Raissa in conversation as usual.

Rose, Robert's mother, observed them together one day as she was passing and confirmed what she had been told: that the unlikely pair were firm friends.

Once Robert had gone, she returned to the shop and introduced herself.

'And how are you finding your life here?' she enquired.

'I am very happy. It is very interesting. And now that the weather is less like a damp freezer, I am enjoying it very much.'

'I hear you and Robert are great friends. Perhaps you would care to come and have tea with us some evening?'

Raissa, taken aback, said nothing.

'What about this week some time? It would be company for you both.'

'I don't think that would be possible.'

'Would you prefer him to ask you?'

'No, it's not that. I would be very glad to come and meet you. It's just that it's impossible.'

'You mean there is some objection?'

'Yes. It's not something we do in my culture.'

'But if you live here, don't you think you should try to integrate a bit?'

'Yes, I would love to.'

'Would you like me to speak to your parents about it?'

'No. It wouldn't do any good.'

'Maybe you'd rather speak to them yourself, then?'

'No. I don't have to ask. Some things you know instinctively.'

Raissa suddenly looked distressed and Rose felt sorry for her. Surely there must be a solution to this dilemma? People should be able to come and go a bit, especially if they had just arrived in a strange place.

'There is so much help and real pleasure your family could receive if only you were open to it.'

'I know. I have experienced it at school. It is wonderful. I feel so privileged. Some of the teachers are terrific.'

'Then why?'

'It's our culture. The things we believe. The rules and regulations. They are so different from yours.' And Rose saw the line of fracture in this family— like a fissure opening in the ground just before an earthquake— one of whose members was attending school with all that implied: of meeting new customs and ways of doing things as well as new ideas, while the others were still acting as if they were living in a dusty, desert, community under a blistering sun with tents to be folded every morning at dawn before they rode off on their camels to some point on the far horizon. But the fracture had to be on one side or other of the girl. And suddenly, Rose feared for her.

That evening, she mentioned it to Robert at dinner.

'She never goes anywhere,' he replied. 'She is either at home or at the shop. That's it.'

'Doesn't she even get to the pictures or a dance?' said Margaret, who had observed the goings on in the bus every school day but never sat near her elder brother but with other girls of her own age. 'That can't be good for you.'

'No, I agree,' said Rose. 'But I don't think there's anything we can do about it.'

'You could ask her out.' said Jane.

'I don't think she would want that,' said Robert.

'Well, I have an announcement,' said Hector. 'I sold a painting today. To a yachtsman in Kinoidart. It was hanging on the wall of the tea-room and he bought it.'

'Oh, well done, Daddy,' said the girls and everyone smiled.

'And that's not all. While I was there, I learned about a boat that is for sale. It's a day-sailer with a half deck fore and aft with a centreboard so it will do in shallow water. It has sails and oars and even a small outboard. What do you think? Should we buy it?'

'Can we afford it?' said Rose.
'The money from the painting will just about cover it.'
Everyone thought this a good idea. 'There is just one thing' added Hector. 'Everybody must take lessons on handling the boat. I don't want it capsizing. After the trouble you have been to us getting here, I don't want to lose anybody.'

After dinner, the two men walked into the village to collect the boat and sail it back home and Robert enjoyed his first taste of handling a sailing boat.

And so there were voyages of ever increasing distance around the coast among the islands and picnics in secluded places with white sandy beaches on which hardly a human foot had trod. The entire family went, or parts of it, as necessity demanded. Rose never really took to the sea and usually remained at home to do her domestic chores. The children, even the youngest, soon became proficient seamen and often went out themselves, if the weather was good, which, for a month that summer, it was exceptionally.

A fortnight passed before Robert went into the village to see Raissa and when next he did so, he sailed.

Seeing his smiling face, tanned by the sun to a light mahogany, her expression lit up with pleasure. 'Where have you been? I missed you,' she told him. 'I missed all our talks. I thought perhaps you'd given me up. Found a girl-friend or something.'

Robert laughed and told her about the boat and how he had been learning to handle her. 'That's my girl-friend.'

'Can I see it?'

'Sure. Come outside. She's beside the jetty, just a few yards away.'

Leaving the shop unattended, Raissa and he went down to the jetty to see the new boat.

'What is it called?'

'It's not an it. Boats are always 'she'.'

'Well, what is 'she' called?'

'My little sister, Jane, has baptised her Matilda.'

'What is baptised?'

'Cracked a bottle on her bow. There was a ceremony with a bottle of *Babycham*. We had to pick up the broken glass afterwards. We haven't painted the name on her yet.'

They stood for a while on the jetty looking down on the little boat.

'Did you know that Einstein sailed a boat like this near Princeton?'

'I didn't know. Is that in America?'

'Yes. He was at the Institute for Advanced Study. The loch was not far away. It seems to have been his only recreation apart from the violin.'

If the boat had been interesting before to Raissa, it now took on the significance of a sacred object. She looked down upon its trim decks and furled sails with longing.

'Would you like to go for a sail?'

'Yes, I would. I would very much like to. But I have to mind the shop.'

'Then sometime when you are free we'll sail together. What do you say?'

'I am not sure how it could be managed,' she said, with regret.

'Do you never do things you are not supposed to?'

'Never.'

'Well, life must be very dull. Everybody here does what they want most of the time. Why don't you ask your Dad?'

'Some things you don't need to ask.'

'Well, you must do it in secret. Then,' he said, with an inspired insight, 'you will be just like Einstein,' the scientist above all that Raissa admired, 'wafting around Princeton Loch in the breeze.'

'If I wasn't minding the shop, I would come with you right this minute. But I can't. Not now.'

'Tomorrow, then? When would you be free?'

'I can't wait that long. What about this evening? About seven?'

'Will I meet you here or collect you out of sight round the point?'

'Round the point would be best.'

'At seven this evening, then?'

'Yes.'

And so by seven o'clock that evening, Robert had sailed the boat up the channel towards Kinoidart and beached her on the other side of the hill that protected the village from the wintry gales of the Atlantic. A path wound downwards to the beach through the woods and there he waited.

'You climb in and I'll shove her off,' said he, when she arrived, dressed as ever in her usual costume. 'I don't suppose you would be able to change into something more appropriate without giving the show away?'

'No, but it is warm, too warm for these.'

'Well, if you make a habit of this we'll have to fix it. Your habit, I mean.'

'My clothes?'

'Exactly. Anyone sailing will know who you are from the clothing. It would be better if you were dressed more normally. Then no one would say anything.'

'I don't have any other kinds of clothes here. The school uniform is kept in a locker there.'

'Then we must acquire some others. If you like it, I mean. Sailing.'

'I love it. How could I not?'

'You feel like Einstein, don't you?'

'Yes, except for the violin.'

'I can provide that.'

'So you can. I have heard you playing. At school.'

'Between the pair of us, then, we can feel like Einstein.'

They sailed seawards, tacking past the house and outside the sea loch altogether and then they beached the boat. As he helped her out, Robert said, 'Margaret would lend you something to wear. You are about the same size. What would you agree to wear?'

'The same as you, I expect.'

'You mean shorts and a shirt? You would need gym shoes or something like that which can get wet and dry off.'

'If I gave you money you could buy them for me.'

Robert agreed and they talked sizes for a time. Raissa would never be in a position to go shopping without her mother in close attendance.

A couple of hours later before dark, Robert deposited her back at the foot of the Mound and she walked home without incident or enquiry. When asked, she merely said she had been out walking.

A few days later, Robert appeared at the shop with a plastic bag. 'I brought your clothes. They are to be a present from my family. If there is nobody about why don't you go and try them on?'

Raissa did so and soon emerged in a pair of pink shorts, a yellow shirt and a pair of blue shoes. 'How do I look?'

'A touch colourful. It was my dad's idea. He thinks you need to be easily identifiable, in case you fall in. He is the same about us. We are to wear yellow life jackets. The shoes are proper yachtsman's with flat soles that give a good grip.'

'Where will I store them?'

'Either in a bag in the woods or on the boat. Whatever you think best.'

'I might be seen changing in the woods or an animal might interfere with my clothes. I wouldn't want that, now that I've been given them. I really like them, you see; like the uniform. I like it too. People have been very good to me. Please thank your family for me.'

'You can thank them yourself. You'll meet them next time we go out in the boat. I'm to sail you home for lunch or tea, whichever seems best.'

Raissa wasn't so sure about this and showed it.

'How can it do any harm to come and meet my family and have a snack?'

'Well, our food is supposed to be of a certain kind.'

'You mean like the Muslims? Halal food? That's no problem. Just eat what you can and don't if it offends your regulations.'

'But I might not know what it is made of and it would be embarrassing to have to ask for all the details every time. That's why we don't mix. We never eat pork, that's the main thing. Pork has worms.'

'Not nowadays, it doesn't. Never mind. How would sandwiches do? With egg or tuna-fish filling?'

'I think that would be all right. We eat bread. My mother used to bake her own but now she just uses the kind in the shop.'

'Well then, it's settled. Off course, you'll drink the aquavitae?'

'Water of Life? Yes, I expect I could drink that. I also take tea and coffee.'

Robert merely smiled.

A few days later, Raissa managed, as she expected, to be able to escape the confines of the shop, pleading the need for a walk in the woods. Her mother was happy to do a turn, with the youngsters playing around her on the floor behind the cash desk. By arrangement, Robert was waiting for her at the other side of the Mound. 'We can go ashore somewhere and you can change. There is a secret beach just around the headland past our house. I believe it is ideal.'

And so they sailed and Robert gave Raissa instructions about the set of the jib and the need to duck when gybing.

Around the headland just to the north, was a short swathe of delicate white sand, so soft, your feet just sank into it. Best of all, there was a stretch of water right behind the rocks on one side into which the boat could be moved, still in the water, and concealed behind them without having to beach the boat and pull it ashore.

Robert got out and pulled the boat through the water until it lay hidden from the sea and under the high cliff and so also protected on the landward side. 'It really is a perfect place, isn't it? Let this be our special place. What do you say?'

Having come ashore with the boat still afloat in the small natural channel, Raissa was looking around herself with wonder. There was a cave carved out by millennia of high tides and storms and the sand continued all the way inside. She soon found she could stand up in it for several yards. Here again the sand was as if swept clean by a besom, it was so smooth and pure. Then, going outside, she noticed the flowering plants that grew upon the sides and crevices of the cliff above them. There were whites and creams and pinks and the powerful yellow of the gorse that stood protectively at the top of the cliff.

'It is a magical place. No one has been here before, I think.'

'Then we are the first. You could change in the cave, if you like.'

And she did.

'What will we call this place?'

'Our place. Or the place. What need of a name.'

'Come on, we must get home. It will soon be lunch-time.' Raissa boarded, Robert gave it a push and the sail was soon up and carrying them back the way they had come.

Raissa sat on the foredeck and listened to the water as it swished past. It was to be her favourite place on the boat, a place of contentment of a kind she had never known or imagined. But the best place of all was the smooth, silky, sandy, pure white beach.

In a fresh breeze they were soon at the house on the spit and they walked up to it in a happy silence.

Robert introduced everyone formally and they shook hands. 'Come, Raissa, join us in the dining room and sit here among us. Before her on the table-mat lay a white object, the same colour as the object on every other place. Everyone smiled and put on their paper hats. 'You are supposed to do the same, Raissa,' said Robert.

'But it's not the same as the others.'

'That's because yours is special.'

Wondering, and a trifle nervous at these unexpected developments, Raissa put on the hat. It was different in having a very broad brim with a string underneath.'

'She looks wonderful, doesn't she? I told you,' said Robert to the others. 'This is a present from me myself. The floppy hat will conceal you from prying eyes and the string will keep it on, even in a gale. I hope you like it. It's a good fair weather sailing hat, I think.'

'Can I see it in a mirror?'

'Certainly', said Rose who was dressed in a Laura Ashley, heavily patterned in mauve tones. 'There's one right behind you.' Raissa turned and looked and smiled and then turned to Robert and said, 'Thank you very much, I am very pleased.'

Jane passed the sandwiches and soon everyone was talking at once— except Raissa, who was not used to any of this.

'What will you have to drink?' said Hector who was wearing a kilt that day and a white shirt.

'Robert mentioned you had aquavitae?'

Everybody laughed. 'That's whisky,' said Hector. 'I wouldn't drink that myself at lunchtime. I'd never do any work afterwards.'

'If you would really like to taste it, I am sure we could make an exception,' said Robert, mischievously.

'I don't think your religion would approve,' said Rose. 'It is very strong alcohol.'

'I'll drink tap-water, then. I understand you are an artist,' said Raissa, as Robert poured from the jug. 'That's something I know nothing about. What is it that you do?'

'Try to do, for now at least.' Hector began to reflect on the question, one that was rarely made in that group for fear of hurting his feelings, for the failure to sell paintings was still a failure and one that affected everyone by depriving them of money they not only could use but needed if they were not to be disadvantaged relative to other students with wealthier parents.

'Every artist has different ideas about what he is trying to do, whether he is succeeding and what the effort is for. The most important thing is to advance the subject— a bit like science, I suppose. If you don't do anything new, you haven't made it, aren't successful. I expect you realise this. I still have a number of conflicting aims which are unresolved— maybe they never will be— I have to believe the creative tension will help me generate something worthwhile. First, there is the desire to create something different—if it's the same as other people's, it's no good. Then, it should be beautiful in some way—if people don't want to look at it what is the point? They'll tell everybody else not to bother. So you're wasting your time. It mustn't be repulsive. So it is to be different, beautiful, something that people want to look at and also something that provokes a response—if it leaves people cold it has failed. It should engage the emotions. People who see it should be changed by what they see, by the experience of standing looking at it— maybe not right then but later, perhaps, when they've thought about it. I think, too, it should have dramatic quality, should attract and engage the viewer. Like a play. Like Hamlet or Macbeth.'

'What about *Look Back in Anger*? said Raissa. 'We read that at school and saw part of it on a video. It was not beautiful. It was angry and lacking in any grace or delicacy.'

'There are you then. It provoked a response in you, engaged your emotions. It did not leave you dead in the water. I bet you were changed by it. You would have seen a slice of life that we don't have around here in this sheltered spot.'

'So it doesn't have to be beautiful in the conventional sense?'

'No. Quite right. It is beautiful in another sense; it is engaging, riveting, I'd say, and it has a message that the world needed and wanted at the time. That's why it was successful: it was new and it was wanted and it expressed things that needed saying and offered a voice that many people flocked to hear. That was art all right.

'And you are right. I should be trying to do these things too. That is what I suppose I mean by provoke.'

Robert said: 'So *Trainspotting* is worthy because it tells us, those of us who do not know that world, about that world of drugs and poverty?'

'Yes, that's why it is enjoyed. It has a message and it matters and most people did not understand what that world is like until they saw the film. That's why artists often submerge themselves in alternative worlds— at least for a time— so that they understand them better and the people in them and the problems they have, the solutions, or lack of them, that they discover to cope with that world.'

'John Steinbeck stayed with a dirt-poor family for months before he wrote *The Grapes of Wrath*.'

'You've read that, Raissa? Good for you.'

'Dickens's novels had this effect, perhaps more strongly than any art ever did. His depiction of poverty and the real lives of the poor of Victorian England without a welfare state did much to provoke changes in the Factories' Acts and the conditions of the workers. For the first time, people—wealthy people with the power to change things, yet cut off from the poor and unable to recognise their suffering— could see just how miserable and unhappy were so many lives. And it became fashionable to do something to improve their lives. Dickens changed the laws. That's how important his art was. And the laws changed society very quickly. It became unlawful to exploit the workers, to employ children down coal mines and in mind-numbing jobs in factories from morning till night.'

Thus was the first of many visits to that lonely, run-down but charming house out on the spit of land between the village and the broad ocean. Raissa kept her yachting clothes on the boat in a locker in a waterproof bag and changed into them whenever it was convenient, usually in the woods, after collecting them from the boat when Robert met her. Not a word was said to his parents about this arrangement or to her own.

Every day they could, they spent at 'their place': the idyllic little beach with white sand, well-hidden, out on the Atlantic coast. There they would read and think and enthuse, discuss and argue and, sometimes, violently disagree.

Her mother observed them one day in the shop unexpectedly and realised that there was no difficulty, for they were locked in a terrible dispute and, at the time, tearing strips off each other, using every atom of wit and sarcasm in their power to diminish the other's case. The rigorous mind is demanding and causes trouble everywhere around it. Passionate about truth, it gets genuinely angry at the failure, or apparent failure, to understand the insights that seem obvious to it.

This was a boy from school, she realised, and knew from Raissa's behaviour that nothing had changed. All that hot summer they got used to her going off to walk in the woods and high places around the village with a book for company, and it concerned them not at all. This village was as tranquil as they had ever known, as free of everyday difficulties as they could imagine. There was almost no chance of being burgled or robbed or mugged in the street. All they had to do was man the till and fill the shelves. Easier by far than making ends meet in a war-zone in danger of being blown up by one side or other, or one warlord or other, just as bad.

It never occurred to them that their daughter went sailing in a boat or that she had company, especially male company. All was peace and tranquillity, all the more enjoyable after so many years of not knowing if they would survive the next day.

The day after the big bust up in the shop, they did not see each other for a few days but then the Highers results arrived through the letter box and they had an immediate impulse to find out how the other had done. Robert was awarded six A's and Raissa five. They set off to meet almost directly and did meet on the other side of the Mound as usual. As Raissa was coming down the path through the woods, Robert was approaching in the boat. As soon as the keel grounded, Robert was out and running. When they met, their eyes immediately recognised that the highest results possible had been won by the other. Robert put his hands lightly on her shoulders and she did the same. 'Now will you collect your clothing and get changed so that we can get away. What a fine day it is. What a pity to waste it.'

Afterwards, after they had reached their beach and lain down on towels on the sand to read and had read for an hour or more with concentration, Robert laid aside his book and said: 'I'm going to do a sixth year. What will you do now?'

'I don't know. I shudder to discuss it at home. If I say nothing, I hope they will let me stay on too. They will think that is normal. If I say anything, they will address themselves to the consequences.'

'You are going to university, aren't you?'

'I hope to but I'm not sure how it can be managed.'

'What would your parents expect you to do—in normal circumstances?'

'To serve in the shop until I marry.'

'That would be a waste.'

'Yes. I would have to wait until someone suitable was found.'

'You mean an arranged marriage?'

'Of course. My parents would have to approve. A young man will expect a dowry. An older man might pay for the privilege.'

'So there would be no love involved?'

'No, not usually. Sometimes the couple have feelings for each other but love comes later. So at least my mother says.'

'What do you think about that?'

'It's what we always do. What should I have to think about?'

'But you've read Jane Austen and even Barbara Taylor Bradford, for heavens sake. You know what love can do for you?'

'I know the trouble it can cause. Women often fall in love with the wrong person from the point of view of living together. That's why they separate after a few years.'

'So love is not all it's cracked up to be?'

'I don't know. I've never had the experience. Maybe I never will. Maybe it comes after years of married life when care has been taken to make a suitable arrangement.'

'Well, I think the whole idea of an arranged marriage is crazy. I won't marry for anything but love and it will be the enduring variety.'

'How will you know when you have found it?'

'How can I know that? I've never experienced it either. But then my head is stuck in books most of the time. A lot of people our age seem to fall in and out of love by the year or even the month.'

'But they have nothing else to do except moon around each other.'

'Where will you live when you marry?'

'I've no idea. Wherever I am taken.'

'You mean, you have no choice?'

'I shouldn't think so. My father will decide who it will be and that person will decide where I am to go.'

'So you will be a camp-follower to cook and bear children?'

'That's about it.'

'And you accept this?'

'What else can I do? I have no choice. I have no job or means of support— even if I wanted to leave my family. If I don't obey, I will be cast out and then where would I be?'

'You could come and stay with us.'

'No, I could not. It would not be right. Your family has enough trouble. There are five mouths to feed and three people to educate. And there isn't enough money.'

'How do you know that?'

'From things you said.'

'You could still come to us.'

'No, I could not. It wouldn't be right to add to your parent's troubles. They have enough on their plates already.'

Soon after this it rained and all sailing was given up for a time. When they met it was on terra firma, usually walking in the woods above the village, always clutching a book. At that time, Raissa was devouring poetry books in between the better quality true-life romances.

'How can you spend hours reading that stuff when you face an arranged marriage?' said Robert, in exasperation one day. And another argument started.

'I enjoy reading these stories. Why shouldn't I read them?'

'But they're not profitable. They teach you nothing. You can't learn anything from them.'

'Not so! I learn what it is like to be in love and what the problems are. If it weren't for these rubbish romances, as you call them, I would know nothing at all. How could that be better?'

'Better that you don't waste your ability on rubbish.'

'We are not just minds, Robert. We have emotional and biological needs. If we were just minds walking around on two legs we would be pretty boring people. Maybe attending to our emotional needs helps us to attain all that we might achieve. I don't expect Einstein went through life without love.'

'No. He married young and married again and had a mistress, I think, at Princeton. His housekeeper, perhaps. I'll look it up or lend you the book. But, for sure, Einstein didn't waste his time on romantic fiction.'

'I am quite sure he read his share. He was a human being, after all. It is something humans need to know about. Before it happens to them.'

All too soon the summer holiday was over and it was back on the bus each morning to school. Life followed the familiar pattern— except that there was less pressure, for the level of success each had achieved meant that there was no university in the land they could not reasonably expect to attend. When Robert filled in forms for Cambridge, not knowing if he could afford to go, even if accepted, Raissa did the same, having nothing better to do at the time. The idea that she might actually be able to take up a place was too outlandish for her to contemplate, despite the belief among the staff that it would be possible— somehow. A scholarship for both became the joint ambition among the staff and the classes were arranged in part to allow tuition in the kinds of questions students might be asked. It was assumed that Raissa would be able to travel to Cambridge with Robert to attend the interviews and take the papers— if invited. And it was deemed pointless to attack the problems with the parents that were probable until they actually presented themselves and that would only come with success in the application. Because there were two of them in this exalted position, it made sense to arrange things that way by releasing staff occasionally from teaching students outside this advanced programme. What could not be justified for one student could for two—especially two such good students.

Throughout the year, a great deal was gained by the scholars themselves, acting upon each other, as the staff were aware. Robert's early training in philosophy—a training in argument— was invaluable and there was hardly a person on the staff who could take him on. Anyone who did risked the most humiliating destruction, for the young argue to kill and Robert was entirely careless of the scars his razor-blade intelligence could inflict. Raissa learned a lot from her discussions with him but she brought to these a quality less evident in his mind: intuition, allied to a deep insight: close to what the ancient Greeks would have recognised as the first signs of the wisdom expected of the highest class in *The Republic*: The Guardians.

Robert, having far more freedom, began to spend more time among the other adolescents of the area, occasionally collected in their cars, often borrowed from parents and once or twice reaching home a day late, utterly intoxicated after late night celebrations, such as when Oban won at shinty, Scotland at Rugby or England got beaten by anybody. Such is the Scottish psyche for too many. There were even women and parties and a few experiments of a biological nature, as he would explain later, with a straight face to Raissa: 'I never had the advantage of a course in the subject. So I have to make shift as best I can and find out how things are, off my own bat, so to say.'

'Well, what did you discover?' Raissa would reply, also straight-faced. 'Maybe I can fill you in out of my exhaustive studies of the subject in which, as you may know, I am judged an expert.'

Robert would then pretend to give detailed instructions as to how to produce an orgasm in a woman and then add: 'Of course, you wouldn't understand any of that.'

Raissa would blush and reply: 'I doubt that would do any good at all.'

'You mean you don't know?'

'Of course I don't know. I've never done any of it.'

Because of the blush, this was a conversation Robert liked to repeat out of devilment but soon Raissa got wise to this and would wave a finger at him and stride off in the opposite direction as if his company had become offensive to her.

When the time came to attend the University for interview, surprisingly, Raissa was allowed to go without comment and given money to stay overnight in a college.

Because Ahmed continued to wear a turban, he was not much engaged in conversation by anyone: he was taken by the natives as too much of a native himself, though of another kind and another culture. But a few incomers with nothing better to do had passed the time of day and knew that Raissa was considered an academic star at the High School she attended. Word of the possible scholarships at Cambridge had filtered through to them and they only wished they had children of their own who could add lustre to the family escutcheon by winning one. That much Ahmed absorbed. Since there was evidently profit in this activity—though of what kind was not immediately clear— he was for it. Time would tell what profit there might be. If it added to the family name, he would go along with it and he even took a pride in handing over £100 for the journey and accommodation, a sum he judged sufficient. The idea that he or a member of the family might have to travel as a chaperone never occurred to him. She went by bus everyday to school 18 miles away, didn't she? So why should a journey to a university in the company of other classmates be any different? It was just a bit further, that was all. It was under school auspices? That was enough. He had great and probably undeserved faith in the Scottish School System, like many another.

Thus it came about that Raissa and Robert travelled to Cambridge one day, slept in separate college rooms and were interviewed the next day by the tutors of a few colleges.

These were, to say the least, intrigued to receive applications from two such diverse people from one comprehensive school out on the far periphery of the country.

Usually, successful applicants are informed after the students have returned home and after exhaustive discussions have taken place. In this case, the matter was easier. Indeed, the two were such excellent candidates that they were told the outcome together that very day, for there was a perceived danger that they might just be head-hunted by their older rival not far to the west or even snapped up before making a decision about Cambridge.

'We would like to offer you each a scholarship,' they were told. 'Are you happy about that?'

'Yes!' they both cried.

'But, we cannot accommodate you both in one college. So what is proposed is that you, Robert, go to Trinity and you, Raissa, to Emmanuel. How does that sound? At least you will be in the same university. We understand, from your teachers as well as yourselves, how important you have been to each other in your intellectual development. This would allow you to continue in this vein.'

It sounded very well indeed and they said so. Only very much later did the irony of the choice for Raissa emerge: Emmanuel was of course an alternative name for Jesus Christ. Not the most inspired choice of name for one of her esoteric religious persuasion.

And so, after a celebratory coffee in the late afternoon, they made their first acquaintance with Heffer's bookshop and then, on impulse, attended a concert that very evening that was advertised in a board in the shop.

A string trio was playing chamber music and Robert loved it. Raissa thought it very civilised, a judgement she would soon learn to apply to many things or not, as the case may be. On the return journey, they read, discussed, enthused and speculated about what it would be like at Cambridge and then they were home again and as everyone could very well see: nothing much had changed except that two futures were now well-defined and mapped-out. The rejoicing at school and in Robert's home was spectacular; in Raissa's, it was worth an extra glass of orange juice.

6

That was the year that Alexandrovna Katusheva arrived in Oban to teach Russian—her native language—as well as Arabic and Mandarin Chinese. No post was advertised. At the start of the autumn term she simply arrived out of the blue and announced herself. The School Secretary spoke to her in the reception office and was so struck that an interview with the headmaster was immediately arranged. When she arrived in his office, his shock was even greater. Alex, as she explained she preferred to be called, stood about five feet seven inches tall and had a pale symmetrical face with high cheekbones of startling beauty overtopped by a great mane of auburn hair that fell in shining waves about her face. She walked in like a ballet dancer on low- heeled white shoes and sat down in front of his desk without invitation as if she owned the place. She wore a pale-blue skin-tight trouser suit of some soft light material which matched her striking blue eyes and revealed a spectacularly slender shape of the finest sort.

As soon as she began to speak, the headmaster was riveted, for here was a foreigner who spoke English better than anyone he had ever heard. Admittedly, it was English of such perfection that only many years of study with an expert elocutionist could have produced such quality. The words fell from her lips like music. Pronunciation was accurate to a degree he had never before encountered. It was as if the linguistic equivalent of Jascha Heifetz, the violinist, had walked in. Every note was perfect, every move exactly correct. Anyone who heard the language spoken in this way immediately moderated his own to try to match it, as the headmaster found himself doing as soon as he had recovered from his surprise.

Having given her name, she presented herself as a person qualified to teach Russian, Arabic and Chinese and asked for a job. She produced certificates of degrees from three universities on the continent, one of them a doctorate, a diploma from a college of education in England and even, God be praised! one from the Scottish Education authorities entitling her to teach in schools like Oban. All the checks were there in her handbag. The distinction of her appearance and presence was matched by the documents which all told of an exceptional teacher.

And since a language teacher had just left suddenly on maternity leave for a year, and there was a vacancy the headmaster had not expected to fill, it was a miracle.

Laughably, the questions asked were, at first, peculiar: 'Can you give help with other activities? Like sport?'

'I was a gymnast. I represented my school and even the first university I attended. I could teach this. I can also teach ballet.'

'What made you give up gymnastics?'

'I needed the time for music.'

'Oh? Do you play an instrument?'

'Yes. The violin.'

'So you played in a chamber group, did you?'

'No, I was the soloist of the orchestra.'

'The university orchestra?'

'No. The Leningrad Symphony Orchestra.'

'You were the soloist of the Leningrad Symphony Orchestra?'

'Yes.'

'How many times did you perform?'

'About ten times over a few years. I also played in others.'

'Why ever did you give it up?'

'I enjoyed it but my heart was not in it. The idea of travelling the world to play every week, live out of a suitcase and practise several hours a day did not appeal to me. Besides, I wanted to study other things. I left to attend other universities.'

'And so you did!' said the Headmaster, though the effort of translating the certificates was not easy, despite being in Latin.

Everything seemed to be 'summa cum laude' which required no translation, a phrase rarely encountered in the certificates of school teachers.

'And what brings you here? When you could go anywhere.'

'I have been reading about Scotland and I came here to experience it. I like the look of Argyll and I will find a house here and live for a time, I think, if I am allowed.'

Thus was it that Alex settled into a small, very private, detached house in a wood on a hill overlooking the sea and joined the teaching staff—which determined how Robert spent much of his sixth year. As well as mathematics and physics he took lessons in Russian and Mandarin in a class with others and received individual tuition in violin playing.

Dr Katusheva's ear was so perfectly attuned that she could detect in an instant the slightest aberration of pronunciation or playing, which made her continually interrupt until the student had it perfectly. The rigour of this process appealed to Robert, though to few others. Under her supervision his violin playing advanced by leaps and bounds and by the end of the term he played before a spellbound audience in the School Assembly Hall, one of the great partitas of Bach, number 3, in which every melody is heavenly and every alternating one, original genius. The applause at the end was deafening. At the conclusion, Robert bowed a few times, called for silence and then addressed the crowd. 'I am very grateful, thank you. But I am more grateful than I can express to Dr Katusheva, my teacher. And you have never heard her play, that is the pity of it. I wonder if you would agree to hear her play? As a favour to me?'

The move was completely unexpected. Alex was sitting in the front row with one or two of the staff. Without waiting or receiving permission, Robert left the stage, violin in hand, descended the stairs at the side and crossed to where she was sitting. 'Please will you come and play for us?' he asked. And when he received no reply, he stretched out a hand, took hers in his, raised her up and led her back to the stage, at the centre of which he handed her the violin and the bow, stepped back and bowed to her and then went to stand at the side. It was a very mature move for a school-boy and took everyone aback by its suddenness and confidence of execution.

For once, for the first time, Alex was, at first, left with nothing to say. Then, without preamble, she began to play and it was as if Heifetz were playing: everything perfect, every note, every tone, every interval, every hint of colour, exact, never too much or too little and then there was the music itself. It was the opening of Beethoven's concerto—a passage as difficult as any in the repertoire, a passage that had never sounded the same from one player to another or even by a single player alone, on separate occasions, because of the difficulty. It was a solo passage at the start and that was just one of the difficulties: playing such a difficult sequence cold without any kind of help from the orchestra.

She played the whole of the opening and of all interpretations it was more akin to Heifetz's than anyone's. The applause was rapturous. Robert came on to shake her by the hand and together they left the stage.

Many came to shake Robert by the hand and Alex also. After ten minutes of it, Robert dashed off to take refuge in the toilet. The effusions of admiration had eventually almost unmanned him. When he emerged ten minutes later, everyone had departed. He walked out into the playground and stood, holding the violin case and wondered how to get home. A car drew up beside him. It was Alex. 'Get in,' she said. And he did.

'How do you feel?' she asked.

'High as a kite! I'll never sleep tonight. I had to leave, I'm sorry. It was all too much. I thought I would burst into tears.'

'I know what you mean. I have felt it too. What would you like to do?'

'Have a drink. Several drinks! I need something to make me come down to earth.'

'Well, we could go to a bar. But you are wearing a school blazer. They might not serve you. I think you must come home with me. There you can drink safely.'

Apart from a huge garage at one side, the house by the sea had a bedroom, a sitting room, a dining area and a kitchen and bathroom, nothing more, as was immediately plain. But it enjoyed privacy, concealed among trees and this helped.

A bottle of red wine was opened and when that was finished—after excited chattering by Robert mostly, who could not sit still but strolled about the verandah overlooking the moonlit sea beneath—they ended up, once he had taken in over half a bottle, sitting on the rug in front of a blazing fire and another was broached.

'How do you like it here?' said Robert, at last focusing upon the lovely lady beside him.

'I enjoy it very much. The scenery is beautiful, the natives are friendly and I have much to do and am rewarded for it. You cannot imagine how wonderful it is to have a pupil like you to teach.'

'Where is it you come from?'

'Borodino, near Moscow.'

'The scene of the great battle. And you came here? That was extraordinary. Did you fly from there?'

'No, from Tashkent.'

'What were you doing there?'

'Research. I have been all over. Afghanistan, Pakistan, India, Iran, Chechnya, Kazakhstan, other places.'

'Arabia? Iraq?'

'There too.'

'What is the topic of research?'

'It is about my family. I have been following them up, finding out about them, where they lived and what they did.'

'And you came here? Were any of them in Scotland?'

'I don't think so.'

'So what brings you here?'

'Information. People who knew my family.'

'Have you any brothers and sisters?'

'No. I am alone. My mother and father are dead. That is why it is important to me. When my mother died a year or two ago I began to look into their history.'

'What did your father do?'

'He was in the army. My mother too, originally.'

'And they are both dead? So you are all alone. That must be difficult?'

'Yes, I make the best of it.'

'And are you lonely here?'

'Yes, I am lonely everywhere.'

'And is there no man in your life?'

'Only you.'

Robert blushed and had the grace to laugh. 'I'm not much of a man, I'm afraid. Sometimes I feel like a learning machine. Fit only for remembering things or solving problems. I can't tell you how grateful I am to you.'

'You will be a man sooner than you think.'

Alex leaned over and kissed him full on the mouth. Robert was astonished. 'I've never done that before! Another first.'

'You did nothing, Robert. Did you like it?'

Robert sat up: 'Like it? Half the school has been dreaming of kissing you and now I have. It is the first time.'

'I thought so. That's why I took the initiative.'

Robert gulped on a throat suddenly parched with nerves despite the wine. 'Could we do it again?'

'Of course. You try.'

And so an introduction to kissing took place, on top of all the other instruction he had received. Robert proved an avid student at this activity as well as the others.

After a while he rose and said: 'I suppose I must be going. I have far to go and should leave you to get to bed.'

'It is too far to go, especially at this time of night. Why don't you stay here with me.'

'But there is only one bed. I could lie down here on the floor if that is all right?'

'Or you could join me in the bed. And receive the next stage in instruction. I see that you are fully capable.'

And so Robert spent the night. In the morning, Alex drove him home, it being a Saturday. He was careful to get out of the car at the entrance to the track out to the house, to avoid awkward questions.

Before he left, she said: 'I don't need to tell you this must remain a secret. The slightest whisper would finish me, you know.'

'That would be a disaster for us both! Will I see you again? Like we were, I mean, for love?'

'It would be very dangerous not only for me. You would find an affair very upsetting, especially if I took up with anyone else and you were jealous.'

'Do you intend to do that?'

'No, not at all. I hope you believe me. I did not intend to do what we did. It was a sudden thing, caused by the occasion, your success and my own. I had forgotten how much it means, the applause, the passionate intensity of the music—when it matters most—in front of an audience. But this is not something I ever do, as a rule. I have never been in love. Not fully, anyway, and not for a long time. I have other things to do and they come before anything.'

'Teaching?'

'Yes, I find you rewarding. But other things too.'

'Your research, then?

'Yes.'

'Will I never make love to you again? I leave school in six months time.'

'Maybe once your success is in the bag, who knows. Until then, we will be celibate. It suits both our tasks. We will do better without the complication of a relationship which, if discovered, would destroy everything we exist for. We are both us truth seekers, if I am not mistaken. That comes first.'

7

The remainder of the year vanished in a dream. Robert travelled in the bus every day with Raissa and said not a word about his sexual adventure. Classes continued as before without a hint of the connexion between teacher and pupil, though there were times, waking and sleeping, when Robert could not think of anything but making love to her. Just once more! He lusted after her so much, he nearly took to prayer. As he was never alone in her company now, the difficulty was minimised, Seeing how it would affect him, she had insisted he give up violin lessons for the time being. Taking relief from the images that invaded his mind became a daily necessity. But the decision she had forced on him was wise and he knew it. The exams were passed with the expected grades. Robert got drunk with his male classmates and a few females. In the street outside he came upon her, alone and clad in a white trouser suit with a loose pale-blue shawl wrapped about her in the cooling summer evening. But seeing his companions, she would not stop to accost him as she had hoped.

'Alex! Alex!' he called after her in the hearing of his friends and one said:

'How can you speak to her like that? It shows such disrespect. I thought you liked her?'

'I do, oh, I do. Doesn't everyone?'

Not until after the prize-giving did they meet. Everyone wanted him to play again and her. It was decided that they would play together, but this time, she would play the viola and he the violin with the head of the music department at the piano.

Only a week was available for rehearsals. After the first of these, Alex decided it would not do. Robert had neglected his practice and lost his edge. He would play a viola and she would take the violin part. The justice of this was clear to everyone.

And so it came about that after receiving about half the prizes available, Raissa having the remainder, Robert and his teacher Dr Katusheva played, accompanied by the pianist. Again it was a great success, though not as dazzling as before.

Robert did not travel back home by bus that day, the last day of term. Instead, he spent a joyous evening with Alex in her little house by the sea and most of the next day. She drove him home in her car and at the entry to the track that led out to the house overlooking the sea on the finger of land, when he would have got out to walk, she stopped him. 'There is no need to hide. I will drive you all the way to your home just as a good teacher would.'

So up the wide track they went between the trees and parked on the gravel around the house and Robert got out with the violin. Rose, who had heard the arrival of the car and was a little worried by Robert's non appearance, came out and, seeing Alex, introduced herself and invited her in to take some tea before the drive back.

A look at Robert so plainly indicated that he did not wish her to agree but it would have been churlish to refuse. 'That would be very nice, Mrs MacIvor.'

Inside, Rose said to them all: 'Dr Katusheva. This is Hector, my husband, and Margaret and Jane you already know.'

'How did it go, did you think?' said Hector to Robert, when they were seated and Rose went off to make tea.

Robert looked at Alex and said: 'Quite well, I think, but not as well as before. Dr Katusheva was brilliant, of course.'

'We thought so. We enjoyed it very much.'

'You were present?' said Robert. 'I didn't notice.'

'We were at the back. We arrived just before it began and wanted to remain out of sight so as not to put you off.'

Alex said: 'I understand you are a painter. May I look?'

'Of course. Most of these are mine.' Alex got up and went to stand before each of the paintings in turn. At the one over the fireplace she stopped and spent time studying it critically. 'This is the one I like best. You are developing a unique style here, I suggest.'

'That is the latest,' said Hector with a smile. 'Nobody around here can see the difference, so your visit is actually beneficial. You've made my day. That means a lot to a struggling artist.'

Alex was taken on a tour of the garden by Robert and Rose and then beyond, out onto the shore where the boat lay drawn up on the beach. Presently, as they stood and surveyed a very placid sea, Rose asked: 'Oh, before I forget, Robert, where did you spend the night? A hotel? And how did you pay for it? Will we be getting a bill?'

'No, Dr Katusheva very kindly put me up.'

'That was very good of you,' said Rose. 'I hope he was not too much trouble?'

'He wanted a drink or two and it seemed best, like the last time. In a school blazer he would not have been served in a bar. I needed a drink myself, come to think of it. He was company for me. I don't often play in public and when I do I am reminded of what it used to be like. I become excited. Music is like a drug: it induces ecstasy!'

'No one can fathom why you ever gave it up,' said Rose.

'The glamour was enjoyable, of course, but the practice necessary to deserve the applause was too much for me. I just could not envisage playing other people's music for hours every day. Imagine it, Robert? 'Playing every one of the Karl Flesch Exercises every day. That is what it would have meant—without a single day off. And travelling from city to city and hotel room to hotel room, living out of a suitcase.'

'But isn't that just what you've been doing?' said Robert. 'What was it? Tashkent, Kabul, Chechnya, Samarkand and heaven knows where else?'

'So you are well-travelled?' said Rose. 'I've never heard of some of these places.'

'Only in the line of duty. I had to visit them in the course of my research. I did not enjoy travelling very much. But it was necessary. One place led me on to another. It is the way with that sort of activity: one question leads to another and the answer is somewhere else.'

'Dr Katusheva is investigating her family tree, mother.'

'How far back do you go? It is difficult in this country. The records don't go back very far for most people. We have Parish Records and tombstones but in this climate the writing usually washes away.'

'There are not many records for me to look at. Usually I talk to people who are still alive or people who knew of them.'

Later, as she drove out from the house along the track between the trees, she observed how beautiful it was, curling amid the conifers, disappearing behind this wooded hillock and that on its way to the main road, just before the village. But it did not occur to her that this very track would figure in her future. It did occur to her to wonder whether they had believed her reasons for giving up the concert stage. Though what she revealed was not untrue, the reality was that her particular research was the kind of duty that took precedence over everything and anything would be given up for the sake of it.

When the final results were made known, both Raissa and he were awarded the expected distinctions, there was more celebration and in a bar Robert got slightly drunk. In the company of other young men and women, what else was to be expected?

'How are you going to get home?' said one, finally.

'I know a house that will put me up. It is just out of town.'

And so Robert walked to the wooded hillock that concealed the small house by the sea, knocked on the door and was soon admitted, despite his condition. Alex gave him coffee and sandwiches and in an hour or two he was feeling a lot better.

Once again, after a while, they were sitting by the fire on the carpet, Robert in white shirt and flannels, the sports jacket having been discarded along with the tie he started out in.

Alex wore a knee length skirt of pale-blue, which matched her eyes, and stockings with suspenders, as became immediately clear when she hunkered down with her back to the edge of the sofa. Robert had his back to a chair and he stretched out across the carpet full length.

'May I ask you something? Something personal,' said Robert, presently.

Alex sipped her wine and replied: 'You may ask. I do not promise to answer or even to answer truly.'

'Why would you lie— to me? I don't understand. It's something I just never do? It's an intellectual offence, very important to any truth seeker. And you are one. I know that.'

'Perhaps there are times when the truth has to be concealed in order that fresh truths will be uncovered. But what is your question?'

'What would be the point? If you do not believe in answering truly?'

'I did not say I would lie to you here and now. I merely say that it will depend on the question.'

'Well, here goes. You have been here a year. You are very beautiful, a star in this place. Every man lusts after you, from the headmaster downwards. Yet you have never been seen with any of them. And yet I have been allowed to stay here twice and it looks like I will spend the night here again. I don't understand what you see in me. I am not looking for praise for an inadequate ego. I really want to know. It just doesn't make sense. —Any more than your sudden appearance here. Why here? When there are so many more interesting places you could work and be paid far more.'

'Well, I don't deny that I have been invited out by several men and even two women. But I do not want a relationship. I haven't met anyone here of that sort.'

'Yet I am not that sort, *a fortiori*. I am too young and too inexperienced. I know I managed very badly last time but then it is all new to me. Some of the men around here will be very good in bed.'

'Has it not occurred to you that none of the others around here are as clever as you? Or as well educated and appreciate the same things I do? How could I respect an Argyllshire clodhopper who happened to be good in bed, as you put it? What would we talk about before and after? I am surprised you don't see this.'

'You mean you like talking to me?'

'Of course. You have a very sharp mind and a deep insight. You can talk to me on level terms. No other man could, around here.'

'But why here? Why not London, where there is an undiscovered genius in every district. Or Cambridge or Oxford, where they grow on trees?' Then suddenly, Robert saw more: 'If you presented yourself at Eton they'd pay you twice as much and if you don't fancy a boys' school, there is Roedean or Cheltenham Ladies College. Or is it that you have some weird penchant for comprehensive education, stemming from your days in backwoods Borodino under the socialist Russian system?'

Alex laughed. 'None of these. I have enough money for my needs. I admit I like Argyll, its woods and lochs and mountains. I wanted to see it. And when I had seen it, I decided to get to know it. So I stayed.'

'I am not satisfied. It doesn't make sense in your case, psychologically. You love music and you play like an angel. You could and should be playing to large audiences at twenty grand a time. Why aren't you? I just don't believe that you could pass up the chance of playing before the President of the U.S.A. at Carnegie Hall. I can't imagine anybody who can play like you who wouldn't jump at the chance. It's yours for the taking. Why do you turn away from it? You don't make sense, Alex.'

In reply, Alex opened her legs and lifted them and Robert soon forgot that the question remained unanswered.

Afterwards, Alex said: 'You are getting better. Not quite so fast. But you still have a long way to go.'

'Perhaps I could meet you during the vacation?'

'I am going on holiday, far from here. I won't return until you depart.'

'Still researching the family tree?'

'Yes.'

'Will I see you during the university vacations?'

'You will be too busy. You are entering a new world and you will look at this one in Argyll very differently in a few months time.'

'But I would like to go on meeting you! You are wonderful! What am I to do without you?'

'You will meet others far more wonderful and you will forget all about me. You must trust me on this.'

'If I said I love you, would that help?'

'But you don't. We both don't know that. We like and admire each other and that is all. It is enough.'

'Can I write to you? Let me have your address.'

'Better not. I don't know where my work will lead me.'
And so, after an orgy of love and music and good talk, fond farewells were taken and Robert had to be content with this. There was, to be sure, something cool about Alex, some inner strength—the same steel in the soul that had made of her a phenomenal linguist and musician—but it made her less enchanting on close acquaintance, because her severe self-discipline masked her warmth. So at least Robert perceived.

8

The drunkenness was deeply regretted and amplified for the sake of his cover story on his return to Kinoidart the next day, on this occasion by bus. Solemn promises were made on bended knee— even to The Great One—in Raissa's presence— a mock ceremony assuredly—that it would never happen again. A promise often broken, alas. But no great damage was done, as far as she could determine; the loss of an evening's creative thinking and the morning after, perhaps; not more. It was just that in the heat of conversation— floating ideas around in a pub—one forgot one was drinking alcohol and accepted everything thrown in one's direction—so at least Robert explained. It was the place and ambience that was responsible. These were the reasons given and they were not quite fatuous. Nothing was said about where he had spent the night or with whom.

Raissa rejoiced in her own fashion: very quietly. Anything else might easily provoke a reaction which could explode all her plans. So, at least, it seemed to her.

When they went up, they went together. Everybody goes 'up' to Oxbridge, though it is very far south of Argyll and 'down' by any other criterion.

Inevitably, Robert's room at Trinity College in Whewell's Court[8] was the meeting place for the pair almost every day. Raissa's room in

---

[8] Pronounced like 'Hughells'

Emmanuel was, by unspoken consent, off limits to any man, just in case. —In case a parent turned up unexpectedly; or a relative from some desert place, riding on a tall camel, shuffled along Regent Street— as Robert laughingly explained, when it came up in conversation at Trinity, where intellectuals would appear for tea at regular intervals in the late afternoon when everybody needed a break anyway. Then, ideas flew about the room like spitfires and were often shot down in flames by whichever airmen or women had appeared to do battle.

It was a heady experience.

'Why don't you do something different, Raissa, suggested Robert, one day? Something completely unexpected.'

'Why?'

'So that you can try out another part of this amazing world The Great One has made for us?'

'Such as?'

A swarm of suggestions followed from the minds scattered around the room like wasps waiting to sting. 'You could take up soccer', said one. 'What about the footlights?' said another. 'You know, lining up with everybody's hands on someone else's hips, on stage, dressed up or even undressed, singing in some production like South Pacific,'— or 'Maybe it should be North Uzbekistan', laughed a third. Others followed, some of them distinctly risqué. Prostitution was mentioned by one, admittedly rather the worse for wear, an event far from improbable, even at 4.30pm in that place. 'You are too dull! said all three, joined by two others in the chorus.

Raissa responded by taking up rowing. Until Robert objected that it was something she could easily do back home in Argyll. The village was made for it. So, under pressure of the most intense and unremitting kind and because rowing meant getting up at five, she agreed to take up cricket.

Having no training or practice in ball games, Raissa had little trained muscle and even less history of coordination. But she was descended from a long line of warriors who had crossed swords with Alexander's Macedonian Phalanx and seen off entire British armies, so there was a toughness that was innate.

She bowled and bowled and bowled at the nets and became a very good quickish spinner who could turn the ball both ways and alter the pace and flight deceptively. After some instruction, she even learned to keep the bat more or less straight and acquired the timing to play a few exquisite shots. Robert, who took no part in games, always attended her matches and would advise and comment upon her technique during them— sometimes to her vivid embarrassment. 'The wicket is the three sticks in the middle, a chain from the sticks you throw from,' he would announce loudly when she had bowled a wide. 'That is what you are supposed to hit.' Some of her wides were famous. One had almost decapitated the square leg umpire. Bowling leg breaks for the uninitiated is like that.

His only diversion was the violin in which he took advanced lessons and became a very good player.

At the end of the first year when the results were posted they were both awarded firsts and more celebration followed. Robert got tanked up in the tavern, they went on the river in a crowd and he, sailing with a girl, fell overboard when his pole stuck in the mud. The girl soon followed. As such behaviour was normal, no one thought ill of it. Seated demurely in her punt, Raissa observed the pair go off to change clothes without expression.

'Did you shag?' she asked him later.

'What did you think? We went to her place and my clothes had to dry out in front of the electric fire. What did you expect? I had to sit there for hours in a pair of her knickers. Something was bound to happen.'

'Was it good?'

'Not the right word, I think, old girl. G.E.' (he meant Moore) 'would not approve.'

Robert seemed to consider the matter carefully. 'It was all a bit quick, according to her.'

'Did you use a condom?'

'Certainly not. Didn't have one on me. Nor she.'

'You are supposed to. They told us at school. Remember?'

'Who ever has them when they're wanted? I've too much to think about.'

'She might get pregnant.'

'It's not very likely. Anyway, I expect she'll take a morning-after pill. They also told us about these.'

'You should make sure she does. Just in case. And get yourself checked over.'

That was the first serious conversation they'd had about sex—between the two of them, that is. Of course the subject came up all the time in a group. It was just an accepted fact that some people did and some didn't. Raissa was one who didn't— for obvious reasons: religion. Or indoctrination, as some, not entirely seriously, referred to it. And Robert, subject to none of these constraints, behaved as the mood took him. Even then, there were few opportunities and he wasn't looking for them. He had his eye on other matters. But when drunk, women would occasionally view **him** as an opportunity. Clearly, he had talent as well as looks. Like his father, he was over six feet and fair-haired.

That summer, following a suggestion made by his Master over sherry in the Lodge, Robert was persuaded to apply to attend Harvard during the vacation. 'What am I supposed to do there?' he enquired. 'Won't they all be away, like the Fellows here?'

'Not the serious ones. They'll still be around. You can soak up the atmosphere in the maths department. See what they are working on.'

'So I'd be a Cambridge spy like Burgess, Maclean or Philby?'

The Master laughed delightedly. 'You'd need to be an Apostle first. Maxwell was one. Did you know? [James Clerk-Maxwell, was the best ever Scottish scientist, director of the Cavendish Laboratory, also an undergraduate at Trinity and later a fellow.]

But what was Raissa to do? Robert enquired that evening after handing up his application. 'You'd get a bursary, like me. To go anywhere and do anything—within reason. What do you say? Where would you like to go?'

The question resurfaced in the late afternoon at Trinity when friends arrived for tea, coffee, or several kinds of alcohol—whatever the house could provide.

One said: 'What about Paris—the Sorbonne in summer. You could lose your virginity to a budding Picasso or Manet.' Another: 'What about an expedition to Everest? I fancy that myself.'

'It's been done, silly. Food and kit of folk that couldn't hack it scattered everywhere. But you wouldn't need much. Collect it when you arrive.'

'There are crosses too.'

'Would you get money for a guide?'

'No chance. It costs ten grand and they leave you to freeze, if you're not up to it.'

'What about Siberia? You could study the bears.'

'Or Antarctica. Say you're studying leadership. That you mean to enter the House of Commons and be the next Prime Minister.'

'Why there?'

'Shackleton, nitwit!' That's what you need for politics these days: Crisis management.'

'Or you could hang around the Marie Curie labs and get shagged by a scientist.'

'—Or Los Alamos'

'How about Lahore?' said another mathematician. 'Isn't that where the Pakistani lives who solved the Prime Number Theorem?'

'Or go and sail a boat on Einstein's loch at Princeton,' said Robert.

As both knew, Princeton and Harvard were as close as two peas in a pod. Did that mean what Raissa thought it meant? Join me this summer. I would miss you? She thought not. No, this was Robert's perception of her ideal.

'I think I'll take Paris. The left bank. I'll mingle with artists and develop my emotional side.'

'—And get shagged by a Frenchy', said one.

Anyway, that's where she went. Got the money in a few days from the Master, sent a letter home and lit out for Paris on the train.

Paris was hot that summer, full of tourists. There were lectures on art-history, a class every afternoon in the language and solitary meals under awnings on the pavements of one of the most magical cities in the world. There were bookstalls up and down the riverside, Cathedrals to visit and efforts to understand this very different religion that went on there and the Louvre to spend many an hour in. Watching, captivated, as a man in a smock on a tall ladder in the centre of a room copied a painting six feet by four onto a pristine, white canvas. In an hour, an almost perfect replica of one half was achieved by the use of eye, brush and pigment alone. It was a miracle and it said important things to her about art.

Of course there were men. Her clothing screamed 'student' (she had long abandoned the uniform required by her faith) but mostly it was because she had become beautiful. Nearly six feet tall, dark hair swept back in a pony tail, light-brown skinned, slim as a stick and with features that Cleopatra would have died for: aristocratic because delicate, refined, high cheek-boned and bursting with health.

'Hi there!' said the first, a very tall American with an accent that drawled out of the southern states. 'Mind if I join you? I'm lonesome.'

Well, why not? She was lonely too. The man submerged her in the small talk of his existence and then insisted on paying for the meal, after which they strolled by the river and he invited her to his hotel—a very good one, he assured her. When she refused, he offered to see her to her own place and would not take no for answer. Since he'd follow her, she had no choice but to shake him off and led him to the Metro. Eventually, she said: 'I get off here. Thanks. Nice meeting you.' But so did he, saying he'd nothing better to do than supply an escort in such a dangerous city. There was nothing for it but desperate measures. She entered a ladies' toilet and waited an hour. Then had the bright idea of leaving in the company of another female. But he'd departed anyway by then. Next day, she cased the neighbourhood for an avenue of escape and found a restaurant with three exits and a toilet. That would do.

But she missed Robert, there was no getting away from it. It was hard to put her finger on. It wasn't just the shared interests. The deep discussions about things that really mattered. She just knew him. Very well. He was like an old Gladstone bag one took everywhere. It had everything in it one needed. All the medicines and all the answers. All the plasters and bandages for the minor wounds of life and a bottle of water, that too, for times of thirst. Without it, she felt bereft.

And so there was a sadness about her that summer and it attracted a score of randy men. Only one ever got close. They had gone to the cinema and he had fingered her there in the darkness and then, when she got up to leave, followed her and attempted to have her in an alcove on the way out. A very daring manoeuvre and nearly successful because of his skill and strength. Only the appearance of a late cinema-goer put an end to it. She shouted and the newcomer just stood there until the man ran off unzipped.

Three weeks into the holiday, she was desperately trying to locate Robert who had evidently vanished from the Fraternity he'd been registered to—and failed, when the phone rang in her hotel room.

A voice in the clipped tones of a Boston accent enquired. 'Is this Miz Raissa Hussain? '

Raissa gulped. It sounded like bad news. 'Yes,' she admitted.

'Miz Hussain from Argyll, Scatland?'

'Yes.'

'This is Special Agent Starling[9] of the F.B.I. Maybe you heard a' me? No? Waal, I'm jest to tell yew that yore side-kick's been picked for a National Security Think Tank. He's gonna stay over here and quit yore Cambridge for ours. He's at security right now and cain't come to the phone. 'Fact, he's gotta be deBritishized afore he gits in. You savvy?'

'What am I supposed to do?'

'Clear his room at your Cambridge and send off his stuff stateside to ours. The loot for the transfer's been sent and the address. As of now, he's undacova.'

'But I'm in Paris. How can I send things off from Cambridge?'

'Ah doan no, lady. Ah'm jest the messenger boy. Up to you sweetheart.'

He put the phone down on her.

Raissa heard the click, tried the redial, didn't get it for it rang and rang and then stopped; and put down the phone. Then she wept. She sat with her head in her hands and tears streaming down her face, remembering all the happy times, the beach and the sailing boat *Matilda* and the talks on the school bus, in the library and the woods.

And it was as if he had died. And she couldn't attend the funeral.

---

[9] A character in the films: *Silence of The Lambs* and *Hannibal Lecter*

Five minutes passed and there was a knock at the door. She dried her eyes on a tissue, blew her nose and wiped her face before the mirror in the en-suite bathroom. Then she went to the door and opened it.

'Surprise! Surprise!' It was Robert, in a crumpled white suit dancing in upon her clutching a bag.

She was so shocked she wept again and stood there weeping in front of him.

'I knew I was good but not that good. Steady on, old girl.'

'Oh, you rotter! How could you play such a trick?'

'It was easy? Why not?'

'I thought I'd never see you again!'

'Well, that was the joke, don't you see?'

He slung his bag onto the bed and collapsed into an armchair with his back to a window. 'Be a sweety and get me a drink, would you? I've been travelling for hours and hours and I'm parched. I'm also very hungry. What's the number for room service and I'll call down?'

Raissa stood looking down at him severely. 'I should kill you for that. You frightened me near to death! Do you realise that if I hadn't seen you today— if you weren't here now, I might have….might have….'

'—Done what? Thrown yourself off a bridge? I don't believe it. What would The Great One say?'

She laughed and dried her eyes again and then left to smarten herself up in the bathroom forgetting about the drink and when she returned found him fast asleep in the chair.

She sat on the bed looking at him intently, as if she'd never looked before and something in her stirred, something low down and profound and it gave her goose pimples on her arms and legs. She sighed and then continued sitting, content just to look. Harvard had given his face a slight tan. He looked lean and fit— or would do, if he were upright instead of slumped like a corpse.

She decided to bathe and tidy herself up and consider what to do. It was all so difficult. In the bathroom, she stripped off, leaving her clothes in a chair and stepped into the shower while the bath was running, washed her hair and was about to step into the bath when she realised she had left the bathroom door open. And stopped suddenly and cursed her stupidity under her breath, as she was wont to do. 'What is happening to me?' She demanded, aloud, as she went to the door and shut it, before entering the bath, where she lay and soaked, luxuriating in the soap-suds.

Her mind, normally like a well-constructed computer, was sending signals that were deeply worrying. There was confusion. Conflicting images and feelings. And, she realised, no ideas at all. Was she going mad? What had become of her bright intellect?

She lay in the warmth and mourned. This French trip had been a bad idea. It had made her feel incompetent. What had she to show for it but confusion and a woolliness of faculty that was intolerable? She should have stayed in Cambridge. Then she would have been intact, her mind unaffected, still capable of the most powerful concentration and purposeful activity for half a day at a time.

After an hour of it, she washed her hair, got out, dried herself, then dried her hair and, forgetting she was not alone, strolled into the room wearing nothing. Until she saw the figure seated at the window lolling in the armchair. She stepped back immediately, humiliated and red-faced. And then realised that he was still asleep. He would have moved, otherwise and said something. She tip-toed to the wardrobe and took out her best trouser suit, nylon stockings, suspender belt and underwear—the sexy kind she'd bought a few days before on impulse—and then made it back into the bathroom without incident, where she locked the door carefully. When she'd got the underwear on, and the stockings and suspenders, she looked in the mirror at herself for the first time. And liked what she saw. But why am I doing this? she wondered, as the trousers and jacket went on. It was a mystery, as if she were under influences of a mysterious kind never encountered before.

She made up her face for the first time. Mascara and lipstick and blusher and face powder and it seemed an improvement, the way other women looked. 'Well, what now?' she said aloud. And had no answer. I am hungry, she thought. I'll wake up the sleeping warrior and we'll go out to dinner.

When she entered the bedroom he was standing up straight. 'Did I imagine something, or were you talking to yourself?'

'No. I mean, yes. I don't know what's come over me. I feel very strange and I don't like it at all.'

'It will be the air of this place. Didn't you know Paris affects some people very badly?'

'I didn't know. I wouldn't have come if I had known. What do you mean? Badly? How? Is it the water? Or the smog? Or the sanitation? Tell me.'

He laughed. 'None of these. No. It's a place of romance. People have affairs here, fall in love and get married.'

'Well, I don't think it's any of these,' she said with evident relief. 'I'm hungry. Are you rested enough to join me for dinner?'

'Certainly. Lead on MacDuff. You know the area. Take me away to your favourite bistro. My treat.'

And so they walked out and took the lift to reception, the tall fair headed man in the white suit and the dark-haired, brown-faced young woman in the pale-blue trouser suit. But in the lift, he said: 'I hope you don't mind my saying so but you look different somehow.'

'How different?'

'Painted up. You know? Dolled up. It's just that I've never seen you this way before.'

'I'm sorry. Don't you like it? I could change it?'

'Could you?'

'If you wish.'

But he was reluctant. He stopped to study here intently. 'So this is the new you, the frenchified you? I suppose you better stay as you are.'

'Really, I'll change it if you'd prefer.'

'I don't mind. It's just different, that's all.'

'I better change,' she decided and headed for the Ladies on the ground floor but he went after her and took her by the arm.

'Don't do that. This is how you want to look. I respect that. It's fine. You look fine.'

And so it was that they walked down the street to the nearest bistro and she stopped and looked at the menu and decided against it. Then moved to another further down and she changed her mind about that one and turned a corner into a different street and headed for yet another. And, to Robert's chagrin, declined it as well. Raissa looked around her thinking where she would agree to go and finally Robert said: 'Look, chum, I'm starving. I really need to eat. Can't we go to some place? Any place will do, so long as I get to eat.'

'I don't know what it is, I just can't settle on any place. It has to be the right place.'

'Why? I don't see why? All we need is food.'

'But there is food and food. Tonight is special. I just feel it. I don't know why. It just is.'

'One of your celebrated intuitions again, eh?'

'No, something else. Something I do not understand.'

Eventually, she agreed to enter an expensive-looking restaurant on a very expensive street. Robert was aghast when he saw the menu. 'I can't afford this,' he complained.

'Never mind, then, it's on me.'

'Couldn't let you old thing,' he mimicked the Oxbridge twang of Anthony Blanche in Brideshead. 'But the credit card will take a beating.'

'What will you have?'

'What can I afford? is the question. Hamburger and fries sounds about right. But I don't see that here. What is the Frog for *hamburger*?'

'No idea. The same, probably. But you can't have that. It's Paris, for heavens sake. Your first night here. You have to eat the local fare.'

When the waiter arrived, Raissa said: 'Nous desire un demi de champagne, premier; et un bouteille de numero quinze suivir. Je desire scallops—coquille— meuniere puis poulet à la maison. Mon ami desire—Well, come on, what will you have?'

'I'm speechless. Do you know what scallops cost back home? Yours will have flown here in a jet.'

'Mon ami, la meme chose,' she announced, snapping shut the menu with a flourish.

'What have you done?' Robert whispered, when the waiter had carried them off out of earshot.

'Ordered a good dinner.'

'A bit different from a tent in the desert, eh?'

'Hush. Tell me about Harvard. Were there many women?'

'Hundreds. Crawling all over me.'

'Hope you used a condom?'

'Never carry them, old bean.'

'Oh, God, Robert, what will become of you? You'll get Heinz 57 varieties. But what was it like?'

'I met Gomes.'

'Never heard of him. What has he proved?'

'He's not one of us. A mathematician. No.' Robert paused to consider. 'He's a small, round, pot-bellied, African-American with short grizzled hair— but then he's old now. They all get like that in the end— even Einstein. I was sitting waiting to go into an office and he was doing the same. He introduced himself as 'Gomes, Peter Gomes'. Nothing more. We shook hands and chatted. It was immediately clear that he's one of the best people I've ever met.'

'Well, I'm surprised. Tell me more.'

'It's hard to explain. He's a man who knows where he's going. His certainty is patent and he knows where you and I should be going. That's the striking thing about him. And he convinces you that you know too.'

'And did you see much of this strange man?'

'He invited me to a party at his house—a large rambling clap-board house on the campus. He's a professor.'

'Of what?'

'Religion.'

Raissa laughed.

'Don't laugh. I went to hear him preach. He was fantastic. I came out treading on air. I felt as if he had led me into a new world of the spirit. I spent the last three weeks reading his books. But it is the man himself who is the star. That was the best thing that happened.'

'Where did you stay? I wrote to the address you gave and got nothing back.'

'Oh, I was at Wigglesworth—it's a dormitory—then I moved to Eliot House. I stayed in G41—where Bernstein roomed as a student. Mail must have got lost.'

'Who is he?'

'Leonard. Composer— West Side Story—you know!'

'What about the maths department? Who did you meet? What did you find out?'

'I was sent to spy on them and they wanted to spy on our place. Full of questions they were. I didn't meet anybody important—they'd all evaporated into the thin air of the Rockies, the Appalachians or Vermont—wherever they go in summer.

'—Oh, I did meet Conway, the algebraic topologist that discovered Surreal numbers[10]. He was doing a summer school. Stays nearby at Princeton. Just likes the contact with students. Probably fucks them. The females, I mean. Still has a family back in Cambridge, I think—our Cambridge, I mean, not theirs. He wore Hawaiian shirts, sandals without socks, a great bushy beard and a huge beer belly. Interesting chap. Very helpful. I liked him.'

'Wasn't he a Fellow at Trinity?'

---

[10] "In the beginning, everything was void, and J.H.W.H. Conway began to create numbers. Conway said, 'Let there be two rules which bring forth all numbers large and small. This shall be the first rule: Every number corresponds to two sets of previously created numbers, such that no member of the left set is greater than or equal to any member of the right set. And the second rule shall be this: One number is less than or equal to another number if and only if no member of the first number's left set is greater than or equal to the second number, and no member of the second number's right set is less than or equal to the first number. And Conway examined these two rules he had made, and behold! They were very good. And the first number was created from the void left set and the void right set. Conway called this number 'zero'…. He proved that zero was less than or equal to zero. Two more numbers were created, one with zero as its left set and one with zero as its right set. And Conway called the former number 'one' and the latter he called 'minus one'. And he proved that minus one is less than but not equal to zero and zero is less than but not equal to one….
'On day 4 the numbers greater than or equal to zero are
0,1/4,1/2,3/4.1.3/2,2,3' See D. Knuth 'Surreal Numbers' pub Addison Wesley, 1974 p6, 59 resp.

'No. Caius first and then Sydney Sussex. He was present when they buried Cromwell's head. Bizarre, it was. Told me all about it. All the Fellows at dead of night begowned and processing to the chapel. No one got to see where they put it in case of a revolution!'

'What made you come back here? Early, I mean. When there's still so long to go?'

'Not sure. I got fed up over there. Gomes only preaches once a week and he was going on vacation. I couldn't think of anywhere else to go.'

'You could have gone home.'

'I thought of that. But it wouldn't be the same without you. Can't sail the boat without crew, what? Would you come? Home, I mean.'

'Not just now.'

'Why ever not? You haven't been back for a year. They'll think you've been abducted to some character's harem and come looking for me in case I'm involved. What weapons do they use? Do you keep in touch?'

'Not much, no. A letter now and then. Everything is so different. I don't want to go back, not right now.'

'And the weapons? What am I up against?'

'AK47's are preferred. A GP machine-gun if they can steal one. Then there's the Molotov. They learned it from the Russians. It takes out tanks. The grenade launcher, that too. Just aim and shoot. It's very accurate.'

'Well, I'll have to get a room. Maybe your place will have one. Would you mind?'

'Not at all. You should have arranged it earlier.'

When the champagne arrived they drank a toast to Paris and then another to themselves and that was the bottle empty. Courses came and empty plates went.

'What will we do. Tomorrow, I mean?'

'Did you think of staying on?'

'Why not? See the city, that kind of thing.'

'I could show you.'

'What about your classes?'

'I could skip them.'

'Could you really? You, the great attender? I'm astonished. I thought you never did wrong.'

'I expect it's the air here.' They laughed.

'What will you say in your report to the Master?'

'I will tell lies.' They laughed again for that was unthinkable, as both knew.

The bill when it came was a fright. Robert insisted on paying with his credit card. 'Couldn't let you, old bean. Just wouldn't do, don't ye know?'

'What is all this Anthony Blanche[11] talk about?'

'I don't know. It started this morning. God knows where it came from.'

'Well, I'm not sure I like it. It's as if you're hiding something.'

'Me? The open book? Impossible.'

'—Or gay, like him. Is that it?'

'No, not a chance.'

The stroll in the balmy air was pleasant, the streets quieter now. At the hotel, another room was requested and found on a floor above hers. He escorted her to hers, collected his bag where he'd left it and then stood at the door for a moment, surveying her, standing in the middle of the room looking back at him.

'I should ask what you're thinking but I won't. I'm still jet-lagged. Wouldn't understand the answer, probably. See you in the morning.'

Robert woke early, wanted to see her and then feared to interrupt her ablutions, not knowing her habits. Instead, he went in search of breakfast, found a copy of *Paris Soir* and read it while devouring croissants, buttered, with strawberry jam. And coffee—cup after cup, as if recovering from drought.

Raissa appeared before him, standing. He looked up and blinked. 'You look different again. It suits you, I must say. 'It' was an outfit consisting of a white and pink striped skirt, bare legs and white trainers. 'I thought we'd go hopping on and off buses all day, seeing the sights. What do you say?'

'Fine, suits me.'

---

[11] An effeminate character in *Brideshead Revisited* by Evelyn Waugh.

She sat and studied him carefully. He said: 'What are you looking at?'

'You,' she laughed. 'No signs of syphilis, yet.'

'The Great One must be looking out for me, then.'

She lifted the butter dish to pass to him and he had an almost irresistible desire to touch her hand, very lightly; something long recognised to be out of bounds. The knowledge that this was so, made him suddenly look sad.

'What's the matter?'

'Nothing, still jet-lagged, I expect. Crazy thoughts in the central processor. Pay no heed. Everything will get back to normal, by and by.'

Soon, they were aboard the open-top bus on a tour of the city and then afterwards they carried on to the Louvre where they spent two hours moving from room to room, after which Robert declared he'd had enough and needed a bracing drink.

Coffee and a jug of iced-water were ordered in a café. 'Well, what did you make of Mona Lisa?'

'The eyes do follow you around the room. I tried it. Clever, I must say. Having an inanimate female who pays one that much attention is a rarity.'

Raissa blushed.

'I see. You think you are the same as Lisa? And it worries you! Fear not, gentle maiden. It's just that you haven't had me to argue with for a month.'

'You know, I never once thought of that.'

'What?'

'Arguments.'

'So you didn't miss me?'

'Oh, yes.'

'What did you miss?'

'I am not sure. I've been trying and failing to understand it. Maybe it's like an old coat you haven't put on for a while. You miss it.'

'Especially when it gets cold. It can't be that, then. It's hot as hell here. Well, never mind. Let's go. There is so much to see.'

And several more hours were spent walking here and there, into shops and the many strange sights of a city whose delights were mainly still to be uncovered.

Just before the rush hour, Robert stopped and said: 'My feet are killing me. I think you're determined to walk me to death. And you know what it is I miss? It's the company. I'm used to you being around. It's just not the same when you are not.'

'Well, that's very nice, I must say. I'm like an old bag you keep handy to carry things for you.'

'—I am sorry. I forgot. Here, give me these.' Robert had bought some underclothes and shirts and she had been carrying them since the check-out. 'I am so forgetful! I should have taken them back when I had paid. What is going on? I am behaving like a nutter.'

'Don't ask me. I'm the same. It's the heat, I expect. Let's go back to the hotel, if you've had enough.'

And they did.

Raissa said she would take a bath and meet him for dinner in an hour. When she arrived in the hotel lobby, she found him with a drink, sitting musing.

'A penny for them?'

'—Oh, there you are. I have been sitting here people-watching, estimating the nature of the lives I see around me and their probable outcome.'

'And what have you concluded?'

'That the man in the tuxedo with the red carnation in his buttonhole is a gigolo. Look at his companion. A lady long past the first flush of youth and loaded with diamonds. She is the money and he is there to earn it.'

'I don't believe it. He'll be her son.'

'No, there is no resemblance. He is very good looking, spends a fortune keeping in shape, at the tailor and barber. I bet he smells of some exotic male perfume exuding pheromones by the billion. Let's watch and see if she suggests they go upstairs.'

But they made no urgent move to do so. 'Maybe they've just come from there. Anyway, what are pheromones?'

'You were the biologist. Thought you'd know all that. Something to do with sexual attraction. Women are turned on by them. Like gravitons.'

'Never heard of them. But I gave that up last year. It must be in the next course.'

'Well, no need to worry, I don't have many.'

'How do you know?'

'—Oh, I think I'd know by now. Compared to everybody else, I'm relatively inexperienced. It means I don't pull the women and that's probably why.'

'—Or you're too busy to look for them. Man with head stuck in book has no talent for sticking self into lady.'

Robert's eyes brightened and he laughed and laughed. 'Where did you hear that aphorism?' he said, astonished.

'I just thought of it.'

And so they went off to dinner, though at a much cheaper place and Raissa was allowed to pay on this occasion. Afterwards they strolled again by the river and talked nostalgically of things past and to come. By midnight they were in their rooms reading up, so as to have good ideas to float the next day and impress and entertain the other— an unspoken activity they'd have denied and new to them.

The weather had changed noticeably but it was still dry and Robert said he would go in a shirt and shorts: both black with trainers. By some chance, Raissa chose the opposite colour: pure white. A thin filmy dress that reached her knees, bare legs and white trainers.

They walked and walked and came to Notre Dame and Robert was fascinated by the great cathedral. They entered and wandered around, absorbing everything. Eventually, Robert sat down at a pew and crossed himself. Raissa joined him there. 'What are you doing that for?'

'I wanted to know what it felt like.' Then he knelt and gave every sign of praying to the deity and Raissa was alarmed. She got up and walked to one side and observed him critically. At last, he arose and joined her.

'What was that all about? It's not like you at all.'

'You should be pleased. Why are you not? I was just trying to commune with The Great One. It is the same one. Bound to be. There couldn't be two of them.'

Raissa shivered unhappily and looked around as if there might be a manifestation any instant.

Robert laughed. 'No need to worry. I didn't get through, you know. I never do. I have tried it, like any good scientist. If there is a God he must want me to believe in him. Why would he hide himself from me? It makes no sense, don't you see?'

'You don't know what you're dealing with. You should be careful,' she said, as they walked down the aisle towards the exit.

'On the contrary! I must not be careful. Must throw myself into every area of knowledge for that is what it is to live. I don't have to agree with it, but I am obliged to try it before rejecting it.'

'Do you mean to try heroin and cocaine?'

'Of course not, silly. Some things you don't have to try. But there are a few that one should, for no harm can come to you by it. How could it be harmful to put myself in the way of God—The Great One— as you describe him? If he is really good, it can do me no harm whatever.'

They were walking back the way they had come when it suddenly started to rain and there was not a taxi in sight or a bus and, by the river, few places to shelter. Even the open-air bookstalls closed up. In minutes, the downpour had altered their appearance to that which might have been achieved by a dive into the Seine. They ran in the rain, fruitlessly seeking shelter and then gave up looking and just laughed and drank from the heavens; and the rain continued to soak their clothing so that they were dripping and it stuck to their bodies. Then, just as suddenly, it stopped and the sun came out.

'See, The Great One has given us the Monsoon and halted it just when it was getting interesting.'

'Interesting? Whatever do you mean?'

'I mean, dear lady, that you are so wet, you are now revealing everything underneath that white skirt!'

And so it was! The filmy white material, with little enough beneath and that of the same material and colour, revealed a striking darkness around the crotch that could only be one thing.

'God, Riassa!' murmured Robert, staring.

'What do you mean?'

'Just God! It is enough.'

Robert turned away, ran ahead and then turned and looked again and expostulated. 'Oh my God!'

Raissa was embarrassed and Robert was apologetic. 'I am sorry,' he said as she came up to him.

'For what?'

'For looking! I can't stop looking and I'm so ashamed.' Trying to look away, he said: 'Here, take my shirt. It will help, believe me.' And, taking care to look elsewhere, he began to take it off.

'No, that's the wrong thing to do. It will just draw further attention to me. Keep it on. Come on, we'll run all the way and maybe no one will notice.'

But of course people, who started to come out again now that the rain was off, did notice them running. So Raissa slowed down and so did he. 'I'll walk in front.'

'Nonsense. Walk beside me as usual. Then no one will think anything of it. Take my hand, if you want to be useful. It will make us look like an item.' And hesitantly, he did.

The feeling of that hand for the first time, though it was cold and dripping, was like the first taste of manna, after lengthy starvation. Robert actually sighed.

'What's up? Tired?'

'No.'

They walked on and had to stop at a crossing. It would have been natural to have released her hand for the sake of safer movement but Robert was in no hurry to let go.

He looked at her with dog-like eyes, brows dripping with rain drops and even shook himself like a dog so that Raissa laughed. 'You don't look too happy.'

'Can't help it. How I look. But I am happy—well sort of. Humiliated too.'

At the hotel, Robert went first, closely followed by Raissa and they crossed the lobby in a rush, got into the lift and were wafted to their separate floors without incident or comment.

9

Robert bathed, lay luxuriating for a time in the warm water, became tumescent as he played the image of her through his mind and then cringed with embarrassment. 'How could I do that to her, of all people? Behave like that? Stare at her pubic hair?' But it never occurred to him that he had seen pubic hair before or that any other man, in similar circumstances, would do the same.

The image of her focused on the parts of her, almost for the first time. That symmetrical face and those dark eyes of hers. He looked into them as if he had never seen her before, as if she were a new person he had just met and a warm glow suffused him. Like a man observing himself from a great height, he realised that it was not just the hirsute signal of her womanliness that had stirred him, it was the unfathomable person within. The strength, the warmth he sensed for the first time that lay there and the goodness. The image moved to the breasts— though he had no idea of these except that they were rounded, like grapefruit, and then lowered, taking in the turn inwards of the flanks which he'd passed over in her trousered state so often and thought little of. And now the area at the top of the legs, the area he'd perceived for the first time that wet afternoon provoked by a flimsy dress with an equally flimsy garment beneath and a shower of monsoon rain which rendered them almost transparent.

He touched himself, briefly, and then desisted: it was the wrong thing to do. Suddenly, he too was a changed person. Some things were no longer appropriate. He could not have said why. Perhaps it was that for the first time his sexuality had but one object: to please her. And to take relief from the contemplation of her seemed disgraceful, the pleasing only of himself. And then he rolled in the bath unhappily, frustrated, thinking of how she would react. She—who only ever valued ideas, especially of mathematics and physics—would think his current thoughts as shameful as his behaviour that afternoon.

When I tell her, he thought— and I must tell her— she will drop me like a hot brick. Then the logic kicked in and he told himself he must delay telling her until the information was too great to bear. He grieved for that time, saw it as the end of an era. He dressed himself carefully, as he might for a wedding or a funeral—his own, he thought, wryly; tying the tie with mathematical precision for once, combing the hair until it shone and sat down on his brow with more grace than ever before, he who had taken little interest in the appearance of things, least of all himself.

Finally, looking in the mirror, he sighed and looked miserably at himself for the last time before turning away to the door and the walk downstairs.

Raissa also lay thinking in the bath, luxuriating in the suds. What did the action of the afternoon mean? Had she repulsed him? No, he had been attracted but very upset by it. How would he respond to that? With revulsion? Her brown skin, so very different from his; her dark hair, the opposite of his golden crown, but most of all the revulsion of things of that were not of the mind. When had he ever expressed an interest in women? Once after a fall in the punt. But had he really done anything to that girl? Men— to judge from the others—were such liars. But was he? The truth-seeker. The story might have been a joke or a tease to provoke her. She remembered his several investigative descriptions of the female orgasm, always related with a straight face; and wondered

Maybe he would be revolted by her. It would, she suspected, put him off his work, if it continued. How would he react to that? In only one way: he would shut her out of his life. Robert, like Einstein, she knew, was like a monk in pursuit of the Holy Grail of Mathematical-Physics: the theory of everything. And he would give up everything to get it.

The thought of doing without him shot into her mind like an arrow. She flinched, rose out of the bath, towelled and then studied herself in the mirror. Would Robert like her? Like this? Would he want to have her? If he were embarrassed by her appearance in rain-sodden clothes, what would he think if she were naked? Raissa was suddenly fearful, fearful that the great friendship was about to end.

She put on the suspender belt first and then fresh stockings and then the white bra and then went out to the bedroom to see what were the very best knickers she had and selected a very lacy pair of white ones through which the pubic hair could partly be seen and it never occurred to her to wonder at what she was doing, the choice of garments, the order of putting them on. She went into the bathroom again and studied herself in the mirror and then, satisfied, returned to pick out a dress and chose the green shiny silk one which stood out from her knees because of the stiffness of the fabric.

When eventually the knock came on the door, she was ready, composed even, though her heart beat faster than ever before.

Robert was in his only suit but seemed unusually dapper, as if great care had been taken over his appearance.

'Are..are..y.y.y you ready?' he stammered.

'Yes, if you are.' She attempted a smile.

As they walked to the lift, she added; 'It's not like you to stammer. Are you all right?'

'Yes, yes of course. It's just—this afternoon. I behaved rather badly and I can't get over it.'

'Do I look all right?'

'Yes, in fact you look radiant.' Robert blushed. 'I do apologise. What must you think of me!'

'There is nothing to apologise for,' she laughed, nervously. 'You saw me at a disadvantage. What were you supposed to do? I would have more reason to complain if you'd ignored me altogether.'

'A gentleman would.'

'Only in Brideshead. Not now. Gentlemen are more sensible. They don't conceal their feelings.'

'It..it..it's just that I've never thought of you that way before.'

'—it must be serious then,' she said half in jest. 'I've never heard you stammer like this. Now you really are talking like Anthony Blanche.'

That evening they ate in the hotel restaurant and at first there was an unaccustomed silence between them. They chose their food and when the wine arrived they sipped it nervously, along with water from the carafe.

'You seem very quiet all of a sudden,' said Raissa.

Robert looked across at her as if she had melted him: 'I expect it's just being together so much,' he lied, without noticing. 'We've run out of things to say.'

'Perhaps you've grown tired of my company?'

'Oh, no! Never that!' Robert looked at her wistfully and went on looking as if the sight of her in front of him was a magnet. 'Maybe you get to a point where words are no longer enough. Maybe you don't need to say anything.'

'But isn't that boring for you?'

'No, not at all.'

'You're sure you're not unhappy?'

'No. I am very happy. How about you?'

'I am happy being here with you but you are in a strange mood.'

'We should go somewhere different tonight. A theatre or a cinema, perhaps.'

'You're not in a hurry to leave me here then and rush off to Argyll or somewhere?'

'Far from it. I wouldn't dream of leaving. If y.y.you don't mind my staying on, that is?'

They ate in silence for a time, looking at each other with light in their eyes; but neither saw the quality of light in the other. Some people, even those with great insight are occasionally blind to things in front of their noses. When the bill had been paid and Robert got up to leave, he started suddenly at the discomfort low down, realised its import and flushed; but then continued as if nothing had happened. Outside, Raissa said: 'Is there something the matter? Are you quite well?'

'I feel fine. It's just something that comes over a chap once in a while.'

'Is there something you can take for it?'

Robert smiled, wanly. 'Not as far as I know. It will pass, I expect.'

But of course it did not pass for very long. When they were seated in the warm cinema it happened again and Robert had to surreptitiously try to adjust himself. Sitting so close to her in the cinema was a delicious experience. Several times, his leg or his arm came into contact with hers and it was as if a charge of electricity had passed.

Outside afterwards they walked back discussing the film but all the time, at the back of his mind Robert's was filled with images of Raissa, sensing the presence that walked beside him, as if for the very first time, as a living, breathing being and not just a mind to bounce ideas off.

He escorted her to her room and made no move to enter—something he'd have done without thinking before. The situation was embarrassing and wonderful and frightening all at the same time. He was almost glad to say goodnight and retire upstairs to his own room where he lay on his back on the bed fully clothed for a time, thinking over the events of the evening and what they meant.

Eventually, he undressed and lay naked under the covers and thought of her. Imagined her and played the images of her through his mind over and over; all the time erect like a truncheon against himself, one that might break the friendship of his life if it ever became obvious.

Yet of course it did become obvious to Raissa. as they went around the great city enjoying its attractions.

Once, stepping onto a bus, unaccountably, Raissa slipped and Robert grabbed her to prevent her falling. The feel of her arm was heavenly. She apologised for being so clumsy: 'I'm afraid I feel a touch accident prone,' she admitted. 'Must be the heat.'

Robert, sitting beside her, had been set on fire once more by the contact and this time so necessary to save her from a fall. When they got up to depart, Raissa looked down and noticed but wisely said nothing.

In a bookshop, they found some interesting mathematics texts and stood studying them, Raissa, turning the pages with easy recognition of familiar equations, brushed against his shoulder while Robert was languidly looking at the diagrams without much interest: his mind was elsewhere, conscious, every waking moment, of the magical person right beside him.

She returned the current book to its shelf, turned to walk to a different part of the shop and bumped into him, reacting to her sudden movement. Her breast made contact with his upper arm and shot goose pimples through her. In a daze, she went to the door to the street, forgetting about the other books and he rushed to open it, again colliding with her and then backed off suddenly, as if from a fire.

At the door of a shop where she wanted to buy some toiletries, again he hurried to open it for her and enjoyed the delicious feeling as his hand lay upon her upper back, as he allowed her to go first. It seemed to be a day of small bodily contacts, which Robert began to plan for and improvise as the occasion presented. Once, greatly daring and without any forethought, as she stopped to pick up an unusual leaf that had fallen from a tree, he stroked her hair, very gently, so gently she hardly noticed.

Yet there were intellectual moments too. The next day, a day of stifling heat, when the very streets, pavements and walls of the buildings of the city seemed to radiate warmth, Raissa had dressed wisely in a light, white frock and trainers under her white hat and went bare legged, anticipating the sweat of a day's walking about. Robert was wearing black shorts and a white T shirt, though, given his condition, he had thought of a jacket, at least to carry on his arm despite the heat, until dissuaded by Raissa at the door of her room when she saw him appear there. He threw the jacket onto her bed without comment and left it there.

They were strolling through a park when they came to a large fountain and the conversation turned to the paradoxes of particle physics, like the Schrodinger cat problem.

'Paradoxes seem to be a necessary aspect of knowledge in every age,' said Raissa. 'They are noticed to be present in the theory as a means of drawing us on to a further set of insights whereby the theory will ultimately be improved when they disappear.'

'You mean there are bound to be paradoxes? Yes, I suppose you are right. The approach to certainty, to full knowledge, is asymptotic: there is always a little further to go. But paradoxes occur in other spheres. Take philosophy. Russell's Paradox, for example.'

'What is that about? Tell me.'

'Define a normal class as one which is not a member of itself. The class of all men is not a man; the class of all paintings is not a painting. Define an abnormal class as a class which is a member of itself. Thus the class of all classes is a class and is therefore a member of itself. So it is abnormal. Consider now the class of all normal classes. Is it normal or abnormal? If it is normal, then it is not a member of itself. That is, it is abnormal. If, on the other hand, it is taken to be abnormal, then it is a member of itself. That is, it is normal, for all the elements of the class are normal.'

'I see. So if it is taken to be normal it is abnormal and if it is taken to be abnormal it is normal. What did Russell do about it?'

'Devised a theory of descriptions which explains it away as a problem which occurs in language which can only be discussed without contradiction in a meta language.'

'I see. In the same way as an arithmetical system of the Godel type is only consistent when it is discussed within a meta language outside it.'

Raissa reflected on the matter for a moment and then her eyes shone and she turned to say; 'Oh, Robert, how wonderful that is! That knowledge itself should contain such a paradox is a miracle.' She put her hands upon his shoulders and beamed a smile of that special ecstasy reserved for the finest productions of the human mind that were such a part of their daily lives—had brought them together in the first place and had reinforced the connexion until it had grown into a bond as lasting as the greatest friendships ever experienced.

But Robert turned away from her, so that her left hand slid off his shoulder and he would not look at her directly but continued to turn away with a flushed face and looked into the far distance, saying merely: 'Ah well, it was all very interesting at one time. Maybe the world has got beyond it now.'

Raissa stood rooted to the spot, and her look of ecstasy—about to be shared—changed to one of dismay. He had not returned her hands on shoulders! It seemed to her to be the end of everything. Robert had rejected her! His words seemed to suggest that he had moved on, out of that special world together they had created years ago in a classroom in Argyll and had entered some other place wherein she was not allowed to follow. It was heart-rending! And there was nothing to be done, that was the worst of it. She turned away from him and her eyes flew erratically in every direction, seeking desperately for something she could fasten onto for security, for some fixed point in this suddenly muddled universe. And saw nothing but the fountain and the water spraying onto the surface. Then she turned to Robert and he was actually making off away from her!

What could she do? How could she attract his attention once more, one last time, perhaps, but oh, once more! And saw only the fountain and the water and, without thinking, she reached the parapet in two strides, leapt onto it with a loud shriek and jumped into the water, closing her legs at the knee as she did so, creating an involuntary depth charge which sent the water spouting ten feet into the air in a violent torrent which then rained down, even on Robert himself.

The pool sloped upwards and outwards but where she stood when she straightened, it was about four feet deep. She turned round to look at Robert and found him staring at her, open-mouthed with amazement, still flushed, with the heat, she presumed. Then she began to walk towards him and the water level fell dramatically near the edge and she saw him flinch and flush bright scarlet. She had embarrassed him! People round about had stopped to look. That was the clear message. She tried to get out but her foot slipped on the wet surface and she could not and expected him to come to her and give her a hand. But no! He simply stared and blushed the more. And then gradually turned for the last time and began to walk away. Yet there was something strange about it which she failed at first to notice.

Raissa was furious, wounded by the rejection, and tried ineffectually to climb out but it was no easy matter. By the time she had managed it he had disappeared altogether among the crowds of people, leaving her alone.

What did it all mean? she wondered, as she tried to catch him up and failed utterly to see where he had gone. There were too many people around. No one seemed to mind her state of soddenness or the water that trailed behind her. Everyone was used to the young cooling off in just this fashion during a heat wave. It seemed sensible somehow, especially if you were clad for it. And she was.

Unable to find him, there was nothing to be done but head back to the hotel and change into dry clothing. Arrived there, she phoned his room: no reply. The concierge told her that Robert had not returned as far as he knew.

Raissa decided to bathe and change and lay there in suds, wondering and even crying at the conclusions reached. She had embarrassed him again! By making a public exhibition of herself in entering the water! Throwing herself into the water like that! Worse, she realised, by revealing parts of herself owing to the white dress that, experience had shown, revealed what never should be revealed, when wet. How had she made that mistake twice? It was unthinkable!

But then, lying back in the tub, playing the images through her mind she noticed for the first time the discontinuity. Robert himself had been different that afternoon. Distracted at times. And after the description of Russell's Paradox, worse than ever. Why had he been revolted by her ecstasy? Why had he for the first time not reacted as she did?

The answer was there in the shape, in Robert's shape, just as he turned away from her! She played back the image carefully. He looked as he rarely looked, his form had changed, had changed as she occasionally had observed it to change all that week. For as he had slowly turned away from her at an angle, turned slowly and with obvious reluctance, red-faced, the line of his lower torso was not the straight line of yore, but a triangle! And the apex stood out from his body.

He was aroused by me again! She concluded. And it embarrassed him. And he did not want to be with me! And he thinks me unworthy for having this effect upon him and fears that his work as a thinker will be affected and that is why he ran off like that out of my sight. He did not want to see me, or to be with me!

Some things, some events in the lives of people, Raissa knew very well, are catastrophes from which there is no recovery because everything has changed. And so it was that she wept.

But after a time, she wondered what he would do now. Would he return to tell her he was finished with her, that their friendship was over? Or would he steal away into the night taking his bag and never see her again? Just as suddenly as he had descended upon her and interrupted her summer school.

Then she remembered the jacket which he'd thrown on her bed. There at least was a pretext for visiting him. Whereas she had always visited him at Trinity when they were up at Cambridge, in Paris it had been the exact opposite: he had always come to her room. Why had he wanted to take a jacket when it was so warm? The triangle, that was the reason.

There was nothing for it but to fight to repair the breach, make any promises necessary for them to continue. Whatever he wanted she would give him. If he wanted her to be as cold and indifferent towards him as before, she would manage it—somehow— and wept at having to do such a thing when her inclination was so different.

10

She got out of the bath, dried herself and then changed into the kind of underwear that had become her trademark and put on a knee-length frock of primrose yellow, as if to say: Here I am in my brightest plumage. Please notice me! And made herself up with cosmetics to the highest standard she had achieved.

For the first time that holiday, she went upstairs to his room and knocked, forgetting the jacket. There was no reply. Had he already checked out? She knocked again, more urgently and eventually the door opened to reveal Robert once again in the white suit minus the jacket.

They stood and looked at each other, saying nothing at first, until Raissa said: 'Won't you invite me in?'

'Of course,' he said, lugubriously, stepping aside to admit her.

'We need to talk,' she said and while he closed the door she went to stand by the window, looking out to the street below, wondering what she should say to repair the situation.

Robert closed the door and stood in the middle of the room surveying her sadly.

'Everything has changed,' she said, turning to face him. 'Hasn't it?'

'Yes,' he agreed, with a lump in his throat that almost caused him to gag.

'Well, would you care to explain it to me? I mean, I am not used to being stood up, like that. In fact it has never happened before in all my life. I just c...c....can't...can't take it in. —There, you've got me stammering now.' She was on the verge of tears.

Robert said nothing. He simply looked at her woodenly, meltingly, foolishly.

'It was my making a spectacle of myself at the fountain, wasn't it?'

'No.'

'No? How *No*? That's where it happened for heavens sake! Of course that's what it is.'

'No.'

'Tell me then!'

'It's not you, it's me,' he admitted quietly, sadly.

'I don't understand, Robert, please tell me. We have so much to lose!'

'I am afraid it's the effect you have on me, Raissa'—he did not so much as speak the name as sing it, with a vibrato which gave it added richness. 'Raissa,' he said aloud again, exaggerating the diaresis, as if savouring the sound of it, for the very music of the name thrilled him.

'But.but..but you have an effect on me too! But.. but I don't walk away from you when we are...are supposed to be together.'

'I had to walk away. You see I was an embarrassment to myself. Everybody was bound to notice. My state. My physical state and my mental state too, because of it.'

Raissa was shocked. 'You were embarrassed by yourself? Not by me?'

'Yes.'

'Not by me?'

'Good heavens no.'

'But it was me in the water again, revealing what should never be revealed—in polite society at least. That's what embarrassed you. That makes it my fault.'

'No. I was like that before you went into the water. Don't you see? I have been like this for days and I can do nothing about it.'

'You never used to be like this. What has happened to you?'

Robert turned his head away as if he would rather not say. Taking relief was not something you could communicate to the goddess in your life, especially when that had become impossible because she had just recently reached that status. His tongue stuck to the roof of his mouth and nothing came out but an animal noise of distress. He flushed, embarrassed by his apparent descent to the lower reaches of the animal kingdom. Then he moved his hands and arms apart as if powerless to say anything, looking weak and bereft.

'Come on Robert! Tell me! I have a right to know.' And when he still said nothing, she added: 'Is it so bad? You don't like me any more? You take me to be a bad person. Is that it?'[12]

'No, No, No!' he exploded. 'It's me. I am the one that's changed. Not you! For God's sake, you are wonderful. That's the trouble precisely.'

'Then why all the mystery? Why did you go off like that?'

Robert was in an agony of indecision which caused him to cover his face with his hands which he finally overcame. He straightened up with a new determination and stared her in the face, that light brown symmetrical face which melted him every time he saw it and even when he did not, but read the image stored in the mind.

'I have a confession to make,' he announced quietly, 'and it is this that changes everything. I have fallen in love with you. I am very sorry. That is what has changed. It means—it means many things. I am not at ease in your company any more. My head is a bag of wool most of the time now. The talk about Russell's Paradox was a welcome relief, I can tell you. But as soon as it was over I was back living in my imagination. And every time we touched—and I spent my time looking forward to the next time and planning for it—it would happen again. I had to leave you because of the state of arousal. I needed to get out of that place

---

[12] Those who are offended by the explicitness of the scene which follows should realise that many people, even today, will not understand the details of what is being described unless they are made available. It is the duty of the writer to convey such things clearly. Most of the trouble with our world, especially in connexion with sex, has arisen because of ignorance and guilt about matters that are simple, necessary and hugely desirable in any life. The idea that the imagination should be left to discover these, when there is often no basis for making the discovery, is nonsense.

immediately or go mad. A hundred times I have almost committed the unpardonable and..and..and reached out for you, to clasp you and MATE! —there in public. To force myself on you! Do you see? It's what I have been dreaming about all week! And everyone who had seen us together today would have laughed at my state and not only at me. I could not bear you to suffer in this way for my weakness. It was a thoroughly moral decision.'

'Weakness? Weakness be damned. What rubbish!' Raissa walked towards him slowly and at first he thought she meant to slap his face but her face gradually opened up like a flower in sunshine, took on a warm glow that radiated everywhere. He stood his ground and she came up to him and put her hands on his shoulders and smiled, a smile such as he had never seen in his life. A smile of such warmth that it occurs only once in a lifetime at the very height of ecstasy. 'Oh, Robert,' she said, with tears of happiness in her eyes. And she waited and nothing happened.

'You are supposed to put your hands on my shoulders.'

Robert was dazed. 'Yes, I suppose so.' And he did so.

'Tell me why you didn't do it of your own volition?'

Robert gulped, with the shock of it. 'I hardly dare say.'

'You must! Please tell me.'

Robert stepped back from her. 'Well, if you must know, I would far rather put them on other parts of you. I've thought of nothing else for days, I tell you. I am demented at the thought of you. I am afraid to put my hands on your shoulders. It would not be enough.'

'But I want the same. I am the same!'

His face lit up. He reached out and took her by the hand and fondled it gently in his as if it were gossamer, a thing of beauty and delicacy to be treated with reverence.

With her other hand, she reached out and touched him on the tip of the nose. 'I've always wanted to do that,' she said in a voice that melted him. 'And now I have. How wonderful.'

'But you're only saying that, Raissa. I can hardly believe it. You just want to prolong what we have. You don't have to pretend, you know.'

Going right up to him, she replied: 'I am not pretending. I am absolutely demented too. Obsessed with you.' She grasped him with both arms and hugged him to her. And she put her mouth on his and tried to kiss him and was not very effective. 'Show me, Robert, please. I need to do this and I don't know how. So show me.'

Robert kissed her on the mouth, bending his head so that their noses were not in the way and when he had stopped, Raissa, gasped with astonishment and her legs wobbled. 'Good heavens! I never knew it was like that! Why did you never tell me? Again, please!'

Robert blushed. 'But this is dangerous. I won't be able to stop.'

'I don't want you to stop. I've felt this coming on for weeks and now it has. Why would I want it to stop?'

They kissed together, and somehow tongues explored each other and the soft areas within the other and bodies began to move. There was the sound of materials sliding across each other. A button caught and pinged into space like a missile but there was no laughter, no smile. The event was far too serious. Hugging him to her body, Raissa could feel his length against her and was thrilled by it, its strength, and excited by what it might do for her. Images flashed across her mind, from old biology books and now—here and now—was the real thing in HER CASE! It was wonderful and tears of gratitude fell down, her tears.

'But..but you're crying, Raissa,' said Robert with horrified surprise.

'I am so happy. So very happy. Here let me help you take off all this clothing you're wearing. Talk about mine! It's nothing to yours. I can't wait to get it off. I want to see. I want to touch. I want to know you, every part of you, Darling.'

Robert was astounded. 'Darling? Darling?'

'Of course, Darling! What else? I love you. I have loved you for ages and I've only just realised it. But I think I knew before you did.'

Then they clasped each other and kissed and kissed and he would not let her go. And she had to tear free, panting for lack of breath.

'Breathe through your nose and then you can go on doing it,' he murmured and then did it again pushing his tongue inside her mouth to explore its heavenly softness.

She began to unfasten the buttons of his shirt, inexpertly, foolishly, between kisses, then reached for his hand and put it on her nipple which he squeezed and she jerked as if shot.

Robert could hardly believe what was happening. It felt like winning the Nobel Prize. He seized her buttocks and squeezed and squeezed again and ran his hands up the flanks of her along the curves, feeling the flesh underneath and the suspenders and the belt. She kissed his ear and bit his lobe and then kissed him on the lip and bit there and she took his hand and put it on her nipple again and he squeezed and then bent forward to kiss and bite it, pulling the garment out of the way and she stiffened again with a sudden shudder of pleasure.

She felt him with her hand and kissed him again. He was kissing her neck and nose and cheeks and face. Then he held her head in his hands and studied her as if she were a new person, a mirage that suddenly and unaccountably turned out to be an oasis. Tears formed in his eyes and rolled down his cheeks. He clasped her and felt the back of the bra under the dress and tried to get at the clip and failed. 'Leave it! Leave it,' she said impatiently. 'There isn't time for that.'

'But I want to see you.'

'I am in a hurry. There are more important things,' she commanded peremptorily. But then relented and made as if to unfasten the buttons behind her.

'No, here. Let me do this,' he insisted.

Raissa actually jumped up and down twice with impatience. But eventually the dress was unfastened at the back and Robert managed the clip. The garment fell at her feet.

He stepped back to admire the sight of her, the breasts which lay like grapefruit. 'I want to undress you myself,' he declared, in awe, unable to tear his eyes away.

'But I'll die of starvation before that!' and she laughed with delight—and mischief—that too. But she stood still and let him do as he pleased.

He raised the skirt exposing the stockings and suspenders and the white lacy undergarment and gasped with amazement and turned away as if the sight would turn him to salt. 'Oh! Oh my God!' he said, staring enraptured. 'I never saw anything so beautiful in all my life. I have imagined this and now I have it in front of me and I am allowed to look as long as I want. Is that really so?'

'Yes, yes. But hurry up with your looking. I have things to do also.'

Delicately, clumsily, he pulled off the dress and then felt inside her remaining garment, running his hand down the hard front of her until he found the hair that had first induced his final metamorphosis. 'Oh, that's lovely, so lovely! I never believed I would be doing this! It's wonderful. I'll never tire of this, never!'

'I hope so,' she replied. 'Oh, I do hope so!'

The rest of the clothing came off very quickly and it was Robert's turn to stand while Raissa undressed him. First the shirt buttons and then the trousers fell, revealing the triangle except it was a triangle no more. She gasped at the sight of the rod that lay close against his body and tremulously touched it. 'Does it hurt?' she said.

'Oh no. Far from it.'

'I must get to know this. I hope you'll let me. Will you?'

'Of course. Every morning when I waken I will get up and stand to attention for your close inspection, like a soldier at reveille.' They both laughed, tears still coming from both.

His hands were on her thighs and he felt her, felt the place he'd dreamed about for days, moved his hand lightly over the hair and felt its springiness and traced the lines of the two labia and moved the flesh back and forth several times until the wetness came. The scent drove him wild. 'Oh my God!' he declared. 'Oh my Go-o-o-od!'

He inserted a finger and she shook her head. 'No, not this time. I need you there, only you, Darling.' She fell down on the bed askew and held out her arms to him. 'Come on. Do it please.' And Robert made to do so but there was resistance, there was no room, the angles were all wrong. It was the calculation of an instant to see what the matter was: a certain incompatibility of volume and experience.

'Do it, Robert,' she told him.

'But it will hurt.'

'I don't care.'

'But I do.'

'Do it! Do it!' she ordered. And when he would do nothing, muttering 'No, No,' she pulled him into her. 'Oh God!' he muttered, sliding inwards finally because she continued to pull on his back with hands clamped to his buttocks. They felt the membrane break and her head jerked but only for an instant. Then they were still, fastened together but still, examining the sensation of conjunction for the very first time. It was for Robert like being in an aeroplane, high up above the ground, floating, and he knew he had to keep still to avoid falling, for once he started to fall nothing would stop it. There were forces at work of phenomenal power and he was not in control of any of them.

Breaths were exhaled by both, excited, hot, passionate breaths.

Then it was sinuous movement together, slowly, on and on, exploratory, inexpert but incomparable, the greatest sensation either had ever known. And finally, after all too short a time, the aeroplane began its descent and nothing could stop its journey; for Robert, explosive release such as he'd never known or imagined. 'Oh God!' he exclaimed. 'Oh Goddd!' 'Oh GODDDDD!'

It was if he had spent the whole of himself in a few seconds experience of paradise. Afterwards, he lay back like a great white shot seal with a golden head, exhausted. They lay together, silent for a little and then Robert slept.

While he slept, Raissa had showered and dressed and was sitting with a cup of tea looking at him, absorbing all of him, occasionally touching him very gently with awe, as if not quite sure that he was present, recognising that for the very first time she was allowed to touch him and that he would not think ill of her. How many times before had she wanted just to lay a finger-tip upon him; anywhere? He woke suddenly, sat up on the edge of the bed and said: 'I wonder what the Great One thought of that?'

And Raissa's expression of happiness and wonderment changed to anxiety. 'Well, it's not something I'm supposed to do. Not with you, nor out of wedlock.'

'I don't see how he could object. We were not in control of ourselves, you know. If anything controlled us it was him.'

'But you don't believe in The Great One. He's a joke to you.'

'Not exactly. It's a hypothesis— his existence. I am trying to take account of it, for your sake. If it was me alone, of course, I'd never think of it.'

'I've never felt like this before.'

'Well, depend upon it, we are meant to. It would not have happened unless it was what we are supposed to do. No matter what anybody says.'

'Maybe we're not supposed to. That it's a test.'

Robert laughed. 'And we failed it? No chance! Not to do what we did was impossible. I wonder if other people have it like this? Somehow I doubt it. In many cases it will be in a car or alleyway with someone they don't really like very much—or soon will not like. But look at us! We could not be more suited, have known each other for years and have been growing together for years. And we will be able to do this forever. Think of that!'

'Will we?'

'What's stopping us?'

'My family.'

'Hang your family. You haven't thought of them for a year—except for occasional letters home, so you told me. I am so happy! And absolutely starving. Can we go and eat? I need to refuel. I want to do this again. Are you OK? Not sore?'

'I feel a little strange. Wide open. But not sore, not really. It feels as if the wind might blow in.'

And so they went out and dined again in the expensive restaurant to celebrate the epochal change in their lives and afterwards they strolled the streets under the lights, hand in hand, joyously at ease. 'You must go on the pill. Tomorrow. You have a career and it must go the full term.' And then he looked at her as if his eyes would melt with tears: 'And we'll be mates, proper mates. I bet we do even better.'

'Just so long as my father, or more probably my grandfather, doesn't come after us with an AK 47.' Thus said Raissa, levelly, quietly but firmly.

But that evening, it was soon forgotten in the heady experience, once in a lifetime, of first love. They raced into the hotel lobby, ran into the lift, were discovered in sinuous embrace when it reached her floor by a couple who shook their heads in amazement and regret for what once had been their own experience, now decades in the past, and extracted themselves with difficulty. They stood in the corridor, each looking as if the other would soon be devoured, and then, clutching each other tightly, managed to reach the door, fumbled the entry several times and eventually fell inside, laughing, and rolled on the carpet, inexpertly failing to get clothing off and unable to wait.

'Next time, we'll make it to the bed,' she murmured, through a mouthful of ear.

'Oh, God!' he said.

'Are you taking The Great One in vain?' said Raissa, half seriously.

'Certainly not! I am asking for his aid to enable me to accommodate what is happening to me. And expressing gratitude too. What else could I say that made better sense?'

'But you don't believe in him.'

'It is all I can think of to say. Maybe there is something in that. Anyway, I don't suppose he would mind, assuming he exists at all. Why would he mind? Wouldn't he be happier at my using his name than the name of some other god? Or take the humanist stance: and say instead: 'Oh, my value system!' It doesn't have the flavour of amazement at all. No,' he concluded, 'I am definitely saying the appropriate words, even for me.'

11

Two weeks were spent profligately, joyously, seeing the sights of the great city, walking the streets and lanes, by the river—often—in and out of galleries, museums, churches and shops, mostly bookshops but dress shops too. Robert became insistent about purchasing dresses. They would pass a clothes shop and he would notice a dress in the window and insist on entering to try it on her and then buy it with a flourish of the plastic, as if he actually had the money.

'But how are you going to pay for it?'

'Do you doubt my earning capacity? Have I not a brain? I am one of Besicovitch's[13] boys, remember? That should be good for 100 grand a year.'

'But you'll need a loan, just for tuition and board etc.'

'You're forgetting the scholarship.'

'That won't cover everything.'

'Then I'll apply for another. Win a prize at something. Tell them I need the money. I've just fallen in love with the most beautiful girl in the world and I must have it, if the country—the world, by God!—is not to lose, for my creativity depends upon my happiness and that is in her hands.'

---

[13] One of the leading mathematicians of Cambridge. To be tutored by him you had to be outstanding.

Robert turned to a statue and addressed it as if it were a judge, with hand crossed over chest clutching lapel: 'M'Lud, if it please your lordship, the accused stands here guilty as charged of misappropriation of plastic funds. He deeply regrets this and urges mitigating circumstances. To wit: one female, devotee of The Great One, whose charms have appropriated his wits. Should he be given a prison sentence his creative river will assuredly dry up and the universe will be deprived of the galaxy of theorems he is about to unleash. In accordance with the Code Napoleon, M'Lud, might I suggest a suspension of the repayment until just one of these theorems has won the renown (as well as the cash) which is an inevitable corollary?'

Raissa laughed delightedly.

Then there were the meals. Meat pies and coffees in paper cartons, eaten on the hoof, ice-creams and lolly pops and more substantial affairs consumed in restaurants with wines by the bottle.

Once, in the street, Robert ran across first, getting separated by traffic, leaving Raissa behind. Seeing this apparently desperate approach to her, a prostitute who assumed he had been attracted by her pink hot pants and precious little else, engaged him in preliminary negotiations. As Raissa, blushing with embarrassment, drew near, under the eyes of a crowd of bystanders, some of them in similar negotiations, and not quite sure if she was about to be ditched in favour of the competition, Robert bowed to the Lady of the Night and declared loudly: 'My Dear, I do not love thee

    And perusal of thy charm
    Sayst that to mate with thee
    Wouldst do me only harm.'

The prostitute was furious at losing the client to a competitor, as she judged, and, as they strode off arm in arm again, swore venomously after them.

The Eiffel Tower was a favourite. They went up four times, kissing and embracing and once almost copulating until other mountaineers protested at the obstruction on the stairway to the top.

They made love before and after dinner. Before breakfast and once in a toilet during lunch. It was a time of delicious sensual madness.

Finally, there was no time left. The new term was due to begin. 'But I don't have an air ticket?' Robert admitted. And when efforts on the phone to get him on the same flight as Raissa came to nought, dressed in the white suit, he sat down in the chair in her hotel room and complained: 'Well, we'll just have to go by train—if they'll have us. I can't bear to travel without you.'

'But it will cost so much! It's just an hour or two,' she replied, sitting on the bed facing him in the white dress that had dried out.

'No good. Not letting you of my sight, Darling. Some tall, dark Arabic person might see you and snaffle you. Carry you off to his harem. You don't get out of my sight. Promise?'

And he insisted until she did.

'But what will you do? About work? To make up these debts? And all the others I see on the horizon. What have you in your creative pipeline?'

'Plenty! We've spoken of it, have we not?'

'Not recently. Nothing that would earn enduring fame and big bucks.'

'Well, what about economic theory. Make a mathematical model of the changing financial climates and their outcomes.'

'There are loads of these already and they don't work.'

'Mine will. I'll take a period, or probably periods, one by one, describe the circumstances prior to the main change and derive the theorems that govern the outcome.'

'I bet that's been done.'

'But not by me and not exhaustively. I can do it, Raissa, believe me. With you behind me, there's nothing stopping me.'

'What if there are no laws that can be used as predictors?'

'There are, depend upon it. There is a way. I know it and I will find it. Maybe I'll have to invent some things to do it but I'll do it. You'll see. The least thing can affect the direction of change. I'll use the new supercomputer to compute all the possibilities at the speed of light. The Mathematical Prediction of Change, that is what it will be—a new science. It will effectively foretell the future based on a detailed description and understanding of the present and past.

'A lovely dream. But it might be impossible!'

'But nothing is impossible.'

'Not so! What about Godel's Theorem? A self-consistent system of elementary arithmetic is impossible!'

'Then, if stuck, I will join the cipher group at Cheltenham and make a truly unbreakable code and break everybody else's. Or head for Langley and the intelligence development unit.'

'And if they won't have you because you're attached to a foreign national of indeterminate religion, presumed anti-American?'

'Then I'll just have to settle down and win a Fields Medal for the remaining Hilbert problems or a Nobel prize. '

'Physics too?'

'The Schrodinger Cat problem. I'll solve that and clear up Quantum Mechanics. The paradoxes are outrageous. "Just calculate and shut up^{14}, indeed! These were made for someone like me.'

So whatever the difficulty, love would conquer all.

And, with the irrepressible confidence of youth, they set off for the train station, Cambridge and the future. But as the coach slid across the Channel, Robert turned to Raissa and enquired: 'I think I must go home for a few days, to show myself. What about you?'

'You go yourself. But don't say anything about us. It might get back to my family.'

'But I must! I'm dying to tell them. They deserve to know. They'll have to be told sometime.'

'But not yet.'

'Why won't you come?'

---

^{14}^{14} The philosophy {attributed to Dirac and (almost certainly wrongly) to Feynman} of many of the physicists (such as Andersen of Copenhagen) who are content that sub atomic predictions can be made and who do not worry about the paradoxes still in the theory. Such as: that you only know where a particle is when you measure it and it is somewhere else if you don't. **Or that a vacuum has a great deal of activity within it**. * Or that there is a force which will pull together a pair of parallel metal plates set apart in a vacuum, despite the absence of magnetism or electric charge. And the Schrodinger Cat problem which makes the cat simultaneously alive and dead, a variant of the measurement problem. A solution, according to the GRW scheme, is suggested in Roger Penrose: *Shadows of the Mind,* p334. The cat is a massive object with a vast number of particles. The first hit of the photon 'would localize the cat's state as dead or alive.' Fig 6.3.   *SEE p199!!

'My family will never understand. I don't think I could go home now. I'd have to put on the tudong and all the other stuff. The truth is I've become too used to this western dress and this western lifestyle. I can't go back to the other. But if I go back home, they will make me.'

'They can't force you.'

'Yes, they can. You don't know them. How they were, in the desert.'

'But they're not in the desert now.'

'They think they are. It's just the same to them, except for the rain.'

'So that's why you were never keen to go back in the holidays?'

'Yes, and my family have put up with it because they have confidence in me—that is in the tribe— and they think I'm on some kind of new adventure and that I'll appear on the doorstep once again in my swaddling clothes with a suitcase of money and presents.'

'—And a bearded chap with a turban on your arm?'

'No, that would not be expected. If I came back with a man on my arm they'd assume the worst. He would be grilled and I would be banished to a back room where I'd be examined by the women.'

'—And then?'

'Depends. On what took place and was he suitable?'

'And what would that take?'

'The right background and enough money. They'd want money for me. A lot. Even a young man—good from every point of view—would be expected to pay for me.'

'You used to think it might be an old man with cash?'

'That was before I went to university. No matter that they do not understand what goes on there, they still see it as an asset, a feather in my cap. There's value in that. I am valuable. That's how it would be.'

Raissa was staring out of the window into nothingness and Robert saw the sadness there for the first time. He took her hand in his. 'We'll get over this. You'll see.'

'I can't see how.'

'Life moves on. Maybe your family have. Living in Argyll may have had some beneficial effect.'

'You don't know them. They don't mix—they are not supposed to mix! At all! How could they change? I just hope you're right but don't count on it.' Raissa considered the matter with a worried frown for a time and then turned to Robert. 'I want you to listen very carefully and do what I ask. Do you promise you will?'

'Yes, if I can.'

'You must promise without conditions. Do you?'

'For you, Darling, anything. Yes.'

'When you get home you must only tell your parents and swear them to secrecy. I realise it's asking too much not to tell them. They'd see it in you anyway. But that's all. And don't go anywhere near my family. Don't go to the shop. Stay well clear. And if by some misfortune you run into one of them and they enquire after me, please say that I am doing well and am happy and I will be in touch in due course when I have time. Not another thing more. Can you do that?'

'I suppose so.'

'Not good enough! This is important. Don't mess me about, please. It could affect both our lives in ways you can hardly imagine. I need to know for sure.'

Robert in mock horror, raised his hands as if to defend himself from punches. 'I never realised you were such an Amazon. If you wish it, so shall it be. I promise. Indeed, I solemnly swear to thee and The Great One that it shall be as thou sayst.'

Yet, after a pause for reflection, Robert added; 'I don't understand, darling. Why all the drama? Anyone'd think your father was Dracula and your mother his blood-sucking wife.'

'You don't know where we come from, Robert. Blood is very important there. In ways you can scarcely imagine. When something goes wrong at that level, they shed a lot of it, usually other people's.'

Thus it was that they went back to London where Raissa kissed Robert goodbye, publicly, the very next morning at the Station on his way to the north, while she waited for the next train to Cambridge to get back into her books at Emmanuel.

12

Returning home after so much change in his life was a strange experience for Robert. The train stopped in Glasgow Central and then he had to walk over to Queen Street for the train to Oban. Very little had changed. A few shops sold different goods, the faces were different but Miss Cranston's was still there and he stopped to have lunch, read *The Herald* newspaper and wait for the train.

At Oban he thought of heading for the school, realised that he would be lionised—for the success in the first diet of the Tripos[15] might be common knowledge—and headed for the bus station instead. The idea of calling up and asking to be collected had occurred but he wanted the visit to be unexpected.

Thus, he climbed off the public bus just short of the village and walked up the track to the house, Tigh-na-mara, out on the spit, which he'd taken so often since boyhood.

There was no sign of the car in the drive but the door opened when he turned the door-handle and he stood again in the hall and laid down his bag. 'Anybody home?' he called.

There was some noise above and presently his father was standing on the stairway, palette in hand, brush in the other, unkempt, in brown corduroy trousers and crew neck sweater, both stained with dried paint. Then, descending, he laid them down on a side table, took a rag from a pocket and began to clean the paint off his hands.

---

[15] The examinations at Cambridge: Part I is taken after a year and Part II after 3 years.

'So, the wanderer returns. Let me look at you. Turn round.' As Robert did, Hector said: 'A little taller, maybe. You look older too. Or is it shagged out?'

Robert laughed, embarrassed. 'Never heard that word in here before.'

'Isn't it what everybody says now?'

'Yes, I am afraid it is. At Cambridge, anyway.'

'Why afraid?'

'No reason. It seems to diminish the act, somehow.'

'So it was love then?'

'Is there no one else here?'

'No, why should there be? Why does it matter? Your mother's in the town, the kids at school.'

'I have a secret to tell and it must be a secret that only you and mum get to hear. No one else. You will understand why later.'

'Ok, but it's no secret. I believe we both know.'

'What? You couldn't know.'

'It's Raissa, isn't it?'

'How did you guess?'

'There had to be something keeping you away and that was the obvious answer. We could read between the lines of your few epistles. We know you would have come home sooner.'

They both absorbed the news, staring at each other.

'She's not with you, is she?'

'No, she's afraid to come home. Can't bear to put on these silly clothes.'

'Well, you'll have to tell them sometime.'

'What do they know?'

'Not much, I think. They keep themselves to themselves, just as before. They're quite pleasant but they don't mix at all.'

'What about services: doctors, dentists, that kind of thing?'

'Couldn't say. Maybe not much wrong with them. You just never see them much. They stay indoors, mostly—with occasional trips to Lochgilphead. Then the whole family goes. Though sometimes the old man stays home to look after the shop. But he doesn't manage our money very well, though his English has become very good—because he watches so much TV.'

'Have I disturbed you at your work?'

'No, I've finished for now anyway. Come and sit down and we'll debate the nature of the fatted calf now that the prodigal has returned.'

They went into the sitting room, Robert sat on the sofa and Hector got out the decanter.

'You don't often use that.'

'It has the best of stuff in it. Caol Isla, 20 year old, they said. Fell off a lorry somewhere between Mallaig and Fort William, if you get my drift.'

'I take red wine now, or beer, occasionally.'

'Still looking after the brainbox? Good for you. So how did you spend the summer?'

'Harvard, to start. Then Paris.' While Hector uncorked a bottle, Robert gave an edited version of events.

'So Raissa remained at Emmanuel and you came up here sworn to secrecy?' said Hector, handing over a bumper of red.

'That's about it.'

'What are you going to do if her family won't allow you to marry?'

'People don't bother nowadays.'

'But hers will, depend upon it. They might cast her out, of course. Disown her.'

'Raissa doesn't think that's an option. Once they find out, the fat's in the fire.'

'You think they might stone her or worse?'

'She thinks so. That's why it's so important that the matter be kept quiet.'

They sat opposite considering the matter, Hector on a matching sofa, with the fire on his left.

'You know,' said Hector, thoughtfully, 'I am not sure it can be kept quiet. If we know or thought we knew, others in the village will have drawn the same conclusions. One of them is liable to spill the beans in the shop one day and that will put the cat among the pigeons.'

Robert contemplated this prospect with alarm. 'Nothing can be done about that. This village is a mine of gossip. If I said anything to inhibit a remark like that it would be made quicker than ever. You know what they're like.'

'Yes. I'm not sure what to advise.'

'Obviously we should stay away as long as possible. Avoid them like the plague. That way she won't have any trouble. That is a major concern. She has to be left in peace to do her work and pass her exams with the distinction she deserves. I should never have come home at all.'

'Won't they go and look for her? Why haven't they been already?'

'I think she writes regularly and they have such confidence that they don't expect anything untoward—like this. I mean, her and me.'

'But don't they miss her or she them?'

'I suppose they must. But they are stoical, tough, I guess— from what she says— used to deprivation, disruption and so on. She does miss them, I know, but she is very afraid that they will haul her back into the fold. She doesn't like the fold at all.'

'So what are you going to do?'

'Leave first thing in the morning. I have to get back to Cambridge anyway, to attend lectures and see my tutors. They will have assignments for me. I'm one to one with Besicovitch in two days time and I have to be ready.'

So that evening, when Rose and the girls returned, they enjoyed a special dinner, talked until late and Hector drove Robert to the station the next morning for the journey to Cambridge.

The term passed in a whirl of lectures, tutorials, reading, questioning, absorbing and revising while writing exercise after exercise; above all it was about developing the problem solving tool in the mind, focusing with ever greater intensity, seeking depth and speed and building up the list of auxiliary problems to enhance the stochastic effect of the search for new answers. It was a heady experience under pressure to get all the work done and there never seemed to be enough time. They worked together, ate together, walked in the parks by the Cam together, attended occasional concerts together and made love in Robert's room at Whewell's Court. Mostly, Raissa returned to spend the night at Emmanuel.

When the university broke up, the problem reasserted itself. They had nowhere to go and little money. How were they to spend the vacation?

'We could get jobs,' suggested Robert, in December.

'But not together, I bet.'

'Well, we could rent a cottage or a room somewhere.'

'Using what for money?'

'Plastic. I could take out another loan.'

The problem was kicked around the group who collected for afternoon tea. Eventually, a cottage was found at St Ninian's Bay in Bute where somebody knew somebody who had one there and it was unoccupied most of the year. The journey was a revelation, across a narrow sea and then a bus several miles across the island and a long walk out to a small white house stuck out on a peninsula all by itself, one that required wading because of the high tides which temporarily cut it off from the island.

The first day of miserable cloud and rain was spent hiring bikes, stocking up the panniers and rucksacks with provisions, especially coals for the fire and paraffin for the lights. Then, in a rain-storm, clad only in the thinnest of plastic macs, they cycled all the way back from the town.

Cold water was got out of a rainwater-butt, heated in a pot on the open fire Raissa managed to light—being used to desert fires—and then used to brew that first cup of tea after the misery of soaking in the rain and wading across the channel with the stores. It was a haven shared as they stood in the damp room with windows looking out onto a bleak expanse of sea hidden by low-lying cloud and even fog. In time the room heated up, the dampness disappeared somewhat, and they unrolled the sleeping bags onto the concrete floor in front of the fire, there to sleep the sleep of exhausted travellers who had come 500 miles in a day.

They awoke to the cries of seabirds which collected shellfish, rose in the air and dropped them on the rocks below. Then to swoop and gobble up the innards.

Two islands lay before them. A low-lying one in front, Inchmarnock and, further out, another, Arran, with snow-capped jagged mountains reaching to the sky. A magical place it was.

Getting things to work and improving their dwelling was the next priority and then breakfast: cereal and eggs. But soon, they were catching fish, mackerel and cod, and even mussels which Robert, who had lived by the sea all his life, knew how to cook: steamed with a little lemon, cream from a nearby farm and white wine. Then they found the upturned boat, 2 oars inside the shed attached to the house and they went fishing in earnest.

Every day they caught something. Mostly they studied, shared knowledge and insights and argued occasionally. Cut off from everyone out there it was a happy time. And when the food ran out they rode to town, replenished the stores and went to the pictures in the evening before going home in the dark.

On Christmas day Robert spoke to his family, one by one, on the phone, described his situation and swore everyone to secrecy. Raissa sent a letter, knowing hers would not easily understand where she was and would not find them if they did, for they were strangers in a strange place, hardly ever seen about the village.

And so they survived. And the next holiday was just as good. They subleased a flat in London, put the costs on their credit cards and took advantage of the fleshpots: theatres, restaurants, the British Museum and Library, the Science Museum and the usual attractions like the Tower and the Art Galleries.

But at the end of May, during the week of the ball, when cameras were outside King's College during a news programme, interviewing people on the street, Raissa happened to be passing the Examination Schools near by.

It was the children in the house above the shop in Kinoidart who noticed on the TV. 'See, Grandfather, there is Raissa!' said one, excitedly. But with surprise, 'She has no clothes on. Where is her tudong?'

The three clustered around the set in wonder until the image was lost. Suleiman considered it for a time: what it signified; and when Ahmed came in after closing up, he told him. The family watched the later newscast and, sure enough, there she was again and they caught all the footage this time. They had no doubt of it! No tudong. No djellaba. None of her clothes! Only the western ones: a white short sleeved blouse which emphasised the bust and a pair of slinky white trousers which fitted her like a glove, revealing every charm in her jewellery box. In one hand she carried a briefcase. She looked happy, beautiful— as they had never seen her before— and confident and more mature than they had ever imagined possible. She was a western woman. She had rejected their culture. What was to be done?

Suleiman was incensed. He got up so suddenly the turban nearly came off. It was a time for action. And he missed action so much, cosseted here in rainy Argyll with all the food of the west to feed on, every luxury and many he had never known even yet. This was a reason for being. One last skirmish, perhaps, before he went to meet The Great One. He spent the night checking his weapons. There was a curved blade about seven inches long which had to be sharpened and a long, silver-inlaid but much battered which had somehow been smuggled across various borders, unseen by customs people: taped to the underside of the lorry they arrived in. This had to be cleaned with a pull-through and every part examined minutely.

A few days later, Ahmad's cousin, Mohammed Bombazine, appeared at the porter's lodge of Emmanuel College. The porter on duty studied him with amazement, for Mohammed could have stepped out of the tales of Scheherazade or at least Lawrence's Arab Legion. His five feet six inches were clad like an oriental potentate in blue turban, white pantaloons and a blue overshirt or dish dash. 'I wish to know where lives Raissa Hussain,' said he.

'And who might you be, my dear sir?' enquired the porter.

'Mohammed Hussain,' was the reply. 'An uncle.'

The number of the room, the building and directions for reaching it were given.

Raissa, clad in white T shirt, green Bermuda shorts and white trainers was sitting at her desk, deep in Complex Number Theory, engrossed in the contemplation of the mathematical implications of Riemann Sheets. When the knock came to the door, she called: 'Come'.

When she turned to look at her visitor, he said: 'It is I, your uncle Mohammed. Raissa, why have you no clothes?'

The shock of this apparition she had last seen in the desert was enough to jolt her into the real world. Here it was in front of her in its most compelling aspect. For was not Mohammed Bombazine so named because of his nature? It was, after all, a nickname. Translated, it meant something like: 'Mohammed-who-prefers-to-dispatch-his-enemies-by-blowing-them-to-pieces-with-a-bomb.'

'Why are you wearing no clothes?' he said again, menacingly.

She laughed, hysterically. 'But I have clothes on. I am wearing a T shirt and shorts.'

'These are not clothes! You are nearly naked. You reveal everything to the world. It is not decent. Not proper. Your family is disgraced. I am here to take you home. But first you must come with me and put off these disgusting things and wear proper clothes. Our clothes.'

The little man reached down with one hand, grasped her upper arm and drew her to her feet. She over-topped him by five inches and was nearly his weight. Yet he was wiry and strong. He attempted to lead her to the doorway. She resisted. 'You can't do this.'

'Of course I can. I am your uncle. I have the orders of your father and grandfather. What will Suleiman say when he learns of this?'

'I won't go! I have things to do. Important things.'

'What things of yours could be important?'

'I am the first one of us to come here and will be the first to graduate. Don't you understand? It is important to the tribe!'

'Camelshit! It is camelshit, you talk. You are to come with me and no questions.'

'But I won't! I won't!' and she struggled to free his hand from her arm but only brought his other into play in a wrestling match. Presently, tiring of this and disgusted that he lacked the strength to overwhelm her—what must they be feeding her on that she had grown so tall and strong?—he knew nothing about the advantages conveyed upon the female anatomy by bowling and batting at cricket—he loosed one hand and sought for the scabbard of the blade, drew it in one swift movement, raised it threateningly above her face as she was in the act of drawing back, wondered what Suleiman would say if he slew her there and then and stabbed downwards and to the side—trying to make an impression, but without dispatching the recalcitrant completely. It was really too irritating that a mere female should have resisted his efforts to follow orders which, everyone knew, were instructions from The Great One himself. By taking off her clothes, uncovering herself in this demeaning western manner, had she not already condemned herself to apostasy? And was the punishment for this not death?

The knife scythed downwards and across her torso, bisecting the filmy shirt like tissue paper and catching her with the point on the very flesh itself, so that a curved red line of blood seeped outwards.

Raissa gasped.

Her hand leapt to her side and she brought it up to see the bright blood upon it. 'Get out! Get out of here!' she screamed, picking up the chair and hurling it at her uncle who, hit full in the face, fell down on his back under the chair.

Raissa ran past him out of the door, down the stair, across the college lawn and out of the front gate, where she stopped for an instant to look right and left. Then, realising that there might be others, she set off to run to Trinity, reaching the main gate of which, she ran beneath Sir Isaac Newton's old rooms, wondering, crazily, as she did so, what the great mind would have made of this? What would he have advised, had he been her supervisor? She took the stairs three at a time, burst through the door of Robert's sanctum and found him absent. He would be attending the Archimedeans, she realised, Trinity's own mathematical society. Besicovitch was lecturing that evening.

Faced with the choice of staying put and perhaps being followed there by others—the tribe did nothing to do with blood by halves—she threw the door open and ran to the room where the lecture was taking place.

Thus was it that Besicovich, in mid sentence, halting to remark: 'You are late, Raissa. You missed all the good bits,' then saw the streak of blood across her torso, noticed the flap of white material which fell down exposing her stomach and the seeping wound and the drops of blood elsewhere further down on the trousers, threw down his notes and exclaimed. 'Oh God! What has happened to you?'—the first time anyone had ever heard him invoke the deity in many years at Britain's most famous college for the mathematically gifted.

In the front row, Robert came out of his focus on the ideas before him on the blackboard, turned his head and leapt out of his seat to go to her and take her with utmost gentleness and reverence, sit her down in it and examine the wound, cooing mildly with alarm and fright. 'Is she dying?' 'Who did it?' 'Is it self-inflicted?' 'Would someone phone the police?' 'Rubbish,' said Besicovitch: 'Find a doctor. Get Shearman. He's a doctor and he's in his room. I passed him not long ago.' So said several people, among other remarks not all as sensible or as stupid.

'Come away, Robert,' ordered Besicovitch. 'Leave it to others who are more objective.'

This was difficult but at last Robert was led to one side so that more rational men and women could attend the patient.

As anyone could plainly see, she was not dying. There was a wound and it seeped blood but it was not going to be a cause of death. When this was made clear and began to be the accepted view, Robert stopped sighing and quivering with fright. And then Shearman arrived, a large avuncular sandy-haired Fellow of the College in a brown suit who told the gathering to hush and, with a sad smile and a friendly dampening wave of the hand, ordered everyone out of the room; and when that had taken place, began to examine Raissa carefully, asking her to describe the attack and the reason for it.

Finally, he stood up and declared Raissa free from imminent danger. She was to go to hospital immediately and might need a few stitches but the wound did not appear to be deep or serious in any way.

While Robert, two students and Raissa's supervisor, Professor Baker, accompanied her to the car park where Baker kept his car, the doctor explained the incident to Besicovitch as he was best able, adding: 'She is in shock, of course. I've given her something for it but they'll take far better care of her at A and E.'

'But what is the cause of it?'

'It seems to be tribal, from what I could gather. She has broken the rules of the tribe by wearing western clothes. That was enough. As you and I know, she has doubtless broken other rules far more serious. What sort of a reaction there will be when these become known is interesting to speculate.'

13

'Well, there is no point in pressing charges,' said the Master of Emmanuel, in his office later the next day when Raissa returned from the hospital. 'As there were no witnesses, it is his word against yours. The question is: what to do about you?'

Robert and she were sitting in front of a huge ornately carved desk of some antiquity, side-on to a bank of mullioned windows that looked out to the lawns in the centre of the college. Around the oak-panelled stateroom were portraits of other masters: scientists, politicians, literary men and divines, ie scholars of the Anglican God.

'The incident is likely to take place again but with more helpers and greater chance of success. So you tell me and I can believe it. I spoke to McAllister, a Fellow at Keble, who is an expert on peoples of that region and he assured me that they are unusually determined in anything they attempt. Evidently, they have slaughtered British armies in the past.'

The Master was sixty, balding, with a tonsure of white hair, clad in a white pin-striped dark-blue suit, white shirt and wearing an outsize pink bow tie which flapped on his lapels. His patrician features shone with health and brightness.

'I've had a word with the Master of Trinity, Robert, and we are agreed that something must be done, at least when you are most at risk—both of you are at risk, I would say. What you should have is protection. But there aren't funds for that, I'm afraid. So you will have to be very careful as you go about your duties during term. Never go alone if you can help it. Keep an eye open for brown gentlemen in turbans. That kind of thing.

'What we are most anxious to achieve is that you both finish the course. Another year is not a long time and the outcome for you both is potentially splendid. It would be a great pity if because of an incident like this you were unable to complete the Tripos next summer. You do need to take these exams and you must achieve the highest level you are capable of. Whatever you do will be a signal to the wide world hereafter and its value must not be underestimated. You both need a first and it needs to be one of congratulatory quality. You are both good enough to apply for All Souls and should do so, all being well, that is. But there's many a slip between the cup and lip. It has all been seen before: bright potential star metamorphoses into comet which disintegrates at the very last moment. Remember the last term. That is vital. Do not neglect it in any way. Be at College. Attend all lectures and tutorials, especially then, for you will pick up all sorts of hints and help about the questions that will face you. Your tutors will want the highest marks for you but it will be up to you on the day. And remember to be well rested. Rely on your native insight, that most of all. It is more important than any quantity of obscure knowledge in deep textbooks. Thinking is everything, as I am sure you appreciate. Having your mind at the highest pitch of efficiency is the key.

'The difficulty is the vacation. Or to be precise, the 3 vacations in front of you. After the Tripos you can go anywhere you like. Until then, you can do nothing. You have to pass the tests everyone of intellectual stature must pass and with distinction. A bare first is not going to be good enough for you. From success in this will come Fellowships, means of support, while you work at your masterpiece, whatever it is to be.

'Here then is what I suggest. In a few days time at the end of term or right now if you prefer, you can go to Dryburgh in the border country. I have a cottage there and it is yours for the vacations. There you will stay and there you should be safe. —Providing, that is, you take precautions about concealing your whereabouts. If your family find out where you are, of course, you could be very vulnerable there. So no one must know. Well, what do you say?'

Their faces lit up and they each thanked him.

'Oh, one other thing. Since you have little money, there will be no rent. In addition, the Master of Trinity and I have agreed to give you each a scholarship to tide you over the summer and the other vacations. This means you can keep up your very good work without that worry. '

Their thanks were effusive.

'There is always money for deserving causes. Just make us proud. That's all we ask.'

As they were leaving, the Master added: 'Just go out and discover something useful. A nice theorem or two which defied everybody up to now, would be a start.'

But how were they to get to Dryburgh without being seen?

Walking around the quadrangle, Raissa said: 'The train and bus stations might be watched. It's what they'd do.'

'Won't we see them? And give them the slip?'

'Not necessarily. They are very resourceful. Believe me, I know them. Remember what the Master said.'

'In that case, we must have a car. Nobody will lend one. It could be set on fire or worse. So I will have to buy one. Something reliable but cheap. I'll get it on the plastic. Take out another loan.'

'I'll pay half.'

Thus it was that they escaped from Cambridge early one morning. Up the A1 they drove, past Isaac Newton's house at Woolsthorpe, where not all the terrors of hell could prevent them stopping.

The house had not opened up, it was so early. They parked in what had been the farmyard and got out and walked around the rather small grey-stone, two-storied building, eventually to sit on the grass under the apple trees—descendants of those very ones Isaac had been sitting beneath when there landed upon the genius brow the fruit that launched the theory of gravitation and the first mathematical system of the world.

The air was cold that morning but they wandered about the grass as if they were treading in the footsteps of the great man himself and felt it not. The inner heat of inspiration provided by such a place was sufficient warmth.

Eventually, the house opened to visitors and they went through it alone. There was the bedroom in which Newton had first opened his eyes to the world and the shutters with the very hole in them through which he had allowed light to enter when performing his first experiments with the prisms which split light and revealed the spectrum. They did not need a guide. While still at school they had both absorbed *The Optics*[16], the first really great work of science written in English which described these experiments in detailed 17th century language, a rustic style, conveyed forcefully like a chisel upon stone. The rigor of this, the first great attempt in English to objectify experiments had been an arresting revelation. Of course they had devoured all the principal biographies[17] of the great man.

'It is a very bleak and simple dwelling,' said Robert, presently, 'but full of an inspiring and unfathomable richness, nevertheless.'

'Do you think an apple really fell on his head?' said Raissa.

'Why not? It is just the thing to call it to his attention.'

'Yes, all it took was something exceptional. He was exceptional enough to notice.'

There were no pursuers. Had there been, they would have been caught at the Manor House. So they were able to linger and the loitering was like a Christian visit to the Holy Sepulchre in Jerusalem. That day, it was not Cambridge that was the centre of their world but Woolsthorpe Manor House.

As they drove away, it was with a real sense of destiny, the ambition to follow in the great man's footsteps, quietly present in each mind, emphasised by having walked over the ground of his childhood.

A pit stop at Grantham for fuel and food was followed by the long trip to Berwick where they began to ease off to the west up the Tweed

---

[16] By Isaac Newton, published 1703.

[17] Six people were given access to the voluminous Newton papers in the 1960's -80's; biographies, each with a different slant, were produced; and several others since. Eg Manuel, FE, A portrait of Isaac Newton, 1968;Westfall, R. *Never at Rest*, 1980; Dobbs,BJT,1975 *The Foundations of Newton's Alchemy*; Christianson, GE, 1984, *In the Presence of the Creator*, Gjertsen, D, *The Newton Handbook*,1986; Hall, AR, *Isaac Newton Adventurer in Thought*, 1992 White, M, *Isaac Newton The Last Sorcerer*,1997; Fara, P, *Newton, The making of a Genius*, 2002. *Newton's Principia for the Common Reader* by Chandrasekhar, S, 1995 is a mathematician's account of the famous work in 'simple' terms: simpler than Newton's version in Latin, at least in using English and modern notation.

valley towards Dryburgh where, after Kelso, they found an old ruined Abbey set in a great park beside a village nestling under the hills to the north. The cottage was a dream come true. Everybody's ideal retreat from the battlefield where too many lives, even those in the high places of Cambridge, are lived.

Every morning they rose early and studied for three or four hours, walked and talked in the afternoon after lunch, fished in the early evening when the rise of trout started, worked some more after dinner and then made love and slept till they arose to start again. On Sundays Robert took to attending churches in the surrounding villages and Raissa accompanied him because she liked the company as much as she feared to be alone. She knew very well that Robert's presence would stop nothing if their whereabouts were discovered.

She wrote no letters home now but on return to Emmanuel in the autumn found many from her family, all with one message: return to the culture, give up the western life she had adopted, especially the signs of it: the clothes she now wore; but, in addition, every habit she had acquired there. No one ever attempted to get in touch by telephone and continue the persuasion. That was never their strategy in matters of this kind, she knew. Sudden, invariably dramatic and often bloody intervention was their style.

That summer one additional event of a peculiar nature occurred: Suleiman and Ahmad presented them at the gate of the College and requested to see Raissa.

'She is not here at present,' said the Porter, who had, like everyone else, been briefed on the situation and how to respond.

'Then where can we find her?' said Ahmad. 'It is such a long time since we have seen her.'

'I do not know where she is,' replied the Porter. 'Only the Master would know and he is on vacation himself.'

'When will she return?'

'Impossible to say for sure. It would depend on whether she is travelling overseas on a scholarship of some kind,' parried the Porter.

'We will return in two months,' decided Ahmad, irritated.

'I do not think you would be admitted,' concluded the Porter.

'We are her family. She is my daughter. Of course she will see us.'

'She is a student of this college and above the age at which she need consider the wishes of her family. She does not wish to see any of you. This has been made clear by her. And we are ordered to follow her wishes, by the Master who is her guardian now.'

Whether the Master himself had left instructions which involved him quite so directly is hard to say. But this was how the Porter interpreted them.

The two turbaned men left in some anger and annoyance at being thwarted on a matter to do with their family. It was, to them, a matter of blood. Few things were as important.

Thereafter, when Raissa returned to College, she would leave and enter by the back gate, always in company if possible. Since her situation was well known by now, everyone was willing to help by acting as protectors, even though they little realised the full implications of their alliance with her. Being killed in the crossfire was a distinct possibility, as she knew from past experience in her early life in the homeland.

Efforts were made to track her down by the family and way-lay her but this was very difficult at Cambridge because of their ignorance of the way of life she led. A watch that did not attract attention upon itself could not be made from a parked car because every street was double-yellow lined and severely policed with instant fines and clampings for offenders. Any brown-faced, turbaned person seen loitering was of course and by routine, reported and subjected to questioning by the police who had been informed by the Master.

And so, the next two terms went by in a rush but with little to distract the pair from their labours. The Tripos came and went and they waited for a few weeks in their colleges for the results. Punting on the Cam became a serious way of spending the time, with a bottle of wine, sandwiches made up in the college kitchens and some novels to read for diversion. Raissa would step aboard with the hamper, Robert would shove off and propel the delicate ship downstream towards Grantchester (or the other way) and they would anchor in some shady bower, eat, drink, be merry and read.

They did so well in the exams that the Master invited them for drinks. There they met the Master of Trinity and a few dons.

'We think you should both write the papers for All Souls,' said the Master of Trinity. 'What do you say?'

Of course they agreed and a week later they set out for Oxford to be interviewed, spend the night and be examined yet again. There were five candidates for two places. As usual, all had been invited. Besides the two mathematicians were a chemist, an astronomer and a philosopher. The decision to take only one mathematician was easily made in such brilliant company. After the examinations and interviews, when it was being decided, the mathematicians consulted—three of them—were asked: 'Who has the best chance of achieving something genuinely original?'

They were unanimous: Raissa. So she and the philosopher were elected.

A week later it was announced that Robert was to be a fellow of Trinity. So that was some recompense for the disappointment of being placed second.

Since Raissa was also named first wrangler as a result of the Tripos and Robert second, this was not unexpected. But as Robert said in the cool light of day after all the congratulations and celebrations were over: 'You do realise, dearest, that the second generally outstrips the first who is often never heard of again? Maxwell and Lord Kelvin were both placed second, the best men of the century.'

'Perhaps if we work as a pair, we will alter that precedent.'

Somehow, amid the parties and celebrations of their success, the problems of the Hussain family were forgotten.

At the end of June they set off homewards in the car via the Lake District where they struggled up Helvellyn, spent a few days walking round Grassmere et al and then appeared once more in Kinoidart. The idea of Raissa returning to her family was never raised. They stayed together at the house out on the spit, celebrated with Hector, Rose and the girls and then, the very next day, set off for Oban where they walked the familiar streets, ate in McTavish's Kitchen again and were, unfortunately, as it turned out, noticed by several former classmates and a few teachers who were soon informed about the unusual extent of their distinctions.

'That means you'll never have to work again, doesn't it?' said one.

'Not quite,' said Robert with a smile. 'We will have room and board at the colleges but not a lot to live on. Not enough to be rich, if that's what you mean. But the assumption is that we will be working all the time and the fellowships give us the opportunity to do so without having to worry about earning a crust.'

'So you're not rich then?'

'Certainly not. Not if you mean wealthy. We are rich in other ways. We can do things. Should be able to do original things.'

The next day, the phone rang. It was the local newspaper. A feature was to be run that week. Would they agree to be interviewed?'

Thus was it that a few days later the front page of *The Oban Times* carried the picture of Raissa and Robert, showing in the background the garden and the sea outside the window, both described as mathematicians of genius—a description both had been anxious to dispel.

'Are you both geniuses?' the interviewer had asked.

'Certainly not!' they both said, laughing.

'But why not? You are the best in Britain, according to your results.'

'Just the best in Oxbridge,' said Raissa, 'not the same thing at all. There are other places.'

'Doesn't that make you a genius?'

'No. Not as Mozart was, or Beethoven or Einstein or Newton. These men changed the world. We have not done anything in it yet and may never achieve anything.'

'But you don't think that, Robert, do you?'

'No. I hope we will achieve something—something big.'

'Something important, anyway,' added Raissa.

And of course with celebrity of that kind, the knowledge that Raissa was even now staying in the house at the spit was immediately clear to everyone in Kinoidart. What did it mean?

14

'Mamma, Pappa!' cried the girls a day later, 'Raissa's in the newspaper and she's not wearing clothes.' For, as usual, the papers had been sold without Ahmad noticing what was on the front page. But worse was to follow. Her name was mentioned on TV and the very next day there was a televised interview in the dining room overlooking the sea at the Kinoidart house. Raissa wore a pair of white trousers, black patent leather shoes and a dark green satin top which contrasted with her brown complexion, dark eyes and raven-dark shining hair. Robert, in grey Oxford bags and open-necked white shirt, sat with her on the sofa and, forgetful of their unusual predicament, did what came naturally and held hands while answering questions.

'And so you are school friends?' said the interviewer.

'Just so,' said Robert. 'We met on the school bus every day and talked over what we had been learning.'

'And are you more than just friends? You are not sweethearts by any chance?'

'We are very good friends,' said Robert, with a smile. 'That is all you need to know.'

'But you are to attend different colleges now. Is that not so?'

'Yes, Raissa will be at Oxford working under Sir Michael Atiyah at St Catherine's and Sir Roger Penrose too, some of the time.'

'They sound very important people.'

'They are. Atiyah is a Fields Medallist and an ex President of the Royal Society, like Newton. Penrose is a world-class mathematical-physicist.'

'And you, what about you?'

'I will be at Trinity in Cambridge also working for a doctorate.'

'So you won't see much of each other then? The friendship will deteriorate.'

'I doubt that. I expect we will travel to meet half way every week at least.'

The interviewer sensed there was more to this than friendship and said: 'What do you say to that Raissa?'

'I would expect to meet more often than that. We get along very well; discuss our work and help each other.'

'So,' said Suleiman, that night, when he saw this, 'she has been lying with this man.'

'No, I don't believe it!' cried Nemissa, her mother. 'Raissa couldn't do that! It doesn't mean this!'

'Of course it does!' said Ahmad, incensed. 'They should have told us this at Cambridge but they said nothing! Just like the British! They are deceivers!'

He turned to his father and said: 'What shall we do?'

Suleiman frowned and reflected. 'If we do anything it will be on the TV— like this. It will be in the newspapers you sell.'

'I could stop the papers.'

'But not the TV.'

'It is already a very great shame. Everyone who saw this TV will know. She wears no clothes and she lies with this man. It is enough. We must act. It is our duty.'

Nemissa cried out and wept: 'No! You must not do this thing! She is our flesh and blood!'

'Precisely!' declared Suleiman, springing up from his habitual seat, cross-legged on the floor in front of the television set. 'That is exactly the point. It is for us to carry out the wishes of The Great One.'

'You will go to prison! Both of you!' cried Nemissa.

'What is that beside our duty?'

'You will rot there all your lives! We will never see you again! How will we live? Who will look after us?'

Suleiman soon began to make preparations. He called up Mohammed Bombazine and told him to contact his two cousins and their sons. They were all to travel to Kinoidart as soon as possible before the pair had fled back to Cambridge or wherever they were going that summer. There was, he sensed, a window of opportunity to remove this shame on the family name but it would not last for long.

With a matter as important as this, every male in the family simply deserted his place of work, armed himself according to his practice on such occasions and set off for the place of conflict: Kinoidart.

Within 24 hours the flat above the shop was full of men armed to the teeth, all of whom arrived silently under cover of darkness, though the only sign of it to the outside world was the array of vehicles parked in the street. But there were also women. This thing had to be done properly in accordance with the law and that demanded that Raissa be examined to ascertain her state. For this, women were needed.

The turbaned men sat around on the floor drinking tea and smoking. Some of them, from a hookah which stood in the middle of the floor. A few preferred cigarettes.

Suleiman, solemn, with the by his side, was in charge. But there was little to say. Everyone knew what was at stake and what must be done. What need of discussion? Eventually, a cloth was spread out in their midst by Nemissa and cooked dishes were placed upon it by the women: of rice, seasoned as they liked with fresh herbs and spices and many dishes of various meats, heavily spiced, and fresh dates of the finest kind and fresh fruits; and orange juice and tea and coffee, lots of each, in silver pots with soaring spouts poured into small glasses. The men were solemn and quiet and they ate with care using their fingers, as was their custom, as if preparing for a great battle and one from which they might not return. Suleiman wore his customary white turban and white robes; the others, different coloured versions of the same.

When it was over, everyone washed his hands in rosewater and dried them on an individual towel, heated for the purpose in the kitchen. When this was done, Suleiman took his weapons, sprang up and announced: 'It is time. We shall go now.'

And so they left the house by the stair, entered their vehicles and drove off following the lead of Suleiman and Ahmad in their van with Nemissa in the back, weeping. When they reached the gravel around the house on the spit, they parked, surrounding it like a laager of wagons on a veldt of Zulus or a prairie in the Wild West. Then, clutching their weapons, four went to the back door and the rest to the front. Suleiman then knocked.

It was Rose who met them there. 'I have come for my granddaughter, Raissa,' he said firmly, in a tone that would not be denied.

Rose was too surprised to do anything but reply: 'Please wait,' and leaving the door ajar, returned to the sitting room where she called 'Hector?'

When Hector came into the hall and saw the open door and the men standing there, he said 'You should have closed the door, as we agreed.'

'How could I? They are related to her.'

'What can I do for you?' said Hector, occupying the doorway.

'We have come for Raissa, our child.'

'She is a child no longer. Not yours. Not anyone's. She is a person in her own right. She is here by her own choice and chooses not to see you.'

'We will see her nonetheless,' said Suleiman.

Seeing the weapons and realising the danger of the situation, Hector said: 'I must close the door now. Good evening,' and began to close the door with his hand. Suleiman put his hand to the door and resisted its closure. Then he pushed violently and it flew open, knocking Hector down so that he sprawled on the hall floor.

Suleiman strode into the hall, closely followed by the men outside. After them came the women.

Within a few minutes, Raissa's family stood around the walls of the sitting room overlooking the loch which could be seen outside, dimly lit by moonlight. They stood, ten of them, around the room—six men in pantaloons, turbans and dish dashes of different colours and four married women, head to foot in dark clothing, overtopped by the dark tudong of a married woman. In the centre, sat Raissa and Robert on one of the sofas, still holding hands in front of the television set. Hector in white shirt and kilt followed Rose into the sitting room where he attempted to lift the telephone on an occasional table. 'Stop that!' Suleiman ordered swishing the like a magic wand and green-turbaned Mohammad Bombazine, in white dish-dash and blue pantaloons, scimitar in one hand, laid his other on Hector's and then raised it and shook it under his nose with a devilish grin.

'When does the killing start, grandfather?' said the youngest, Iskander, a thin brown youth in a scarlet turban and cream robes, relishing the prospect and smiling with anticipation.

Suleiman ignored him. 'Take her away and examine her,' he ordered. The women, except for Nemissa who stood by the fireside weeping quietly, lifted up Raissa by the arms and led her outside without protest because of the shock of it all. Suleiman turned off the television.

Hector, who had remained by the door watching, still recovering from the trauma of landing on his back and feeling himself gingerly with one hand, said: 'This is a monstrous invasion of my privacy and my family. You have no right to do this!'

'It is necessary because you will not yield up our child.'

'She is your child no longer. I told you. And what she wishes: that you stay out of her life.'

'She does not have this choice. She is one of us. That comes before everything.'

'In this culture—the culture that applies in this house and the one you have embraced in coming to this country and agreeing to abide by its laws— the individual comes before anything, before the tribe and even the family. What the individual wants— so long as it does no harm to others— comes first.'

'Your culture no longer applies here in this house because I have taken possession of it for the time being.'

'You are breaking the law of the land and will pay for this.'

'Raissa has harmed not only herself but her family— all of us! By this wearing no clothes. She has brought disgrace upon us all.'

'Where is the disgrace?'

'She has behaved in ways that are inappropriate. They are against our beliefs and customs— the beliefs and customs of centuries.'

'Why can her clothes matter so much?'

'Because hers are the clothes of a whore! They reveal her as no woman should be revealed except to her husband!'

'Are you calling my wife a whore? And my daughters?'

'Yes, since they dress like this.'

'But that is untrue! They are all beyond reproach.'

'How can you know that? They are not under your eye every day. When out of sight you do not know what they do. How can you vouch for them?'

'I don't have to vouch for them. I trust them.'

'Your boy has made a whore of Raissa.'

'Nonsense!'

'We will see presently,' said Suleiman.

At that moment, Raissa was led back into the room by the women and released. She was very subdued and even tearful. She sat down again in the centre beside Robert on the sofa and he took her by the hand and squeezed it, comfortingly, ignoring Suleiman's malevolent stare.

'Well?' said Suleiman.

'She has lost it,' said the aunt, a fiery, feisty, dark-eyed woman in a whole black covering, fit for a funeral,

'So,' replied Suleiman, 'it is just as we thought. She has been violated and is a whore. She must pay and the man that did it shall also pay.'

Suleiman lifted the jezzail and pointed it at Robert. 'Did you violate her?'

'No!'

'Then why has she lost it?'

'Lost what?' said Robert with rising indignation.

'Her woman's membrane. What else?' shouted Suleiman, advancing to rest the muzzle of the jezzail on Robert's chest.

'She didn't lose it,' said Robert, pushing it aside. 'She gave it away. She wanted it gone. That is why it is no longer.'

'You violated her!'

'I did nothing of the sort! I wouldn't harm a hair of her head!'

Raissa arose suddenly, surprising everyone, dominating the room. 'It is true Grandfather. I did it myself! He didn't want to and I insisted. I pulled him into me!'

'He did take it then!'

'No, No! Grandfather! I broke it myself—on him. It was me. Me alone! He would never have done it. I couldn't wait! I wanted him!'

'You are saying this to protect him! You lie for him!'

'No! No, Grandfather! No! I tell it how it was. I do not tell lies. You know that. I never told a lie in my life and I will not start now. Not to save my life!'

'But you ruined yourself! How did you do that? How could you? It means you are a whore. You can never marry. No man would have you! You are fit only for a concubine! You have shamed yourself!'

'No, Grandfather. I fell in love and the man I loved also loved me. Of course I wanted to mate with him. Isn't that what always happens? Who could have prevented it? Who would want to prevent it? What was the point of preventing it?'

'It is the law! It is how we always do things. You know that. Yet you went ahead and did this awful thing.'

'It's not awful! It's wonderful! Don't you see? I am as happy as I will ever be. I was made happy by what we did together, he and I. How could I not be happy?'

'But you asked no permission. Showed no respect to your family. To me.' Suleiman rested the muzzle of the jezzail on her neck under the chin.

Raissa made no move but said: 'You would have given no permission, Grandfather. I knew that. I knew you would take me away from Cambridge. I was born for that place, Grandfather. I love it there. It was paradise, a paradise you could not understand if you thought for a million years.'

'How can this be, Raissa? It is impossible! The Great One has told us of paradise. What is this Cambridge to that?'

—'Everything! Grandfather, look! Behold! What is the paradise of The Great One? It is numberless streams of clean pure water, fountains of it, like old Babylon, and so much fruit on the trees of the oases you could not eat all of it in a lifetime, and women so beautiful and so many—and every one a virgin—as if that were another bounty. How could it be? When virgins are all as tight as the Hookah tube. So tight a man could not even insert himself! What is so confoundedly good about a virgin? Is he supposed to enjoy her the more because of her pain? Where is the sense in this? Oh Grandfather, think! I beg of you. Please think!'

Suleiman was temporarily speechless with amazement at having to argue with a mere female—and one of his own grandchildren, to boot—that he dropped the jezzail to his side and looked away out of the window to the moonlit scene beyond, reflected at the strangeness of life and then turned back again to stare her down.

'Grandfather, the paradise of The Great One is a paradise of the desert traveller, the man accustomed to drought and sand and unbearable heat. Accustomed to privation of every kind, especially sexual when he is at war with neighbouring tribes and must be away from home fighting other men, as men do. The ideal female is a virgin only so that there shall be no fear of disease. Not good enough, Grandfather! Not sensible. WE ARE NOT IN A DESERT ANY LONGER! PARADISE IS DIFFERENT! **We have countless streams of water here all the time! It never stops raining!**'

Robert's head rose and roared with laughter and Hector and Rose and even Raissa. In the midst of all this terrifying danger confronted by weapons all around, they laughed, exploded with it so that their laughter filled the room. Every other face was shocked.

'Is this paradise then?' added Raissa standing with raised arms that seemed to embrace the room and the wide world. 'Is this paradise, this Argyll, because of the incessant rain?

'What would this man here think paradise is, Grandfather?' she continued, turning to point to Hector, thumb first as all pointing in her culture was performed so as to show respect.

'How could he believe paradise is numberless streams of pure water when he has it all the time? For him, Grandfather, paradise must be **a relief** from streams of water! A touch of dryness, now and then would be desirable. It would save him getting wet every time he pokes his head out of doors! Sunshine! Lots of it! Even Rose, his wife would like that.

Then her flowers would grow—instead of being drowned in rainfall—rainfall that is exceptional. Hundreds of inches a year!

'—And he doesn't want a virgin! That's the last thing on his mind! How would a virgin contain his manhood, a huge man like that? It would injure him, Grandfather!'

Raissa paused for breath and then added levelly, quietly but directly: 'It would injure you too, Grandfather. What good is a virgin— a narrow, tight female without any experience? Impossible, Grandfather, that this is an ideal— for you, for Hector, for Robert— for anyone!'

Raissa laughed loudly, adding: 'Robert didn't enjoy my virginity, he hated it. It hurt him! I saw how it hurt him. He never wanted my virginity! Refused me because of it! I used him to take it from me. Because I didn't want it! I wanted to enjoy him and I was prepared for him to hurt himself so that I could enjoy him. What then is his crime? Or mine? I loved him and love him still and expect to do so for the entire duration of my life and I think he feels the same about me. Where, Grandfather was the harm?'

There was a dead silence for a time as everyone tried to absorb what had just been said. Raissa sat down and took Robert by the hand and they each squeezed the other. Nemissa collapsed into a chair by the fireside, quietly sobbing to herself.

'Can we do the killing now, Grandfather?' said Iskander, the youngest male present with a grin of genuine relish.

15

The atmosphere was electric, could have produced arcs of lightning from one weapon to another which for a few moments seemed the likeliest outcome: that guns would blast the air and sharp edges descend upon innocent heads spurting blood in every direction.

The men standing around the walls of the room put their weapons into the attack mode: an Ak47 was cocked, an M16 carbine and an HK 70Z semi automatic pistol, likewise; a scimitar was drawn and a sabre. Only the
jezzail did not move. But it was in Suleiman's hands, already cocked and primed to fire. Hector and Rose stood impotently, frozen with fear; terrified that if they so much as moved a muscle it would unleash a torrent of bullets.

It was Rose who broke the silence. She crossed the room to where Nemissa was sitting in a collapsed heap in the chair by the fireside, turned away from the conflict as if it would burn her to death to face it.

Ignoring Suleiman who stood in front of the fire still wielding the jezzail pointed at Raissa, Rose stooped, took Nemissa by the hand and said: 'I wonder if you might care to help me? I believe we could all do with some tea?'

Nemissa's face, crumpled and clouded over by the disaster taking place around her, suddenly lit up: 'Yes, yes of course! What a good idea.'

'And we can talk at last. And get to know each other,' added Rose, leading her out of the sitting room into the kitchen where she filled the kettle and set it to boil and found a couple of trays and showed Nemissa where there were cups and saucers; and found some spoons and then thought of food. 'Should we make sandwiches? Would that be a good idea?'

'Yes, yes, they would like food. If they ate together it might make a difference.'

'What would be suitable? You must advise me. I wouldn't want to offend.' Rose opened a cupboard and pointed to the tins inside. 'I expect they came from your own shop, some of them.'

Nemissa pointed to the corned-beef tins and the tuna fish. 'These would be liked, I think.'

'And they would not offend? That is very important.'

'They would not offend. They also like eggs.'

'I have eggs. I could boil some and make sandwiches of them too.'

'That would be very nice.'

And so, with half an ear to the menacing silence which persisted next door and an eye to the hatch which gave a view of it, as the men and women studied each other, stern-faced, the women made piles of sandwiches and two large pots of tea and set off for the sitting room where they laid them down on occasional tables and poured it out into cups. Somewhere during the course of the preparations, Rose said: 'Your daughter Raissa is very beautiful and very brilliant. You must be very proud of her. We are very proud she is our daughter-in-law.' And Nemissa enjoyed this. And then, haltingly managed to admit that: 'Your son is a very noble young man. And so clever, everyone says.'

Suleiman absorbed this additional information about a marriage having taken place with interest but decided that, as it would be a Christian ceremony, it hardly counted as significant and need not distract him.

It was Rose, of course, who handed up the first cup of tea and it went to Suleiman. In his white robes and white turban, he stood unmoved for a moment, viewing it and her with his usual inscrutable expression and then leaned the jezzail against the arm of the armchair and accepted it and even began to sip it, carefully at first, as if it might be poisoned. Then he judged this unlikely.

'Would you like sugar? Or milk or lemon, perhaps?'

'Sugar, yes. Lemon if you have some.' And Rose soon supplied both. Suleiman noisily soughed a draft of tea contentedly and the tension in him seemed to diminish.

Rose and Nemissa both handed round cups of tea. Rose to the women and Nemissa to the rest of the men of her family, each having different priorities. Raissa and Robert were served last, almost as if they were the least important persons present. As the tea pots were soon emptied, the women retired to refill them.

Hector said: 'It might be helpful if you all sat down somewhere.' He fetched a chair which stood against a wall and brought it to Suleiman and invited him to sit in the centre, in front of the fire. Suleiman was glad to do so. His old legs were unused to standing for long periods. He sat down gratefully, holding the jezzail between his legs. Hector went to fetch some more chairs from the dining room but when he returned he found that the others, men and women, had arranged themselves on the floor around the walls of the room where they seemed comfortable; their traditional position, Hector realised.

'I was just saying to Nemissa that we are very proud to have Raissa in our family,' said Rose, returning to the room. 'She is so beautiful and so brilliant. It is a great honour to us.'

—'Honour?' shouted Suleiman, rising and putting the cup and saucer down on the mantelpiece none too delicately so that it almost rattled to breaking point. 'Honour!' he said again hoarsely, as if enraged within his very interior like a cauldron of bile. 'He', pointing with the jezzail, which he lifted, 'has dishonoured my family! Our family, swinging the jezzail around the room to include the other members of it. We are disgraced by him! As well as by her,' he added, angrily, pointing at Raissa.

Robert stood up. 'Where is the disgrace? I see no disgrace. She loves me and has married me. And I am worthy. A Fellow of the best college in one of the finest universities in the world. How is she disgraced? I will never have to work again. Never have to take a job to support my family. How many men can say that—ever in their lives—

and ours has hardly begun? I have earned the right to marry better than anyone of my generation throughout this country. I am admired in Cambridge. Everywhere I go there I am known and spoken to with respect. I can live there as long as I choose and in some comfort. I am admired here in this neighbourhood. You must have seen it for yourself in the newspaper. No one in this region has achieved such success. In marrying me, Raissa is honoured and her family, including you, by it. Everywhere you go—and your family goes—in this country, you will be able to say that your daughter is married to me and you will be respected and admired for this. It will help your sales in the shop, for sure. Everyone around here will prefer to buy from you rather than journey to Lochgilphead. If you open other business ventures—providing you continue to treat people well—they will flock to your service. That is the clear evidence of the honour that this marriage brings to you.'

Ahmad, who had until then played a relatively silent role for the injured father involved, being a personality of lesser weight than his father, saw these advantages for the first time for what they were: momentous! No more crawling around this country of whites like a small brown worm struggling to make small profits in a small shop in a wilderness far from the cities where real profit was to be had. Instead the image flashed into his mind of a great emporium in a great city like Glasgow, stuffed full of goods which constantly entered by the back door and left by the front leaving only banknotes by the bundle in their wake for him to count. And then factories and hotels sprang up in his fertile imagination! All this was now possible. Within his grasp! How he had dreamed of owning a Merchant Bank! Even that would be possible.

'Father!' he exclaimed. 'He is right! Do you see what this means?'

'It means,' replied Suleiman sternly, 'that he has taken her membrane! It means he has violated her! It means we are disgraced among our own people.'

'No! No! No!' cried Robert. You have chosen to live among *our* people, The Scots. Among them you are honoured. You left your own people behind in the Eastern deserts. They know nothing about you. How can you be disgraced even in their eyes? They know nothing about you! But if they ever do hear about you it will be because of me and Raissa and the great things we will achieve together. Not because we fell in love and married in ways that are outside your customs.'

'Our customs demand that you both be beheaded.' Suleiman signalled with his hand and Mohammed Bomabazine passed across to him the long scimitar that gleamed in the firelight. Suleiman laid down the jezzail against the chair and felt the edge of the sword with a finger and then lifted it to show the blood that flowed.

Robert said: 'Raissa has the finest brain of her generation. One of the finest on the planet. And you propose to cut it off? Are you mad? Have you any idea how much good she has the power to do within that one head that you yourself are partly the author of? How can you even consider for an instant the destruction of the one person you created, the one event in your long life which is the most worthy by far of any you ever did?

'And if you do it, you will be reviled in every quarter of the world—even back in your own Eastern desert. Men there will get to hear of it and you will be disgraced most foully for all time. *There is the man that cut off the finest head in the wide world*, they will say. The man who was so stupid he could not see what harm he did.'

Suleiman, for answer, said nothing at first, but seeming to inwardly vibrate with fury, laid the point of the scimitar on the neck of Robert and glared as if preparatory to drawing blood.

Around the room there was a collective intake of breath. Followed by a silence. Which Suleiman ended: 'You take me then to be a fool?' he roared. 'Is that it? How can I let you live after such words? Why are you not already dead?'

'Yes, yes, grandfather! Kill him! Kill him!' shouted Iskander.

Maybe it was this untimely intervention—itself a further slur on his authority that stopped Suleiman. With the point still on Robert's neck and a thin stream of blood falling down his shirt front, Suleiman said: What are these honours you speak of to me? I know nothing of such things. I do not honour things I know nothing of. Give me one example, one thing this head that is the finest in the all world—if it be so—has accomplished. Or is it all talk, the talk of deceivers and liars. To save their lives.'

Very levelly and quietly, Robert said: 'She has solved the problem of anything. Why is there anything at all? Why is there not just nothing at all? It has defied the world ever since humans walked the planet. Raissa saw the answer last week. She was the first in Cambridge to see it; probably the first in all the world!'

'Huh! You are lying again! Trying to speak of things that are impossible, to escape your fate.'

'What must I do to convince you?'

'You could try giving her answer.'

'I am not sure it will make sense to you. You would need prior knowledge.'

'Give it then or die!'

'Very well, then. Here it is. The Physicists have just discovered that even a vacuum is busy with activity, particles and antiparticles, especially, continually in reaction. What Raissa was the first to realise is that the state of nothingness is impossible! How could it be possible when it can only be occasioned by the interaction of particles and anti particles and others galore? Their very existence ensures that nothingness is an impossible state.'

And Suleiman did see! His eyes gleamed and he drew back the sword and gradually lowered it as the light of understanding grew in his face.

'It's like Newton's treatment of motion. Every body is in a state of motion all the time and is never at rest because there is no fixed point in the universe which might be used as a universal reference point. So it makes no sense to ask where a body is at any moment. Instead, you have to ask where it is in relation to some other body.

'The question: why is there not nothing disappears in a similar fashion because nothing, the state of nothing is actually impossible. To achieve it, there would have to be particles and anti particles galore to provide it. That is a contradiction for it means that there are many things present just the same in this nothing!'

Suleiman looked at Raissa with delight. 'And is this so? Are there really particles in a vacuum? In empty space?'

'Yes, grandfather. They have to be there combing and separating to create the empty space.'

'And you understood this first?'

'Yes, grandfather.'

Suleiman stood back and was in a mixed state of shock and pleasure that one of his family had made such an achievement.

Robert approached Suleiman and, ignoring the scimitar which had fallen by his side, embraced him. 'Raissa has brought you much honour. Her marriage to me has brought you even more honour. And I am very happy to have brought this honour of mine to you and to your family!'

Suleiman was stunned into silence for a time. The scimitar fell from his hands, landed on the carpet and he made no effort to pick it up. Robert stepped back and sat down.

Finally, sitting down again, Suleiman said: 'Where were you married?'

'In the college chapel,' said Raissa.

'A Christian place then?' replied Suleiman, with a hint of a sneer. 'It does not count.'

'We made our own special service, Grandfather. I prayed to The Great One first. We both asked his blessing on us and our union. We gave solemn vows to each other and exchanged rings, as is the custom. I pledged all my world goods to Robert and he to me. I promised to serve him as a loving wife till the end of my days and he did the same, as my husband. We said these things in his language and in mine. What more could we have done? It was right and proper conduct.'

'How could it be so?' said Suleiman angrily. 'Your family were not present. There was no discussion and negotiation beforehand. No bride price. No arrangements for afterwards. No discussion about the education of the children or their upbringing. Or where and how you would live.'

'Well, you know why that was, Grandfather. You would have killed me and my husband rather than see it happen.'

Hector said: 'Would it help to discuss the bride price now?'

'What is your offer?' said Suleiman venomously, as if the very idea were ridiculous, 'for this female with the finest head in all the world?'

'What currency would you expect?' said Hector.

'Ten camels is usual,' said Raissa. 'A hundred, exceptional.'

'Then I offer a hundred camels for Raissa as bride for my son.'

'You don't have any camels,' said Suleiman, dismissively.

'I will buy them and bring them here if it suits you,' said Hector, with a smile.

Suleiman pondered. Ahmad said: 'It is fair, father. A hundred camels is a great price.'

'But not for the finest female head in all the world.'

'How many then?'

'A thousand,' cried Suleiman, angrily. 'It is scarcely enough to take away the shame!'

Ahmad was amazed. 'Where would you keep them? They would die, father. In this place'—looking around him and imagining the rain falling— 'they would drown here, father. And what would they eat? None of the food they eat is available here.'

'Five hundred camels,' said Hector, grimly.

'You would really pay five hundred camels?' said Ahmad with surprise.

'Of course! To save my son and daughter-in-law. Why would I not?'

'You do not mean this,' said Suleiman with disbelief. 'You do not have them to give and you cannot buy them in this rain-soaked country. You would have to send to the east for them and even then they would die on the ship.'

'Then the money which would buy so many camels. What about that?'

'How much is a camel worth, Raissa?' said Robert.

'Depends on where it is and what condition.'

'But roughly, dearest? Quickly, we have a solution at hand.'

'Ten English pounds would do it.'

'Well, then,' said Hector, 'I will pay five thousand English pounds as a bride price. What do you say?'

'That you do not have so much money,' roared Suleiman.

'I will arrange to borrow it from the bank tomorrow. It will take a few weeks to arrive. Not more. When it comes you shall have it. What do you say?'

'You do not drive a hard bargain.'

'I don't care about money.'

'But I do care about camels.'

'Well, I don't have any and as you rightly point out these would be no use to you here even if they could be delivered.'

Suleiman was discomfited, felt he had been outwitted and showed it. How had it happened? After all these years!

'I do not think this arrangement will work. I do not think you are serious. And there are so many other matters which must be discussed.'

'We are serious!' declared Robert, firmly. 'Deeply serious. We were never in this house—any of us— ever so serious about anything in our lives. What still troubles you?'

'The Great One. Did you really pray to the Great One?'

'In this country we call him God. I did pray to him.'

'How can you be sure it is the same person?'

'It has to be. There is only one God. You know that. There cannot be two of them.'

Evidently Suleiman was satisfied for he did not contradict this.

'What about Raissa wearing no clothes? That is unseemly. It is against what we believe.'

'Raissa lives here in this country and does the things that are appropriate here. Of course she must dress appropriately. Her credibility would be affected if she insisted on wearing dress that is foreign to this culture. To take full advantage of all the honours she has won for herself and her family— that is you and her father, among others— she must adopt the clothing of this country. The honours are not available to you without western clothes!'

'Would you accept her if she insisted on wearing the clothes of our culture: the tudong and the others?'

'Of course. She is far more important to me than any clothing. But I know she would prefer to wear western clothes.'

'You could make her wear her own clothes, our clothes?'

'I think so. I am sure she would do it to please me. But I would never ask her for I know it does not please her. And it does not please me.'

'Would you order her to wear the tudong to please me?'

'I might, if I thought it made sense.'

'What if I did not agree to this marriage unless you did?'

'I might agree.'

'Why would you do it? Out of respect for me?'

'No, out of respect for her. I would want what is best for her and what is best for her is to be on good terms with her family.'

'How would you manage this, then?'

'I would ask her—if she thought it would help— to wear the tudong in your company and not to do so when she is among westerners.'

There was the hint of a sigh among some of the visitors, the women, as if an important compromise had been reached.

'What about your beliefs? Would you agree to worship as we worship?'

'When we are together your family and me, I would try to go along with whatever rituals are normal. When I am in your house, say. Eating with the fingers, without knives and forks. But when you are in mine, I would expect you to respect my customs. I think that's fair. But I don't mind if you eat in my house with the fingers. So that is more than fair.'

'It might not be fair to me and the Great One. Would he think it is fair, is the question?'

'Well, if The Great One ever strikes one of us down, then we might get an inkling of his views. Until then, I doubt anyone can know *what* he thinks.'

'But you do believe in The Great One and his importance?'

'I do not believe in the Christian God, at least as a person, so I suppose I would have to admit that there is a difficulty over this. Yet I did pray to your Great One during the marriage ceremony. I asked him to reveal himself to me. I always do when I attend a church or temple of any kind. Unfortunately, he never has.'

'Maybe he does not think you deserve his blessing.'

'Yet I have done nothing to offend him and many things which ought to please him.'

'So, as well as being a man of this Cambridge, you are also a perfect man? Is that what you are saying? A man with nothing to confess?'

'I have the small sins of ordinary men. I have done nothing I am ashamed of. All my sins are of little consequence and there is nothing I can do now to amend them. Yet I do consider my conduct at the end of every day and I try to do better the next. I make mistakes because I am human and it is human to do so. I do not regret that I am a human. So how can I regret my sins? I try to be as good as I can be. Some people think I am a fairly decent example of a human being.'

'Well said, Robert,' said Raissa. 'I am one of them.'

'You are biased,' said Suleiman, waving his hand dismissively.

He sat before them surveying them as they sat together holding hands on the sofa and then arose. 'There is nothing further to be done tonight. We will depart to consider these things and above all this bride price—whether it is sufficient to remove the stain of disgrace on this family. Whether we will allow you to follow the path that you have chosen which is away from us and our culture. What does The Great One think of this? That is the question.' To Rose, he said: 'I thank you on our behalf for the food and drink.' And to Hector: 'I regret that we came upon you like a force of brigands out of the desert. It must have been hurtful. It seemed necessary at the time. Our family, our tribe, has always responded suddenly to insults of our blood. You will see us again, count on it.'

When they had departed without another word, each man and his woman in his car or truck, Hector, who stood with Raissa staring out at the lights as they sped away into the darkness towards the village, heaved a noticeable sigh of relief and said: 'What now? What does it all mean?'

Raissa wept tears of relief: 'I don't know. It is so unusual. I've never seen anything like that before.'

'What would the usual outcome be?'

'My head and Robert's rolling on the sitting room carpet. If you had resisted, yours too. Maybe they would have torched the place to remove all the signs.'

'But they'd never get away with it here.'

'They'd try to. Straighten every blade of grass on your lawn and scrape every tyre mark on the gravel, if it would help. And if it didn't, or they worried that they had missed something, Mohammed

Bombazine—the little man who cut me—would lay a series of bombs and blow the whole place sky high.'

'But forensic scientists would get to the bottom of it.'

'Not if the pieces were very small. There wouldn't be a trace of DNA after a thing like that. Without it, they'd prove nothing.'

Inside, Robert said: 'Mother, you were wonderful. If it hadn't been for the request for help to make tea I think we'd all be in paradise.'

Rose said: 'That old man is certainly no angel Gabriel. He's used to acts of atrocity as a means of settling scores.'

'How can you tell?'

'It's just in him. How he is. He must have been a devil in his youth. The kind of man who would shoot first and blame it on The Great One afterwards.' A prescient remark as events were to reveal.

'Should we phone the police?' said Rose.

'Waste of time,' replied Hector. 'The nearest cop is at Oban. They'd never come down here at this time of night. Anyway, what would I say? That we're frightened we're going to be killed?'

'Right, Dad. No offence has been committed yet. They'd do nothing. They haven't even said they are going to. They just look as if they are.'

Raissa said: 'It certainly won't help matters if the police knock on the door in Kinoidart. It would be seen as a great insult. An interference.'

Robert and Raissa looked at one another and Robert said: 'They might even kill the policeman.'

'It would do your cause no good, Raissa, if we went to the police,' said Hector, finally. 'Your family would hate us worse than ever.'

16

Back in the family home in Kinoidart above the shop and overlooking the anchorage, the men arranged themselves on the floor while the women saw to the production of meals, looking after children and the thousand-and-one other things that constituted their well-defined duty in that society.

It was the young man, Iskander, who raised the question in most minds: 'But Grandfather, I thought we went there to kill them. Why didn't we? Why aren't they dead? Did he not violate our Raissa? Did he not marry her without permission? And has she not behaved in ways unbecoming to one of our tribe? It is not just that she wears no clothes. Grandfather, they have been in close contact for years! Anyone can see it. They behave as man and wife. They hold hands in public. They share the same bed—not once but for years! What are we going to do, Grandfather? Why have we not done it already?'

Suleiman sat silent for a time, considering the implications, not just of the unexpected return to the family home with the task undone but of this insolent presumption by a mere stripling hardly yet weaned and certainly never having engaged in the acts that matter to men most of all: fornication and killing.

'We are not in the desert, now, Iskander. But in Argyll, a very different place with many people. The wind will not blow the sand across our tracks here. The men in blue would hunt us, I think. We must be careful. What is the good of performing our act of revenge when it will come back upon us in greater measure?'

'But we never thought of this before, Grandfather. Why do we do it now?'

'That man, Hector, is an important figure here. Anyone can see that. He wears the skirt. We would have to kill him and the rest of his family or it would come out. And they would hunt us and even if they proved nothing we could not live here any more. They would buy nothing in the market. They might even drive us away, the whole lot of them. They could do it, you know.'

'But how, Grandfather? These people are not used to killing. They do not even carry a dagger, never mind an AK47. They go around smiling or swearing at the rain. It is all that concerns them.'

'You do not know them, Iskander. The most dangerous ones are wiry and very hard. I met them once, many moons ago. They go by the name S.A.S. A few of them will be here or hereabouts. This is the kind of place they come from.'

'What is S.A.S, Grandfather?'

'I expect it means "Supernatural Army Service." Or something like that. An acronym, I think you call it.'

'How may they be recognised, Grandfather?'

'The ones I knew wore coloured skirts when off duty—like Hector's. We killed a couple in a café in Kabul once. They were drinking the rotgut.'

'Did they die well, Grandfather?'

'Not very. One minute they were alive and the next they were dead.'

'But if they died so readily, Grandfather, they cannot be much good.'

'They died because they thought themselves among friends. They were on our side. They were shot by mistake.'

'And they were drinking the rotgut?'

'Yes, that too.'

'Have you ever tried the rotgut, Grandfather?'

'No, but since the men of the S.A.S. like it, I should like to try it.'

'But it is proscribed.'

'Yes.'

'Well, then?'

'Maybe some things that are proscribed should be tried if only to see whether they should be. Maybe they are worthy.'

'But The Great One, Grandfather?'

'Maybe The Great One does not know everything. And old men like me who have not long to live should take the risk of his displeasure to make an experiment—the thing they do at Cambridge—there is a great tent there, men say, where they do this all day and all night. It is called The Cavendish.'

'But uncle, what do you think? Is this bride price enough for so much disgrace?'

Ahmad said: 'I think it makes good business. It is a lot of money. With such a lot we could rent another shop in Lochgilphead and if they are right and our name is good because of this marriage they would all come and buy from us. That would be good for the family.' Then an inspired suggestion occurred to Ahmad: 'You could come here to live, Iskander, and serve in the shop.'

'I am not sure I would like the rain. And there is nothing to do here.'

'What is there to do in Leicester?'

'Many things.

'And all forbidden to you, I expect,' said Suleiman, sagaciously, knowing exactly what would appeal to a youth like Iskander. Had he not lived through that age himself? His blood had been stirred by women, awake and asleep. It would be the same in Leicester, except far more opportunities. None of the women wore clothes for heavens sake! It was an incitement to fornicate all day long!

'But what are we to do about this violation,' insisted Iskander.

'They say it was not as we think. They say she wanted it. That she violated herself.'

'But that makes no sense, Grandfather. It is always the man's sword which performs the violation.'

'Not here!' said Suleiman. 'At least, according to Raissa. She pulled the man onto her. The man did not want her, did not want to violate her and break the membrane. He is not responsible.'

'Is that possible, Grandfather? I don't believe it.'

'You don't know enough. Evidently you have yet to explore Leicester fully. It is possible that it is as she says.'

'Then she is guilty. She has broken the greatest taboo of the tribe, Grandfather. She should die. She should be already dead. These are the rules we live by.'

'And yet we must hesitate. These are the rules of the desert. Are they the rules of this rain-soaked place?' Suleiman stood up and walked to the window where, as so often, sheets of rain fell on the anchorage and the boats moored there.

'Surely, the rules, are the rules—anywhere. Is that not what we believe, Grandfather?"

'I wonder if they do not have to change when we live in a place so very different from what we are used to? There is a place in the far north, I have heard, where there is no sand and no rain. Where it is ice all year round and people die of starvation and cold. They live in tents made of snow, would you believe?'

'What is so special about that, Grandfather? You mean the Eskimo, surely? Some call them Inuit.'

'When there is no food the old are left by their children to die. Can you imagine any of us behaving in this way? We would eat the children. And make some more when favourable circumstances presented themselves.'

Mohammed Bombazine, feeling left out of the conversation, said: 'Many and wonderful are the ways of The Great One that he permits such barbarity as leaving the old to preserve the new when it is so much more sensible to eat the children.'

Suleiman sat down again to think. He was clearly puzzled. 'What is your feeling about this matter?' he said to the whole group.

'About killing the old or eating the children?' said Iskander.

'About what we should do and why we should do it.'

Ahmad said: 'The marriage is good for business. We will all live happily ever after in this place if we accept it. We must adapt, father, or we will surely die in this place—all of us.'

'What about the rest of you?'

Mohammed Bombazine said: 'I could blow them all up tomorrow night when they are asleep. There isn't even a dog to rouse them when I do my business in the middle of the night. That would settle everything.'

'And then what?' asked Suleiman. 'When the men in blue arrive, what will you say?'

'I will smile and say nothing.'

'And then the men in white will come and they will put on their white gloves and go to their tent in Cambridge and take every atom of the explosion and tell the world that it was Mohammed Bombazine who fashioned the bomb, for it bears his hallmark. What then? They will come for you and you cannot hide in the temple, for no one protects those whom the men in blue seek. They will draw you in chains into their court of law in The Old Bailey and they will expose all your doings and all your fornications will be broadcast to the wide world and then what? They will put you in a dark, damp prison for the remains of your life. Do you want that? Is that a suitable price to pay for exploding your bomb? Well, answer: is this satisfactory to you?'

'No, I suppose not.'

'What about the rest of you?'

Raisuli, a tall thin man with a long dark beard, streaked with grey and spectacles in wire frames, laid down the hookah tube, coughed, and answered: 'If we were back in the mountains or the desert, we would kill them all. I do not see how we can act differently in this place. Why should a lot of rain make a difference? She has lost it, She wears no clothes. She has rejected us. We should kill her and all these whites who took her from us.'

'The difference is the rain—imbecile! Don't you see? You have the mind of a camel! The rain tells us that Paradise is not what we thought. Not what the Holy Book says. It cannot be countless streams of clear water because we have them here already! The Holy Book can only be true if we are now in Paradise. Do you believe that? That this is Paradise?'

'No.'

'Well then, be silent. And remember the virgins. Did you ever try a virgin?'

'Yes, my wife.'

'And what was it like?'

Raisuli was a slow man and took time to reply. When he had remembered and made up his mind, he said: 'Like pushing into this hookah tube. It is just as Raissa says. I hated it. My wife screamed. I don't think she has ever quite forgiven me for the pain of it. Anyway, I have given it up. She's never been any good. Concubines are better or captured wives in a raid. Except there are no raids in this rain-sodden place.'

'Do you understand, then?'

'I still think we should kill them. It's what we are used to do. What difference does it make if it rains here? I don't care. I don't care about anything nowadays. Ever since we came here. I wish we were back in the desert. It was simpler there.'

'You would be with The Great One then, I think. He kills fools quicker than most. They are no good in new places.'

Ali Tolomaius, a little round middle-aged man, the most pious of the family, said: 'I think we should all pray now and ask for guidance. And The Great One, may he be at ease, might tell us what to do. Whether we must change our rules because we now live in a society with rules that are very different.'

'I don't see how we can do that,' said Iskander.

Rahendra, Ahmad's cousin, a tall, burly figure in a brown robe, said: 'How can we change all of a sudden just because we are here in this rainy place? The Great One could not approve. The Holy Book—have you forgotten it—tells us what to do in every circumstance.'

'But,' snapped Suleiman, 'the Holy Book—progeny of a scorpion—does not cover living in a place where there are numberless streams of water—water so frequent and so copious that it is a problem just to remain dry! And where no man wants a virgin because disease has been abolished—except for those who stupidly insist on going without the rubber protector. And anyway it is painful! It really is! When you get around to trying it, Iskander, you will see for yourself how unsatisfactory it is!'

'Are you saying The Holy Book is not right, Grandfather?'

'Yes, that is what we have learned this night. It cannot be correct. We have just heard why not. In the desert it might work. But not here. And I have to admit that it does not even work very well in the desert either. I never liked virgins! I was always too big for them and they were always yelling and crying because they were so small and tight. What pleasure can a man take in a woman like that who is yelling and crying as if the sword were killing her? The Holy Book was designed for men who were tiny and thin as sticks.'

—'And men who did not live under streams of water, as here!' said Ahmad, joyously, seeing the argument run in his favour.

'Maybe I myself must take the AK47,' said Iskander, 'and go out to that place and put a bullet in that golden head. Then there would be no difficulty.'

Suleiman was shocked. 'You would do this? Without permission? Anyway, you don't own the AK47. It is Rahendra's, not yours.'

'A scimitar, then, in his long guts. That would bring him down to size.'

—'You would need to cut his head off to make him your size,' said Rahendra.

'Have you designs on Raissa, yourself, is that it?' Suleiman enquired. 'Is it jealousy, Iskander?'

'I would like to marry her,' admitted Iskander. 'And as she is my cousin twice removed that should make me favourite. At least we will remain within the family and not join up with barbarians.'

'You can forget that,' said Ahmad. 'She's too big for you, too beautiful and far, far too clever, if what they say is true.'

—'And she would never have you,' declared Suleiman.

'If I cut the head off her lover she might look my way.'

'If looks could kill she might manage that if you did,' said Suleiman. 'Did you not see how they looked at each other? She could never think of you that way. Look at yourself! Beside that man you are a runt. One swing of that fist would kill you.'

Iskander rose angrily. 'Grandfather, I think you are deranged to speak this way of your own family. I should kill him just for that. I can hardly believe you think so ill of me! He would not have a chance against me! He is not used to killing.'

'Neither are you. I tell you: that man has balls, bigger balls than he knows. He stood up to me and all of you when we were on the verge of taking his life. That took balls! You would have been a quivering, snivelling infant, if we had done it to you.'

With a face purple with fury, Iskander got up and left the room.

'We will sleep on this and talk of it again in the morning,' decided Suleiman, going off to his bedroom and leaving the others to make do as best they could on the floor.

17

In the house, Tigh-na-mara, out on the spit, when the four adults had collected in the sitting room, the children upstairs having been inspected and discovered asleep, Hector said: 'I don't know about you folks but I need a drink. What will you have Raissa? Rose?' And to Robert: 'I don't need to ask what you want.'

Riassa shot a worried look at Robert: 'Is it safe, to drink? They might be back.'

'How should I know? You're the expert on your own family. You tell us.'

'I really don't know. I'm just astonished that they left us like that. It was so sudden. So unlike them! I am really very surprised that we are all alive.'

'They came here to kill us, then?' said Hector, with amazement, hardly over the shock of the intrusion.

'Oh yes! They don't pick up weapons for nothing. They will be bitterly angry at not having used them.'

'Why is that?' said Rose. 'How extraordinary!'

'They like using their weapons. That is what they are for. It makes them feel like men— warriors— the people most admired in our culture. You might value footballers and pop stars. They value killing. The best man is the one still standing at the end of the fight.'

'Well, I'm lucky to be alive, then,' said Hector, trying to make light of it. That calls for a double shot of the best Islay malt. What do you say, Robert? Will you take a chance that they don't come back tonight?'

'I think I need something, after all that. But I'll stick with my own poison: a glass of six per cent red wine.'

'No such thing, son, not in this house.'

'Yes, there is. Mix 0.5% and 12% and you get 6.25%. That's what I do. It allows me a couple of glasses without appreciable effect. It's like a single glass of normal wine.'

'And you Raissa?'

'The same please.'

'Well, that's fine, Rose, you and I can get drunk and leave the defence of this fort to these sober shanks.'

'I will have a small G&T.'

And so they sat around the fire, companionably, still recovering, still adjusting to the time of terror—which might or might not be over—trying to put a brave face on things, talking over the events of the evening.

'You were a star, Raissa, declared Hector. That remark about there being too much rain in Argyll for your Holy Book to be correct was devastating. If paradise is unlimited streams of water, of course we have it here already and need not go to any trouble in this life!' Hector laughed again and the others joined in.

Rose said: 'Does it say this in this Holy Book of yours?'

'Of course.'

'And they take it seriously, then?'

'Yes, they read from it 3 times a day during the prayers. They learn it by heart or try to. This is very difficult as it is quite a long book. Where I come from they even have competitions at reciting it.'

'Seriously?'

'Yes. I took part in this myself once. I wasn't very good, fluffed my lines. I never have managed to recite all of it at one time.'

'How can this be, Raissa? You of all people? Such an intellectual star.'

'My memory is not that good. Only when I am learning things that make sense. The Holy Book never did make sense to me.'

'What does it say?'

'Some good things, for sure. The value of consideration of others is stressed. The value of living at peace with one's neighbours. Being kind to them and to strangers.'

'Not much different from the Christian book, then?'

'It is like the Christian book in condemning every other religion and every other book, though far less tolerant. We are not supposed to consort with Christians or Buddhists or Hindus in case we get affected by their different rules, for example. Actually, I think it is really to prevent us being affected by their philosophy more than anything. If people never meet others from different religions it makes one's own more secure. It is when they do meet and talk that the falsehoods in one's own religion become apparent. Like this evening when my family were all turned in their tracks and left without killing us.'

'How can your Holy Book encourage consideration of others and kindness to neighbours when your people came to kill us tonight and nearly did?'

'Because you are of a different faith.'

'But you say that your family have done this before in your own homeland. That must have been against people of the same faith. Were they?'

'Oh yes! They believe at the same time in kindness to neighbours and in killing them if they are offended by their behaviour. If I had made love with a man in my country without marriage and the permission of my family, I would have been killed and him too. In practice, the kindness only applies if the people you are kind to obey all the rules. If they don't, you don't need to be kind. You can go and kill them. In fact they actually believe that it is a duty to kill them if they disgrace the family.'

'So by being kind to strangers, you mean people that you don't know but who are in the same faith?'

'Oh yes. You must not be kind to people from other faiths. Since you are not supposed to have anything to do with them, how can you be kind to them?'

'So if you find a Christian in the desert without water you are not supposed to save his life in case he infects you with his heresy?'

'Yes, I'm afraid so. Many Christians who could have been saved will have been left to die of thirst. But then, many will have been saved just the same. Some of our people are not so callous. Humanity can sometimes triumph over religious prohibitions.'

Robert said: 'What is the status of your Holy Book? For example: who wrote it and when?'

'A prophet. About the ninth century, I think.'

'You only think? Why is this when the Christians, Muslims and others can all put exact dates to things?'

'My people are not scholars. There is some dispute. But long after these other religions certainly.'

'Mohammed wrote in the sixth century, didn't he?'

'I believe so.'

'Your Holy Book is 3 centuries later, then?'

'Yes.'

'What is the status of the Holy Book? I mean, is it subject to interpretation?'

'Not at all. It is the literal word of The Great One, to be followed without argument or discussion.'

'Does your religion have a name?'

Raissa replied: 'No, we don't give it a name. That would distinguish it in ways which are unnecessary. What's in a name? It would be attacked then, by unthinking people who knew nothing about it. Only The Great One has a name. Everyone knows what this means. Even he has no name. Only the phrase.'

'And is there a concept of Holy War?' asked Hector.

'Our men go to war to fight wrongdoing. It is everyone's duty to fight wrong things in the world. And those who lay down their lives doing the will of The Great One will spend eternity in paradise. And paradise, as we have seen, is plenty of food of the best kind and numberless streams of water to drink and many virgins to enjoy. It is a man's paradise, assuredly.'

'So what if a woman dies fighting in a Holy War?' said Rose.

'She goes there too. But presumably it is different,' answered Raissa with a smile. 'I never found out what. Perhaps a place full of male film actors and other celebrities, like footballers. But maybe not: warriors, probably. That is what our women are taught to admire.'

—'And all of them sexually available to the lady who died valiantly?' said Robert.

They all laughed. 'And the men would not be virgins!' added Robert with glee, 'because, if they were, they wouldn't know what to do! They would have to be expert lovers to be worth anything in paradise! Know all the tricks of the trade, all the ways of pleasing women—whatever these are!'

'But women do not go to war in our culture. So it really is the man's paradise that counts.'

'Does that mean that women cannot enter paradise, but men can?'

'No, women can get there if they are good enough and they would at least enjoy the unlimited supplies of food and water of the best kind.'

'Where does your people come from?' asked Hector. 'Arabia?'

'No, the deserts of Tajikistan, mostly.'

'So you are Tajiks then?

'No, we are not indigenous. We are nomads who wandered across many countries and we have taken some things from the religions of these countries.'

'And your Holy Book is mostly rules for governing behaviour like some other religions of that area?'

'Yes, there are certain things we do not eat because it is not safe, like pork, because of worms. And if there is a food shortage so that some will surely die, we kill the children and eat them, for more children can always be made when circumstances improve. That makes good sense, don't you agree?'

'No!' the others protested with one voice. Robert admitted: 'But I see that it makes some kind of sense or the race might die out. It is a way of preserving it which we Christians do not have and could do with—at one level, anyway. If the adults remain they can make more children. Children would not be old enough to make more of themselves. But what if the wife is barren?'

'If your wife is too old for children and you need some more, you can take other women to wife.'

'And there is a limit to this, like some religions?'

'No, you can have as many wives as you can afford to support. Some men have many wives. Some have none. Only concubines.'

Hector said with sudden insight: 'What is wrong with religions in general is that they are all rooted in a particular geographical area of the planet. And this area is special in some way: it is a desert with water shortages or it is like Argyll and has far too much water or it is like Labrador and there is too much snow and ice. And the region—its very peculiarities!—determine the rules of behaviour. But that means the religion does not travel very well when it comes to other regions with very different conditions. This is why the idea of a desert paradise of countless streams of water is so stupid seen from the eyes of those, like us here in Argyll, who are already inundated with water. And why, in a disease-ridden society, virgins are so desirable. They are completely undesirable from every other point of view.'

'Exactly,' said Raissa, 'all religions are defective in that they cannot be universal for they all involve rules which were generated in particular geographical conditions which apply nowhere else. Indeed, they make no sense in other very different sorts of places on the planet!'

Robert said: 'Isn't Christianity universal? It has taken root in many parts of the globe? Why does it travel far better?'

'—Because its idea of paradise is unstated!' answered Raissa. 'Its strength is its lack of definition! Had it been a paradise devised in Britain it would certainly not be one where numberless streams of water were a distinctive characteristic. The Christian heaven is open to imagination and interpretation: it can be anything you desire. And since the Christian Bible is a book written down by men it is subject to interpretation, which means it cannot be attacked when it falls down in some way, unlike my Holy Book or the ones of other religions because these are taken to be the literal word of God.'

Robert said: 'So the very fact that the Christian Bible is not the literal word of God as such is a great strength! When it is wrong, it is the men who wrote it who got it wrong. That's why Christianity travels so well.'

'Yet, some of the things in paradise which one might desire are intrinsically unworthy,' said Raissa

'Right! Like virgins and unlimited quantities of good food.'

'What is unworthy about that?' said Rose.

'Because virgins are not what men really want at all!' said Robert. 'That is another mistake in your Holy Book, Raissa. They are virgins in paradise so that men will know they are free of disease. That is the only reason for them being virgins. Since the invention of the condom, virginity has never been an asset. A hindrance, rather.'

'So Christianity has spread across the world because of this?' queried Hector.

'Because the Christian idea of paradise, of heaven, is undefined,' said Raissa. 'And the values of Christianity really are universal—the values of the Sermon on the Mount at least: they apply anywhere, especially loving your neighbour and that should include your neighbour with different beliefs. And even the complete foreigner in a neighbouring country, or even one far away.'

'—And because very devout believers took it to all parts,' said Hector, 'and died smiling if they were taken by savages who did not understand the special value of the concept of helping the stranger. There would come a time when the men doing the slaughtering would notice that there was no slackening in the number of messengers, even though they were going to be slaughtered. It says a lot for the message.'

'Some concepts are genuinely universal, however,' said Robert. 'The idea that if you blow yourself up while waging a Holy War— and a lot of others too of course—you go to paradise. That is a concept that applies everywhere.'

Rose said: 'But the lesson of explosions of that kind is that many innocents are killed and nothing achieved.'

Robert countered: 'Are you saying the Northern Irish problem would have been solved without the bombings? Of course they would not. It was the bombings that made possible the recognition by opponents of the IRA that Catholics had to be treated equally. Without the bombings it would never have happened.'

'But what about all the deaths?' said Rose. 'In cases like that everybody with any sense realises that it will have to stop sometime. The killings in Cyprus and Palestine when the British were on their way out, are like that. You'd think they'd all come to their senses sooner and save all these many lives. I'm thinking of the Haggenah led by Prime Minister Begin and the Enosis terrorists led by Archbishop Makarios.'

'Like the Al Qaeda bombings? Thousands have died of these but what good will it do?'

'A compromise will be found if it continues,' said Rose. 'And it will continue until it is made.'

'What kind of compromise? That is not a religion which ever compromises.'

'Once they have blown up half the world along with themselves, they will—perhaps—realise that not only is there no paradise to go to but that there will soon be no world of humans at all.'

Robert laughed. 'That won't bother them! They think they'd all be in paradise then! The world itself would have become paradise because they had blown it up!'

'They'll never get rid of these suicide bombers. They think they're going to paradise. That's why they do it.'

'Well,' said Hector, 'we've just seen tonight that the idea doesn't travel. So it is not universal, it cannot be! That means it isn't what they think it is. Is the suicide bomber who lives in rain-soaked Argyll supposed to have the same idea of paradise as one from the arid Arabian desert? Impossible! Therefore it is nonsense. And people—any people— should be able to see that. The fact that Raissa's Holy Book is the literal word of God and that paradise is a place of numberless fountains of water is a contradiction here. So is the idea of the virgins in paradise. It is a contradiction for this time in any civilised society—one at least supplied with condoms. And since there is no shortage of food, at least in the West, that aspect of paradise is also false: it is not universal but applies only in a desert.'

'Haven't they just misdefined Paradise?' Asked Rose.

'No, The Holy Book is the literal word of god, not subject to discussion or interpretation, so the description of Paradise is crucial, cannot be altered. But if the description is clearly mistaken, it means that what happens to them after death in a Holy War is not the Paradise they expect. The Holy Book is wrong about that. In which case, no one should agree to blow himself up in a Holy War because there is no guarantee of going to the Paradise promised.'

'But maybe, though different, it is a Paradise nevertheless.'

'Since the Holy Book is wrong about this, how can we expect anything worthwhile instead? Because it is wrong, we are obliged to disbelieve it is any kind of place that is desirable. In other words, there is no Paradise. Indeed, whatever definition were given, it would not suit some people from esoteric lands and with esoteric views of what Paradise ought to be. For the Eskimo it would involve an absence of snow and ice. For the people of Argyll it would be an absence of rain and for the people of the desert, countless streams of water.'

'One day,' said Rose very wisely, 'Osama bin Laden will take tea with the Queen of Great Britain at Buckingham Palace.'

Everybody else laughed with derision except Raissa.

'I see what you mean,' she said. 'Prime minister Begin and Archbishop Makarios, heads of terrorist groups who blew up British soldiers, did. And Gerry Adams and Martin McGuinness, heads of the IRA, have been at Buckingham Palace. At the time no one could believe that these things would ever happen. But they did. Why should Osama be any different?'

18

In the morning, the situation over in the flat above the shop in Kinoidart was less hopeful and less optimistic. The men sat around waiting to see what would develop and their women served them food and drink from time to time. There was general irritation that they had not been allowed to use their weapons. Life in Britain so far apart from other members of the family had drastically reduced the number of occasions when weapons might be employed. In fact, apart from Mohammed Bombazine, they realised, no one had drawn a weapon with intent to use it, since they had arrived there.

'This life with the British is not what I expected,' said Rahendra, who had slept wrapped in his brown robe, dispiritedly. 'It is not like the old days. The call would come. We would leap on our camels and tear off into the desert in pursuit of some fleeing persons, usually of another tribe who had injured one of ours. Life is tame here. Look at us! We are sitting around here when we should have killed last night. And what is stopping us? The British men in blue. Well, I am not afraid of them.'

'—And the men in white,' said Suleiman. 'And you are a fool if you are not afraid. Do you think they would let you cut off some heads without punishment?'

'I do not fear their Old Bailey or their Barlinnie.'

'That is not the main difficulty,' answered Suleiman with a snarl. 'The men in blue have men with long rifles with telescopic sights. People like you, holed up in a building, say, they would not bother to take to their Old Bailey. They would shoot you instead. Why waste the time on this scorpion, they would say to themselves?'

'I might shoot them first.'

'You do not have a rifle that shoots so far. You would never see them. And if you shot one, he would be replaced by ten others.'

'What about the S.A.S., grandfather?'

'Them too! They attack in groups of four, men say—sometimes double or even treble that number. They are the men in black, black from head to foot. If they attacked us here in this house we would all die. "A double tap," they call it.'

'What is that, Grandfather?'

'Two shots in the head.'

'Well, it is all very boring this place, sitting around waiting,' concluded Rahendra. 'Maybe we should return to the desert. It was more fun. There was always something to do. Someone to fight or terrorise. I enjoy a bit of torture now and then and the rape of some fresh women. That would be fun too. Remember how we roasted that woman like a sheep? She tasted very good even after we all used her.'

'You had no water in the desert. No medicine if you fell ill and you had to steal food to avoid starving. That was the desert. It was very hot. Have you forgotten?'

'Well, I think I could die of boredom in this place. There is no excitement. When are you going to make up your mind?'

Suleiman said: 'What are the choices? We can ask for a higher bride price. But that would be unwise for the man, Hector, might have difficulty borrowing so much money. And if he did borrow it he might fail in his payments— and we might have to bail him out— he would be one of the family, then. Their Laws are most curious, remember. We could go out there and blow them up or cut the heads— but it would need to be all the heads. We couldn't leave any alive. And if we did that, the men in blue would get us—or the men in black, far worse. Every one of them is a James Bond, licensed to kill. They would come in the middle of the night and kill us all— even the wives of every one of you. Do you want that?'

Suleiman paused so that everyone had opportunity to absorb his reflections, then said: 'Or we can take the bride price—which is far too large anyway— and you can all go to your homes and get on with the task of learning to live in this new country which is so full of numberless streams of pure water, like the fountains of Babylon.' He laughed. 'I never thought I would see the day that I actually lived my life with so much water that it depressed my soul just to have it landing on my turban and running down my body in rivulets every time I step outside. I can never quite get the turban dry!'

Ahmad said: 'Have you not considered that since this place **has** numberless streams of water, maybe it is paradise? Maybe in other ways too? There are certainly virgins here, even if nobody wants them and the food can be picked off the trees or even the shelves in my market.'

Ignoring this as nonsense spoken by someone with an obvious vested interest, the old man looked around him, mournfully, as if he feared the decision they would make. 'I could order you but I will ask your counsel. What do you say?'

'What about our expenses?' said Mohammed Bombazine.

'The bride price will supply generous expenses. Without it there will be no expenses. Everything they have will be blown up. Carry anything away as treasure and it will be used to track you.'

'How much expenses will there be?' asked Raisuli.

'Two hundred English pounds each. Ahmad will receive a thousand, as the father.'

'What about the rest?' said Mohammed Bombazine.

'I will keep it for now.'

'What for?'

'To use in the best interests of the family. Probably to buy another shop in Lochgilphead, as Ahmad wishes. We could become rich in this Paradise.'

By a small majority they were in favour of the bride price. 'That accords with my own view. We are agreed then? We will take the money?'

When all assented, they got up to leave and Ahmad said: 'This is a wonderful day! It means we are on the road to riches, at last! We can stay here and make a proper home. We don't have to run away because we have killed. We will have money and admiration because of our new family connexions and we will become millionaires!'

'We will have to tell them,' mourned Suleiman. 'I hate the thought of that.'

'I could tell them,' offered Ahmad. 'I could simply tell them next time one is in the shop.'

Suleiman reflected for a time and then concluded: 'No, that will not do. It would not be very manly. I must do it myself. These men would never make such a weak response. We will go out there once more, you and I, and I will tell them face to face, as a man should.' And, as he rose slowly, for his old bones were aching after so much unaccustomed disturbance, to see the rest of the family off the premises, he added, 'Maybe I will drink some of this rotgut the men of the S.A.S. thought so much of. If it is offered.'

'But The Great One?' said Ahmad, with a worried look.

Suleiman was slow to reply. He got out into the street to wave to the departing members of the family before he put out his hands and felt the rain drops falling incessantly as ever: 'I am too old to be troubled by Him and I don't think it will matter so much now. Paradise is not what we thought it was. If it was, we would be enjoying all this water that constantly descends. Instead, we have to go and dry off the turbans.'

When the single vehicle was heard on the gravel outside the house, next morning, there was at first alarm and then relief when the inhabitants realised that there was not a squadron flying in the rear.

Hector, dressed in the kilt, met them at the door. 'Good of you to call. Please come in.' And, as they entered the sitting room where Robert, Raissa and Rose were seated around the fire, he said: 'I hope you don't mind, but I put on my kilt again. It seemed appropriate in some strange way.' Then, tentatively, he suggested: 'Can I offer you some tea? Or perhaps something more Scottish? We usually have some whisky at a time like this.'

Raissa said: 'We are not allowed to drink alcohol, father-in-law.'

'What a pity,' said Hector. 'What will you have, then?'

'I think we might take some of your brew,' said Ahmad. 'In fact, before I left the shop, I collected a bottle. I hope it is suitable.' He passed over to Hector a brown paper bag containing a bottle which Hector removed with care and studied with interest.

'How very kind of you!' he beamed. 'Talisker, 20 years old.'

'I heard it was better if it was old. This bottle has been in the shop for years. Since we took it over, as a matter of fact.'

'I wonder why it did not sell?' remarked Suleiman.

'Nobody could afford to buy it, I expect,' said Hector. 'Anyway, we'll christen it right now if you are agreeable.'

'Certainly,' said Ahmad. 'My father is anxious to try this Scottish drink, even if it is proscribed.'

'Oh, wherever did you hear of it?' said Hector, going to fetch glasses.

'In Kabul. The men of the S.A.S. used to drink it. They said it put hairs on their chests.'

Everybody laughed politely, the tension having risen.

Invited to do so, Ahmad and Suleiman sat down on chairs which Robert and Hector fetched and drew into the circle around the fire. 'There we are now,' said Hector, having poured drinks for everyone. And then fell silent. What was it to be? The bride price, an increased price or a refusal or something worse, which the lack of armed attendants had been arranged to conceal.

Suleiman sipped the drink and his eyes lifted with shock at the unaccustomed warmth in his mouth which grew all the way down his throat. He blew out his cheeks. 'Now I see what the little men of the S.A.S. meant,' he said, lifting the glass to study the amber fluid within. 'This would keep you warm on a cold night in the desert. I expect that's why they value it.'

Hector laughed: 'If only that were all. No. They drink it anywhere. We all do, this side of the border and even across it and across the pond too. In America, I mean. They sent shiploads to the gangsters in the prohibition years. There were 34 distilleries in Campbeltown alone, just down the road.'

Suleiman cleared his throat and announced: 'We have decided to accept your bride price and'—looking at Robert— 'matters will be as you say,'

There was a palpable sigh of relief from every one of the household. 'Then,' said Hector, rising to his feet, 'we shall, in accordance with tradition in this place, be upstanding and toast the happy couple: 'Riassa and Robert.' The pair of whom, as everyone rose to drink, looked at each other with sudden uninhibited joy and squeezed hands which is what each instinctively recognised the situation called for and not what was traditional.

They sat down and everyone sipped slowly and faces softened and souls mellowed. Presently, Hector brightened: 'You know, I can't believe it has turned out like this. It is a miracle.'

'You have miracles in your religion?' asked Suleiman. 'Yes, I had heard that. Your TV is very instructive. I have learned many things from it. How different everything is here. It is making us soft, all this food and drink and soft furnishings. Do you know, until I came here I had never slept on a bed? I hear that some of them provide heat in cold weather. Now that really is a miracle!'

Raissa smiled: 'But there are aeroplanes, Grandfather. And motor cars and trains and even rockets to the Moon. Now these are miracles. The electric blanket is a small thing in comparison.'

'Is that all it is? A blanket that gets hot by itself? Who would have imagined it?'

'It's the electricity, Grandfather, you push in the plug and switch on and the current flows and makes it hot.'

'Did you learn that at Cambridge? Well, well, who would have thought it?'

'I learned it at school.'

'What is it that you do for a living?' asked Suleiman of Hector.

'I am a painter. I painted the pictures you see around you, most of them. But it is not a living, not yet anyway.'

Suleiman arose, taking his drink, and went to look at the paintings in their frames arranged around the walls, standing before each one and viewing it carefully. Hector joined him.

Before one canvas depicting a blazing sunset, Suleiman said: 'Yes, I have seen such things before in my homeland. Is it not amazing, our world? So many colours and sights to see. They are marvellous to men's eyes. The Great One is the greatest miracle of all for making so many others we can enjoy. Even the electric blanket.'

'That was an invention of men, I think,' said Hector, gently.

'You don't believe in The Great One, then, like so many in this region? Your temples do not have many worshippers, I think?'

'Well, I don't believe the world was made by a person and that he is still around to oversee its progress.'

'What then, do you believe?'

'That this world was always here and men have arisen in it by chance and evolution and they have invented things like the moral values that make living possible.'

'I don't understand this evolution, though I hear the word on your TV. But what is your purpose?'

'I might ask you the same question. I have a duty to contribute to the world as best I can, as well as feed my family and educate them.'

'And these paintings are your contribution?'

'Yes. They're meant to be provocative, beautiful and original things— things no other can do. That's what I aim for, anyway.'

'How are you doing, father?' said Robert.

'Not well. I work every day and I make many canvases and some of them I am proud of but I don't sell very many. I do feel I am getting better. Maybe that's what matters.'

'So you are not like Ahmad, here, who only does a thing for the money it will bring?'

'No, Suleiman. I believe I can say important things and that this is how I should spend my time.'

'Even if you cannot feed your family?'

'I do that well enough, I hope. It is not an issue—yet at least. Maybe I will sell some paintings. I hope so.'

'The Great One would approve of that, better than Ahmad who is trying to become a millionaire.'

'I've never had any sign of The Great One. I presume you have?'

'It never occurred to me to question him. Until now.'

'What do you mean?'

'Until I learned that Argyll is full of running streams of water without end and yet it is not Paradise for I do not enjoy so many streams very much. And that there can be no virgins in Paradise for they would not do at all. What men want is very different. It means our Holy Book is suspect.'

'Well, I am surprised!' said Hector. 'But then Raissa must have got her brains somewhere. I see it was from you.'

'I would like to explore this new religion of yours,' said Suleiman.

'There is no religion and no church—no temple of worship. What you might do is attend the local Church of Scotland and see what happens there.'

'And would you come too?'

'Yes, why not? I am sure we could have classes together with the minister who would explain the doctrine. That is his job, after all.'

Robert laughed: 'Why would you go to church now, after all you've said against it, Dad?'

'I believe it might help you and your marriage if the men involved got together a bit and came to some understanding and, perhaps, common ground.'

'Would you like some more whisky, Grandfather?' said Robert.

Suleiman turned suddenly at the appellation, reflected for a moment, and said with eyes that suddenly shone: 'My old heart is warmed by this.' He turned to Hector and held out his glass. 'Yes, I do believe I could enjoy some more of this drink the men of the S.A.S. enjoy, for it warms the soul.'

'Then we must make it a small one this time,' said Hector, kindly, 'If you are not used to it, it can have surprising effects.'

'I think I would like to get used to it,' said Suleiman. Ahmad was astonished. When both he and his father had received a further libation, Hector said: 'Slainthe mha', It's what we say on such occasions,' he explained. 'It means *good health to you*, or something like that.'

'What is this taste?' said Suleiman.

'It's the peat,' said Hector. 'This whisky comes from Skye, an island to the north, which has lots of peat and the streams are affected by the peat.'

'Ah,' said Suleiman, with sudden insight, 'So these streams might be the very streams of paradise since they are used to produce drinks like this?'

Robert was appalled, Hector shocked at the loss of so much that had been achieved. Seeing this, Suleiman laughed, a full-throated laugh and soon everyone joined in.

He added: 'I see the Holy Book must be rewritten to account for these phenomena.'

Evidently, he was serious, for in a little while he asked: 'When can we go to this temple of yours? I am looking forward to it. And will no one take offence?'

'Certainly not!' said Hector. 'They will be absolutely delighted to see you there!'

'How should I dress?'

'Any way you like.'

'Would these clothes do?'

'Certainly. They will look a little odd but no matter. You will be made very welcome.'

'But you do not go there, do you?'

'No, but they will be glad to see anyone. Even me.'

'Especially you!' said Robert

19

And so it was that Suleiman went to the Church of Scotland in Kinoidart accompanied by Hector MacIvor, known atheist/humanist. And they both enjoyed the experience so much that they went again and again and again. After a fortnight, Hector presented Suleiman with a gift-wrapped package. Suleiman grinned and opened it to discover a broad-brimmed, white, leather hat, with a string to keep it on in a gale.

'I thought this might save the turban. The weather here, you known, doesn't really suit turbans. It is waterproof. I did it myself.'

Suleiman was delighted with it and soon wore it whenever he went out. Of course, because of the size of the hat, it was impossible to also wear the turban. That did not seem to matter. Seeing this, Hector gave him another present: a waterproof suit which would cover whatever he was wearing. This too, Suleiman took to wearing at every opportunity and he was clearly delighted to receive really useful presents which helped him settle-in to his new surroundings.

Sometime during all these visits it occurred to Hector suddenly to say to his new friend: 'I wonder if I might make a suggestion? I do not wish to offend you but it would be a very great privilege for me to try to paint your portrait. What would you think of that?'

'What would I have to do?'

'Come out here every day for a time and sit in my studio upstairs while I commit your face to the canvas with paint.'

'Why would you want to do this?'

'Because I have never until now thought of painting a portrait. I have a feeling it might herald the start of something important in my development as an artist.'

'You told me your aim was to provoke thought; to do something original. What would be original in this?'

'I am not sure. If I knew that, I wouldn't have to paint anything. I just don't know why this seems a good idea, I just feel that it is.' And then after stopping to consider the matter more deeply, Hector added: 'I think it has something to do with our two cultures. They seemed so different at one time; yours so alien, if you will forgive me. I expect mine seemed just as alien to you. Now, we seem to have hit it off together—something I would never have believed. I think I want to celebrate this in the only way I know how.'

'When would I have to come?'

'Every afternoon, about 4 o'clock, say. That gives me all day to paint before you arrive. I can modify what I've done. About an hour or so would do, I think.'

'Very well, I agree. I will walk out to your house here every day at that time. The exercise will do me much good.'

As he was leaving, Suleiman added with a chuckle: 'Do people who sit for portraits receive glasses of whisky to keep them warm?'

'Of course, and artists too.'

And so it was that one day when the painting was nearly finished, Suleiman was just entering the track which led out to the house on the spit when a car drew up. It was a fine sunny day and he felt as much in harmony with the new world in which he lived as he could ever remember. So many new ideas he had learned, so many new things seen. He was reflecting upon these changes and how enjoyable they were becoming. Though he had never yet seen the painting, he knew it would be a very good likeness and that it would do him credit, for the painter was an expert and had become a valued friend whom he liked very much. Suleiman looked down into the front seat of the car through the window, which opened suddenly as if by magic. Inside in the driving seat, was a lovely young woman with a pale face and auburn hair, dressed in a black trouser suit. Through the window, she said to him: 'Would you like a lift? I am driving out to the house. It seems silly that you should have to walk when I am going there in this car.'

'I enjoy the exercise, but thank you all the same,' he replied, smiling at the lovely track through the trees that beckoned him to his new friend and the glasses of the whisky he had learned to expect and enjoy.

'Well, would you help me, then? I am not sure of this road. It is potholed and I might get into difficulties. I really would be grateful for your company in the car. In case anything happens.' Suleiman was too happy in himself to refuse.

'Well, all right, if you insist,' he replied, thinking what a very good-looking young woman she was. 'But I assure you that the road is not very bad. I walk it every day.'

When he was seated beside her, she did not immediately drive off but insisted he strap on the seat belt and said: 'I notice you wear a white turban.'

'Yes, I am being painted in it. Often now I wear a white hat.'

'I wonder if by any chance you have ever been in Tashkent?'

'Yes, I have,' he answered with surprise. 'Many years ago.'

'And have you also been in Kabul?'

'Yes, indeed. I lived there for several years but that was a long time ago too.' Still dazzled by the wonder of such a fine day of sunshine and real heat for once, Suleiman was only half attending to what she was saying. He could feel the heat entering his bones and his aches and pains lessening.

'What about Kandahar? And Rawalpindi? And Samarkand? And Kashgar? And Krasnoyarsk?' she continued.

'Yes, indeed, all these places. But why do you ask?'

'Is your name Suleiman Hussain?'

'It is.'

'That makes me very glad for I have been trying to find you. I have a gift for you. I do not know what it is. It is wrapped up and my instructions are not to open it. I am to deliver it in person.'

Suleiman began for the first time to pay close attention. 'Who is it from?'

'An old friend.'

'Where is this gift?'

'At my home. I would be willing to drive you there and when you have your gift I will drive you back here. How would that do?'

'It will not do. I would be late for my appointment. I am being painted.'

Expecting a refusal, the woman lifted a syringe she had in her right hand which she had been holding out of sight on her right side, leaned across, stabbed the point into Suleiman's neck and pressed the plunger.

He jerked back in the seat as if receiving a jolt of electric current—too late! Managed to utter the words: 'What are y ..o ..u— do.....' before his head fell senseless on his chest.

The woman turned the car and drove Suleiman up the road for many miles towards the town to a small detached house hidden among trees by the sea, parked the car in the drive and then got out, opened the garage door and put the light on, for there was no window within. Then she returned to the car, drove inside and closed the garage door. Since the garage had a door into the house there was no need to show herself again. Even so, no one could have seen her, so private was the house which was situated on a hill and wooded everywhere around. The garage was huge, large enough to take two cars.

When Suleiman became conscious, he found himself on the smooth concrete garage floor, flat on his back, lying on a large thick black plastic sheet. There was no sign of the car which had been driven just outside. He felt groggy but not cold and he realised that the garage was heated. He found that his hands and feet were tied by ropes to ring bolts screwed into the concrete floor. His arms were fixed at right angles to his body and his legs were as wide apart as they would go. He was quite unable to move. Above, he could see that the roof, as well as the walls and floor, were of concrete, a very solid prison then and without a window. A fluorescent strip was all the lighting the garage possessed and it was sufficient. Apart from himself, his ropes, ringbolts and a petrol can, there seemed to be nothing else inside.

The woman returned and stood over him and stared down. 'My name is Dr Katusheva,' she said. 'You may have heard of me?'

'I have not, never.'

'No matter. Do you remember my father? Colonel Arcady Katushev?'

'No, I do not know that name either.'

'You should do, you killed him. Or is it that you killed so many you have forgotten their names?'

'In any event, I do not know who or what you are talking about.'

'Let me refresh your memory. My father was in a jeep on the road from Kabul to Kandahar with one other person driving. You and four others intercepted him. You shot the driver and the jeep crashed and turned over. You took my father out of the jeep and away from the road into a nearby valley, safe from travellers on the road who might have noticed. There you tortured him slowly until he died. You cut off his penis and stuck it in his mouth and forced him to swallow it. You cut off his scrotum and stuck that in his mouth and forced him to eat that too. Then you stuck the point of a dagger into one eye and let him scream some more. And when he became unconscious, you stuck the dagger into the other eye to waken him up. Then you cut out both eyes, severing the nerves. You bandaged his wounds so that he would not die too quickly. And you gagged him so that he would not disturb your sleep. In the morning, you poured petrol into his eye sockets and into where his genitals had been. And when you'd finished, you set my father alight and watched him burn. And there you left him.' Alex paused to let him absorb these things before saying very levelly but firmly: 'Why did you do these things?'

'Why do you think that I did this?'

'Because the others with you told me what you did and what you ordered them to do.'

'Where are these others now?'

'They are dead, of course. I have been tracking your group and you are the last remaining member: the leader.'

'I do not know what to say to you except that I am not responsible.'

Alex laughed. 'I know you are responsible. It is too late for denials. You are the man in the white turban, the man who has been in Tashkent and Samarkand and Kabul—which you admitted— and the other places. And you have the name—also admitted. How could there be any doubt?'

'Other men may wear white turbans and visit the places you say. And there will even be many men who have done these things with the same name as my own.'

Alex laughed. 'That is what they all said— at first. To make me put them out of their misery they all admitted it in the end. Don't you understand that you will do the same? It is just a matter of time.'

'No matter what I admit under torture, that doesn't make it true.'

'Then we will begin with your lunch. Have you ever eaten penis for lunch? Not cold, surely? Not your own, I feel certain.'

Alex took a long fish-filleting knife from a bench nearby and in a few swift strokes had sliced off Suleiman's clothing exposing his penis.

'Why don't you imagine a lovely woman about to make love to you? It will provide your last erection?' When Suleiman said nothing, Alex slowly undressed in as lascivious a fashion as she could imagine. Eventually, she stood above him stark naked. Still there was no effect. Then she stood over him so that he looked upwards towards her vagina and she moved her labia with the fingers of her left hand so that he could see the reddening channel open up beyond. Then she changed the object of her touch to the clitoris and she massaged it tenderly until it stood out red and engorged, widening the labia with her hand sufficiently for him to see. Suleiman's eyes glazed over and his penis began to rise despite his desperate circumstances. Alex bent down over him and grasped it and manipulated it with her left hand until it strengthened.

'Will I make you come, just one last time? Would you like that? I will do it for you if you wish?'

'Yes, anything, please,' he croaked. 'Just draw out the moment as long as you feel able.'

'You don't beg,' she remarked, as she manipulated him. 'Why is that?'

'What is the point?'

'You could scream for help—though it will do no good. This house was carefully chosen. I thought it was you when I came here, though not where you lived exactly. It took time to find out and I had to make many additional trips to be absolutely sure it was you. Now that I have you here like this I feel like enjoying it.' She laid down the knife carefully out of his reach and set to work on his penis with both hands. The erection became gross and he started to sweat.

'Would you like me to suck it and make it truly huge? That is what happens, you know. It becomes so swollen with blood it is painful. It is the effect of the tongue which is like a rasp. Would you like that?'

'I would like anything that prolongs my self and my life.'

'But you won't beg? Why is that? The others all begged.'

Suleiman said nothing.

'You are brave then, a truly brave man. We will see just how brave, by and by. What I really want to know is why you were so cruel to my father? I do not understand. Would you please explain?' She said this gently, in a compassionate voice, as one fascinated by this man's motives and determined to understand his cruelty.

Suleiman said nothing.

'Will I give you your last orgasm first? Would you like that?'

Suleiman said nothing.

'Why will you not answer?'

Again there was no reply.

'Well, I shall just have to cut it now,' she added and lifted the knife to strike, still holding the end of the penis in the left hand. 'But it's going soft again.' Alex laughed.

'I see I must suck it if I am to get it really big. I wonder if I can do that? I'm not sure, all of a sudden. This was never part of the plan. I've been planning this for years, you know. You might think you know a thing or two about revenge, but in my family the matter is taken with a seriousness so deadly you could not imagine it. Kill one of us and you condemn yourself and all those who aided you. And if there is any possibility of a come-back we will kill all your loved ones also.'

Suddenly she stood up and released him. 'I feel hungry and there is no particular hurry. I think I will make a meal, a proper one. Would you be able to eat if I made you something? I expect so, if it prolongs the inevitable. I would like you to answer me, you see. But if you frustrate me I will just carve you up all the sooner. As you see, I have a gallon of petrol'—pointing to a container in the corner—'to do the necessary when you are still alive, just as you treated my father.'

As she went to the door into the house, still naked, but carrying her clothes, she turned to say: 'Think about it please. Why did you kill my father in that particularly horrific fashion? I want to know and only the truth will do.'

After a leisurely lunch, she returned fully dressed again in the black trouser suit—having forgotten his lunch, it seemed at first. 'I have decided not to suck you. I would get angry and bite it off. God knows what bacteria are around it. So I am going to cut it now unless you tell me. Why did you do it to my father? Why did you abuse him so badly?' Her voice rose into a shriek finally.

'I did not know it was your father.'

—'It had to be somebody's father!'

'I saw a Russian soldier. My people had been killed by Russian soldiers. I saw them burned and tortured, mutilated, disembowelled and murdered by the score—by the hundred. Men, women and children, all of them raped—if alive—even the children. And for what? Because we were in the wrong place at the wrong time. What harm had we done to Russians? None!'

'But why didn't you just kill him? That would have been an act of war.'

'This was an act of revenge. I needed the punishment to be terrible to try to assuage the wrong.'

'And did it?'

'No. It was not terrible enough.'

'And is that your final word? All you have to say?'

'No.'

'What more is there?'

'These last few months, when I have been attending church, I have learned about Jesus, the prophet who spoke of the value of love without conditions and of forgiveness. I have begun to wonder if I should not instead have released the Russian and forgiven him for the evils of his countrymen.' A tear slowly formed in one of Suleiman's eyes as if he was genuinely regretful of his conduct.

'Jesus would tell us to lay down our arms and embrace the Russians. That was his message. Maybe it would have worked. Instead, many were killed on both sides before it ended. And it soon started up again.'

Alex laughed. 'If you had disarmed yourselves and embraced the Russian bear it would have mauled you all the more fatally.'

'I don't think so. I think—because it is not an animal but a human— it might have been impressed. How could a human go on killing other humans when there is no resistance of any kind with expressions of kindness on every face that died?'

'I think you have become naïve, old man. Have you forgotten the Holocaust?'

'I think I have suddenly recognised something important.' Then Suleiman sighed deeply. 'This Argyll is a strange place, full of streams of pure water—so that you can hardly move for them and there is the water that comes down from above every other day. And nobody wants to be a virgin— so there aren't any, and good riddance to that loss, I say. And so much food that people even die of it. But a man, even a man like me, can learn things here.'

They looked at each other for a while, until Suleiman said: 'I regret the death of your father and every man I ever killed. And even the tortures I inflicted. I did not know any better at the time. And there is nothing I can do about it in compensation, except to say that I am sorry. I met a man recently, a local man—he is not a highlander but he has lived here many years. And he has become my friend. He is the first real friend I ever had in my life for I have always been the chief and chiefs have to be above even friendship when justice commands. From him I have learned many things. About forgiveness—that most of all. I forgive you for what you are about to do.'

'Forgive me?' shrieked Alex. 'What right have you to forgive me? I would rather you hated me and feared me.'

'Well, I don't. I am sorry for you.'

'SORRY FOR ME? I am about to cut off your cock and balls and you are sorry for me?'

'Yes. You are a person in torment and my death— no matter what you do— will not lessen the torment. You see, I once was like you and I know what it is like.'

When Alex said nothing, Suleiman continued: 'Your personality is warped by your experience. You have been made hard and heartless by your sufferings— for which I admit I am responsible. But it means that you can never find love, not the love of the body but the love of the mind, the kind of love I have for my new friend in whom I take great pride. You are like a bird condemned to fly above the earth with a shot wing. You cannot fly level and have to struggle just to stay in the air, so your view of the ground beneath is necessarily distorted.'

'You would speak to me like that? You are unbelievable!'

'To see the planet as it is, you need to mend that wing and that means you need an epiphany— I believe that is the word. I heard it on the TV: an experience in which you are cleansed of your rancour and that can only happen when you can forgive. The prophet Jesus really was wise.'

'Will you beg for your life?'

'No.'

'Well, then go to your hell!' And in one movement as swift as a falcon in flight, Alex leaned down and severed the penis. Mindless of the blood which spurted everywhere, Alex lifted it and stuffed it into Suleiman's mouth. All the other things she had planned were carried out in succession. Throughout, Suleiman did not so much as utter a murmur. Probably, he died of shock soon after the horror began. He was old, after all. So Alex's plan was thwarted, at least in part.

The fire was fiercer than expected, partly because she poured petrol liberally over the torso when it was apparent nothing could be gained by delay: he was already dead. Because of the heat and smoke, she eventually went reluctantly into the house and shut the door. When it eventually ceased after an hour or two, she found the fire had burned a hole in the plastic sheet. The plan had to be modified: another sheet had to be laid down on the floor and the remains lifted onto it. But this was easily accomplished because some of the edge of the first sheet survived. It was a case of folding and shovelling and lifting and rolling, that too, on one side onto the new sheet and then the second sheet could also be folded and it was strong enough to bear the remains: solidifying fat, charred bones and roasted flesh, mostly.

This was the dangerous time and Alex was keenly aware of it. She did nothing in a hurry; thought everything through very carefully. A third plastic sheet was arranged in the back of the estate car. She opened the garage door, looked around and listened carefully for signs of unexpected visitors. There were none. She reversed the car into the garage beside the bundle, closed the garage door and then carefully transferred the bundle to the boot to lie on the sheet there and then sealed it with the zipper. There would be no appreciable smell in the car because of it. This achieved, Alex closed the boot, drove the car out of the garage, and re-entered the garage again to clean the floor very thoroughly, loading the cleaning kit also in the estate car's boot when she had finished. Satisfied eventually, she began to paint the entire garage inside. By then the places which showed signs of the fire had cooled enough to begin. She unscrewed the ring bolts and cemented over the holes with filler which soon hardened. Everything inside the garage was then painted white.

Leaving the garage door wide open to clear the air of smells of burning and of paint, she drove into the wilderness to a previously chosen spot up a rarely used track behind some tree-clad mountains and there dumped the bundle in the zippered plastic sheet and then started a second fire. This time, the petrol was liberally applied and the blaze was intense. She stood beside it till it went down and then walked over and around it, raking it over until every atom of the contents of the third plastic sheet had been crushed to ash. Anything that would not burn such as parts of the zipper, she carefully collected in a small plastic bag which she kept to dispose of later in a different place along with the cleaning materials and painting kit. Her final act was to scatter the ashes widely using a broom and when she prepared to depart there was hardly a sign that anything unusual had taken place. In a day or two, no one could know that there had even been a fire there at all. As the track was mainly gravel and rock, she noted with approval, and the weather was dry, there was little indication that a car had travelled there.

Two days elapsed before any search of the environs of Kinoidart was made to try to locate Suleiman and another fortnight before he was officially posted missing. No one could believe he had disappeared. He was just not the type to go walk—about, was the view of everyone who knew him. And by that time Alex had sold her house, obtained the money and left for Dover where she sold the estate car. But no one ever looked for it. Why would they? She had resigned her job a year before and gone travelling in Asia only to return when she was completely certain of her find in Argyll. Once in France, she was soon swallowed up in the metro and quickly away by train under a different passport to countries thousands of miles to the east. Years later, a Sherlock Holmes might have located her in Kazakhstan had he been looking for an unusually gifted teacher of English. But then, he would have been searching for a violinist and as one himself, he might have found her—despite her reluctance to perform in public, aware of her tell-tale distinction. However, alas, he was a character in fiction and his skills were unavailable as well as unrequested.

Alex never did fall in love because she never enjoyed the epiphany that would have enabled her to achieve forgiveness and view the earth and its peoples without distortion.

The disappearance of Suleiman Hussain, lately of Kinoidart and several exotic locations in Asia before that, remained an unsolved mystery, like so many. No one was able to explain it because the person or persons responsible were not telling.

Hector MacIvor lamented the loss of his new friend in whose company he had discovered the values of Christianity in an effort to bring two families as well as two cultures together. The painting of Suleiman hung for many years in pride of place above the mantel in the sitting room, despite what other canvasses had recently been created. It showed a face that had suffered, commanded other men and fought the battles of men in a desert country, often in turmoil. The eyes were blue and lit with intelligence and above them, sat a white turban.

THE END

Note: some of the equations and further information about mathematics and physics are to be found in appendices in *A Bute Crucifixion*, also published at this time.

AFTERWORD

The idea of applying to an agent—without whom, we are told, a publisher cannot be found—and waiting for months to be turned down, because only a couple will be taken out of 1000 applications—most of them never even read—was rejected. This book contains a solution—the only solution—to an important problem of international concern. My duty, as author, is to make it available as soon as possible to the wider world, at least to the limit of my resources. Were I to wait for a publisher, I might—like millions of others—wait forever. And the solution would never be seen. As we know, 19 publishers turned down J.K. Rowling, which means publishers are mostly brainless. Q.E.D.

Of course the solution needs to be widely distributed for it to have a significant effect. If then, any reader knows a publisher better equipped than the other 19/20ths, or has any power to influence one to take up the publication of this work to a wider audience, let him apply himself and encourage that company to contact me. Further, this is a limited edition of necessity. It will be valuable one day. Remember this. At the time of writing (and for years!) <u>used copies</u> of *Bannockburn Revealed,* another book of mine published 8 years ago, are being quoted for sale in Amazon.com for from £34 to £128 and $231, though new signed copies can still be had from me for £25.

Notice this also: no publisher would understand the allusions to physics, mathematics, violin playing or philosophy. He would want these removed in case the general reader was put off. Most books are dumbed down for just this reason. Well mine won't be! And the general reader will get the flavour of the intellectual lives being described and even, from the references, be able to follow them up and join those worlds. No publisher would dream of allowing footnotes in a novel. The reader who dislikes footnotes, it hardly needs saying, can simply skip them; some readers will love them: they answer questions, explain things and open doors to further adventures of ideas.

Also, notice this: many writers will be failed by the child reader at the doorway of the publishing house because of the use of non standard English and unusual forms—regardless of content—as if these must be satisfied for a work to be of value. Instead, the original mind will not limit itself to standard language, spelling or form: why should it, when there is no standard English? How could there be when regiments of people—in Oxford, Cambridge and elsewhere—struggle to keep pace with the changes in their new editions of dictionaries? It is even the duty of the writer to extend and develop the language in any way he thinks fit. The one certainty is that the average publishing house is too stupid to understand the nature of originality, its ambition and its demand for the freedom to make things better or even just different. **This is why every writer seeking to acquire a publisher struggles to obey rules which have nothing to do with the quality of the writing and if he fails in this task of idiotic, unwarranted and unseemly obedience, his writing never gets read.**

In my opinion, there is no possibility that a publisher would have agreed to leave my work as I want it. That is sufficient reason for publishing it myself. Indeed, everything that is original and genuinely worthy is, these days, excised by the editors of big publishing houses for the sake of maximising sales and in consequence the versions they approve of are like mush: bland and bereft of all passion, originality and power. Read them and see. Good writing, the best writing, to which this author aspires, has no concern for maximising sales or profits. How could they notice the kind of excellence which is real originality, insight and dramatic power when all they care about is cash?

Thomas Hardy, a great novelist, had to make many changes to his books because the publisher thought them necessary for sales— a common event. Nor are literary peers a reliable judge. Robert Southey, eventually Poet Laureate, and a friend of Coleridge, in the *Critical Review*, described *The Ancient Mariner* as 'absurd or unintelligible.'[18]. Dr Charles Burney, in the *Monthly Review*, said it was 'the strangest story of cock and bull that we have ever seen on paper.'[19] Yet this poem is one of the finest in the language.

I will not compromise my artistic vision for the sake of publication, celebrity or profit.

---

[18] *Wordsworth and Coleridge: The Friendship*, Adam Sisman, p 272
[19] ibid p273

This book will not be found on the shelves of big bookshops like Waterstones. Why? Because Waterstones want 60 % of the cover price and me, as publisher, to pay the postage to them. ie for writing the book and publishing it they think it is fair to leave me 20%. No thank you. I could publish nothing else if I agreed. Money really is the chief obstacle to the publication of good writing.

What should one do if confronted with a suicide bomber to divert him from his act?

Take him and his Holy Book to Argyll on a wet day and point to the description of paradise in his book: where it says it is a place of countless streams of water. And then point to the countless streams there already. *Is this paradise, then?* You enquire. And when he replies: 'OF COURSE NOT'.
 You say: *There is something wrong with your book then. Maybe you are not going to the paradise you expect. Maybe you will just be fragments of flesh rotting in the afterburn.*
Your Holy Book is the literal word of God, is it not?
 'YES', he replies.
 So it must be true, then?
 'YES', he replies.
But you can easily see that it is not true. So your Holy Book is not correct about paradise.
'AH, BUT THERE ARE MANY VIRGINS IN PARADISE FOR ME TO ENJOY', he replies. Then, you say, *who wants a virgin? That was only worthwhile in time of disease. Now all you need is a condom. A virgin will be all pain for her and even for you. Almost anybody else is better. How could a virgin contain a manhood like yours? Do you want to enjoy her screams?*
And if he insists that paradise contains unlimited tasty food, refer him to *McTavish's Kitchen*, Oban; *Kilmartin tea room*; *Brambles*, Inverary; *The Smiddy*, Lochgilphead or even *Craigmore Pier*, *The Waterfront*, or *Ettrick Bay*, on Bute. And if he is still unconvinced, take him into the supermarket and say: *In a desert, there is no food or water. OK. But here in Argyll & Bute there is enough food to feed you for a thousand*

years and even wine to drink with it. And they will even give it to you for nothing if you are in need.

And if he says: 'I AM NOT ALLOWED ALCOHOL', you reply: *The more fool you. Try the bottled water, then. Small amounts of wine will soften your arteries, keep the cancer at bay and warm your distressed soul.*

ACKNOWLEDGEMENTS for this and *A Bute Crucifixion*

I am very grateful to my friends Rev Jock Stein, Minister and Theology Publisher, Christine Boyd, Primary School Teacher, Tom McCallum, Classicist, Gordon McConnell, Head of Mathematics, David Torrie, Writer and Editor, and Colonel Bruce Niven, Soldier, Mountaineer and Leadership Trainer, who all gave up their time to read my work and very kindly allowed me to print what they thought of it. In a self-published work by an unknown, assistance of that kind is invaluable, especially when there are too many important creative tasks ahead to waste time on marketing or self-promotion. I am also grateful to Linda Mellor for giving up a whole day to travel with me to Argyll to hold a watering can in front of the lens while I took photos for my cover. Of course I could not guarantee that it would rain. And I did need rain to make my point. In the end I made no use of these photos as they were not good enough and chose to exercise my imagination instead; but our trip was greatly enjoyed. Patricia MacArthur in Rothesay Library was especially helpful again and Stephen Standaloft's aid with the software showing me how to make covers was invaluable, as was David Rennie in making the spines. John Dick was very helpful in getting two of my equations into the document of the Crucifixion and Sylvia Jardine with Appendix 2 which was a worry because of the amount of esoteric symbols. Dr Anne Howie was useful in suggesting symmetrically formatting page numbers so that I could finish the typesetting. The photo of the old school after the fire is used with the courtesy of The Buteman. The district logo also used is actually indistinguishable from that of the Royal Burgh of Rothesay, the image I wanted, the Crucifixion novel being set just after WW11. Since the image existed before the councils combined, it is right and proper than a Brandane, doing his best for community and country, should be allowed to make use of it which Janet West, for the council, confirmed. It was Christine who suggested I should publish Crucifixion now. I would not have thought of it myself. Without her, it could easily have continued to gather dust like so many other productions while new ones are written—always the more interesting task.

William Scott, Rothesay, Isle of Bute, January, 2008

From p114: **The solution to the problem: why is there anything?** Can now be seen because of the discovery that even a vacuum is a busy place full of particles.

The solution is like Newton's approach to motion in his First Law: no body is at rest absolutely, every body is in motion relative to other bodies. The question: Where is a body exactly located? becomes meaningless. Motion is the state that is normal, expected; to be at rest is abnormal, impossible if absolute rest, without reference to an observer, is wanted. It is the same here!

Since a vacuum has a great deal of activity within it, absolute nothingness is an impossibility, just as absolute rest is impossible for any body in the universe. Even absolute nothingness, assuming it were possible, would have the activity of a vacuum: the presence of the particles and antiparticles necessary to occasion the vacuum. Just as the question of absolute motion makes no sense, because there is no absolute reference point to which the motion can refer universally, so also, the question: why is there anything? makes no sense. The state of absolute nothingness is impossible, for to achieve it there would have to be particles and antiparticles galore, every one of them a contradiction to the idea that nothingness has been achieved.

That humans have debated this question: why is there anything? For millennia, rests on a fundamental error of perception which is: that nothingness is normal. Instead, the existence of things is normal and expected— as we see all the time—what would be extraordinary would be a state of nothing whatever.

PS I am not aware that anyone else has seen this idea before. It is mine alone. I decided to include it within the novel giving it to the character for dramatic effect.

OTHER BOOKS BY William Scott

The Bannockburn Years published by Luath Press, 543/2 Castlehill The Royal Mile, Edinburgh EH11 2ND £7.95 ISBN 0946487340

'William Scott,..a brilliant storyteller.' Nigel Tranter.
'A stirring and thoroughly researched account.' Scotland on Sunday.
'Compulsively readable.' The Scotsman
'Strong Bute bond in Bannockburn book' The Buteman.

This novel, set in Bute in 1314, which won the Constable Trophy in 1997, was written to discover arguments to settle the question of Scottish Independence. Four arguments were found. The first insights about how the Battle of Bannockburn was fought and where, are in this book. The research exposed inadequacies in the current thinking in the Scottish History Community. The two books that followed were the result of a decade of full time investigation of the battle which answers all the questions about it.

Though the research which followed was used to upgrade the novel in a reprint without increasing the number of pages— a matter of some difficulty, time, effort, labour and skill made at his invitation—the publisher, despite a contract which allowed for this, declined to make the small but important alterations in the second edition. He put profit before the truth.

Bannockburn Revealed published by Elenkus, 2000. ISBN 9780952191018. A 505 page hard back including 70 full colour photos of the battle area and relevant maps. £25 from www.elenkus.com or £30 uncluding postage UK; £35 rest of world. Weighs about 2lbs.

This is a very original investigation of the battle using new procedures which demolished the false beliefs which have lasted centuries. Where exactly the battle was fought and how won is made clear here and shown for the first time. All the written reports of the time are translated and analysed within the book. The conclusions, drawn from a dozen sources, tabulated, are clear and established with overwhelming force.

There was no Scottish cavalry charge as everyone has believed for centuries. The Scots attacked the English on foot, penned them between the two streams in the Carse in which they had camped out of bowshot of Balquhiderock Wood, which was in Scottish hands. And when they got within 60 yards of the English cavalry (which had, expecting a foxhunt of rebels, camped in the van) cutting down the available space to get up speed in a charge, the Scots dug their pike butts into the soft ground (it had been raining torrentially just before) the English charged, were held and then pulled off their horses and killed. Unable to move forward due to the 15,000 Scots present, who filled the half mile between the streams, sideways because of the streams, (swollen with rain and the tide and muddied by an army camped beside them) and backwards because of the press of hangers on, trying to see, the English were unable to manoeuvre and were systematically slain. Unless you have a good map of the battle area, the battle cannot be understood. The map here, was made by excising every change since 1314 on Gen. Roy's map of 1750—a brilliant production for that time. This new map of 1314 took a year to make and involved hundreds of visits to the area. In future, history will have to be done this way: assembling all the sources in one book, analysing them, issue by issue, and tabulating the results. When all the relevant sources are consulted and they are in the book, there is nothing more to be said. The battle area is shown in about 70 coloured photographs.

The above work breaks new ground in the communication of history in other ways. Every issue is decided by facts, photographed and justified by the inclusion of the translated written sources and every relevant map.

What has no one has realised before and the printed sources in the book show clearly, is that Robert the Bruce lined up his men at the foot of Balquhiderock Wood in the Carse and **led them <u>on foot</u> with himself <u>on foot</u> in the centre**! A wonderfully brave and brilliant move. At dawn, he marched the Scots right up to the English cavalry lines and they (woolly headed after a night's overconfident carousal) could do nothing to stop him. When he had closed off the streams his men dug their pike butts in to await the cavalry charge and it was easily held because there were enough Scots and no distance for the heavy destriers to get up speed. Once they were halted, they no longer operated as cavalry, were pulled down and killed. Edward II watched from the Knoll in the Carse and was taken off the field when his capture was inevitable. Two old maps, Roy's c1750 and Jeffries's 1746 show the presence of the Knoll which can still be seen today. [Mining between 1904 and 1985 is irrelevant: the ground restored when it stopped]. In the Brut y Tywysogyon, [MS 20 version; the others are useless] a Welshman wrote soon after 1314 of 'the battle among the pools' at which the Earl of Clare was killed ie Gloucester. You can still see these pools of water in the Carse after heavy rain. I counted 34 one day, one of them 100 yards long and a yard deep. This itself is enough to tell us that the battle was fought in the Carse. The Dryfield is a rounded hill and water there either runs off it or is absorbed. It could not be the place of the battle. It is not called the Dryfield for nothing: it is dry. So, as Barbour tells us, the English camped in the Carse and the Scots came out of their wood at dawn to attack them there and the battle took place among the pools of water which regularly form there even today.

Why have academics not accepted this? Arrogance, laziness, stupidity and vanity: they bury my work to cover up their own mistakes. None of them can even draw the Pelstream accurately. They haven't stood in the Pelstream Gorge and do not know that it is 100yds wide and 100ft deep. They haven't seen all the relevant sources and have never spent any decent time studying the area. What hope have they of understanding this complex matter when they are so incompetent?

Bannockburn Proved published by Elenkus 2005. ISBN 9780952191094. An A4 comb bound book of about 300 text pages plus 70 pages of photographs of the battle area plus copies of every relevant map together with the finest maps of the area in 1314 (12 of them) showing the stages of the battle. There are 6 A3 loose enclosures, one a copy of the first OS map of the area surveyed 1860; another full colour of the Roy Maps joined, c1750 plus The Pont Map etc..Cost £100, add £5 postage UK; £10 rest of world.

This work provides formal proofs of the result that the battle was fought in the Carse of Balquhiderock and how it was fought in detail. There are 8 levels of proof from a sentence to a four page proof which uses quotations from all the sources, an original and compelling technique. The best proof is the last one, where 3 simple propositions are established and these are overwhelming. Only someone very stupid or prejudiced could read this carefully and not be persuaded. Future discoveries in archaeology are shown to be irrelevant,

The maps in this work are different. They are triangulated and the finest ever seen. Errors in Roy's maps due to the lack of triangulation have been removed. A year and half full time, with many more investigations of the entire area was spent on these new maps alone. These maps show the elevations, the woodland, the streams, slopes, buildings, roads and fords as they would have been in 1314 (there were no bridges then: the first bridge across the Bannock burn was not erected until 1516) with great accuracy. Without a good, <u>fully justified</u> map (every detail is explained in a 27,000 word appendix[20]), the battle cannot be understood. This is the first time that anyone made a fully justified map of this important area at the time. All other maps have been unjustified and full or errors that made the reported description as well as the place of battle, in many cases, nonsense.

Reviews:

'You should get a doctorate from every university in Scotland for this. This book, like its predecessor, *Bannockburn Revealed*, is the result of dedicated, exhaustive and patient research and, for one reader at least, settles the vexed question of the site of the Battle of Bannockburn.'
— Irvine Smith, Advocate, Sheriff and Historian.

'William Scott brings to this sequel to his previous book, Bannockburn Revealed… his further consideration of the subject, attacked with the thoroughness and cold logic one would associate with a consummate mathematician. As a classical scholar and student of Ancient History I particularly appreciate his evaluation of evidence, sifting the dross from

---

[20] 100 pages of *Bannockburn Revealed* are about the battle area: the topography, which determines the tactics and is such an important feature of the victory.

the gold. He has challenged the historical establishment and in so doing ruffled many a feather. *I would put him on a par with the young Michael Ventris whose work on the decipherment of Linear B confounded the Classical establishment of his time.* Hopefully, William Scott will in the end gain the same acceptance.'
— Tom McCallum, MA Hons, St Andrews, Classicist.

'William Scott's is the best piece of research on history—not just Bannockburn—of that period that I have ever encountered.'
—Roger Graham, The Greenock Telegraph.

'I found Mr Scott's account quite fascinating…As regards the site of the battle, he demonstrates conclusively that it must be the Carse of Balquhiderock….Indeed, he demonstrates that [the Dryfield] would have been impossible.' Review by Patrick Cadell, Historian, ex Keeper of The Records of Scotland. In *Scottish Local History*, Spring 2006.

'There are two reasons why *Bannockburn Proved* is one of the great publications of the early 21st century. The first is the combination of historical scholarship and painstaking on the ground investigation which shows clearly the true site of the battle, and how the Scots achieved such a notable victory in 1314. The second is that the author has found himself, in a modern context, engaged with the same kind of opposition that faced King Robert, in the guise of a coalition of intellectuals and town councillors who now find their superiority challenged and overthrown by a man who understands the battleground.'
—Rev Jock Stein, Minister and Theology Publisher.

'Thank you for *Bannockburn Revealed*. It's quite a while since I felt overwhelmed by a book—especially non-fiction. A whole week-end was wiped out for me—engrossed in reading and map referencing, with the occasional twenty-minute trip out in the car to check out this landmark or that. Perhaps it was the enthusiasm of the style; maybe the pace and very compelling argument. Certainly I found myself delighted by your invaluable met-analytical approach. It's a storming piece of work. Thank you.' —Dr David Simpson, Stirling.

'The Starting point is a close consideration of the original sources, all of which are printed together, in full, for the first time. This gives you a full opportunity to read them all and form your own views. This in itself is sufficient justification for buying the book…you will learn that there were not four schiltroms but three and why…that there was no Scottish cavalry charge…because none of them fought mounted. There was no heroic appearance by the Small Folk, waving their laundry…and even had they appeared where they are supposed to have done, no one on the battlefield would have seen them. And, most surprising of all, the basis on which the size of the Scottish army has been computed is wholly fallacious. Mr Scott has, I believe, definitively established that the main action took place in the Carse of Balquhiderock. He has reached this compelling conclusion as a result of an in-depth study of old maps and photos of the area, particularly a map of 1750 by General Roy and a team of cartographers who went on to great distinction…All this is combined with an unrivalled knowledge of the ground. The many photos of the area will leave you in no doubt that the maps you have seen in other books are at best simplistic and underestimate its complexity. This is an excellent book which I whole-heartedly recommend.' Review by Chris Jackson, Principal Crown Prosecutor, in *Slingshot*, no 230.

"I do believe that the battle area lay undiscovered for nearly seven centuries until William Scott walked the ground, year in year out, for nearly a decade! He alone studied this ground in minute detail making many remarkable discoveries in the process and I am convinced no one else has ever done this. I believe that no one else has made such exhaustive studies of the eye-witness accounts and other important works associated with this event. His book is quite unique in that he applied scientific principles in his endeavour to find out what really happened. This turns out to be far more astounding than the account I was taught at school. All the Scots, including King Robert Bruce, on the day of main battle, walked to their glory! Not one Scot was on horseback! They walked up to the English camp in the early morning, made their presence known and, as the song says, 'sent them home to think again.'

"How did they do this? All is made clear in *Bannockburn Revealed*, a book of truly amazing scholarship, the first 'scientific' history book I've ever come across. The facts, the evidence, are all presented with great clarity and one is compelled to accept that here is the truth because everything fits into place and makes sense. Sadly, what is truly astonishing, is that this book has not been properly read, understood and accepted by any historians from the academic community. These so called guardians of our national heritage, either through apathy or arrogance, have undoubtedly put one of our greatest national monuments, the battlefield itself, at risk. Their lack of commitment towards upholding what has proved to be the truth is likely to lead to a desecration of the battle site for commercial gain."

Donald Morrison, 2004.

'The earlier work *Bannockburn Revealed* is such an outstanding work of scholarship that every single molecule relating to the event has been exposed. In *Bannockburn Proved* William Scott has taken the molecular level to the atomic. Every minute detail has been re-examined raising the status of this book to a scientifically tested proof for all time. The medieval battle maps alone are outstanding documents justified by exhaustive scientific investigation. This proof was obtained after nearly two decades of hard labour. No ivory towers here but an intense examination of every square inch of the battle-ground. No odd reference to an ancient map but a close scrutiny of all maps ancient and modern. No sporadic quote from an occasional source but a thorough searching of all the sources. No skimming of a few works relating to this event. In the process every strand of evidence has been teased out. Having studied W. Scott's work for many years I have to conclude that unlike many discoveries in mathematics, physics, medicine, astronomy, genetics etc, this work is not a theory but is the absolute truth simply because no other facts will ever be discovered which will discredit this truth. What a wonderful challenge for all the academic historians from every Scottish university to dissect this work and try to find fault with it.

They will find none and only conclude that W. Scott should be appropriately recognized and applauded for his achievement.
'My involvement with W. Scott's work led me to undertake the construction of a 3D model of the battle area based on the Roy maps. Mr Scott has been examining every line and mark on the maps for almost two decades and I am convinced that he is in a class of his own with regard to Roy's maps. I concluded that Mr Scott had confirmed, one hundred per cent, everything of importance on the ground by an exhaustive study of the Roy maps supported by other useful maps of the area and the ground itself.'
     Donald Morrison, 2006, 118 Alexander St, Dunoon, PA237PY tel 01369703006

The Bute Witches published by Elenkus 2007.
ISBN 9780952191070 What caused the witch trials in Bute in 1662, after which six women were burnt, who were responsible and why did one who escaped return 12 years later to be executed then?
344 pages £12, £14 including postage in the UK; £19 Rest of the World. A book which contains all the relevant historical records, analysed, together with a reconstruction of events in narrative form. Obtainable from www.elenkus.com or Elenkus, G/L 23 Argyle Place, Rothesay, Isle of Bute PA20 0BA, UK.

'A masterly piece of writing and a riveting story, based on meticulous research, by award winning author, William Scott. This tale captures the reader and transports him back three and a half centuries to dark and dangerous days, with a compelling solution to the mystery of the witches of Bute.'
     David Torrie, an editor, D.C. Thomson Publications

'I must give you all praise for your imaginative interpretation and fleshing out of the account in the archives. I can't fault your logical explanation of the witches' "evidence" and the return of Jonet McNicoll. Your novel is enthralling and would stand alone as historical fiction.'
     Tom McCallum, MA Hons Classics, St Andrews

'A formidable benchmark.' Craig Borland, *The Buteman*.

'An astonishing true story,' Martin Tierney, *The Herald*.

A BUTE CRUCIFIXION by William Scott. ISBN 9780952191063

A 342 page novel with mathematical appendices: a study of goodness in a small community; including poetry, music, rugby and a rich diet of ideas as well as love, humour, action and two original crimes. Price £10.99, obtainable from www.elenkus.com for £13 post free in the UK; £17, rest of the world.

'Award-winning author William Scott explores the relationships in a small community with sensitivity and conviction and produces a superb novel of power and devastating consequences in a titanic struggle between good and evil.' —David Torrie, an editor, DC Thomson Publications

'What a powerful book! Greek tragedy meets the Book of Job. I heartily recommend it to anyone who as at all pondered the questions of good and evil in the Christian context. It is also a wonderful exposé of life in a small Scots town.'

—Tom McCallum, MA Hons, St Andrews, Classicist

'A riveting read I must say. A modern tragedy with the energy of Coronation Street, the passion of Dickens and the intellect of Carlyle.' —Rev Jock Stein, Minister and Theology Publisher